meet me at the Christmas Cottage

meet me at the Christmas Cottage

CHRISTEN KRUMM

sunrise
PUBLISHING

Meet Me at the Christmas Cottage
Jonathon Island, Book 6
Published by Sunrise Publishing
Copyright © 2025 Sunrise Media Group LLC
Print ISBN: 978-1-963372-89-2

This book is a work of fiction. Names, characters, places, and incidents are either products of the author's imagination or used fictitiously. Any similarity to actual people, organizations, and/or events is purely coincidental.

Scriptures taken from the Holy Bible, New International Version®, NIV®. Copyright © 1973, 1978, 1984, 2011 by Biblica, Inc.™ Used by permission of Zondervan. All rights reserved worldwide. www.zondervan.com The "NIV" and "New International Version" are trademarks registered in the United States Patent and Trademark Office by Biblica, Inc.™

For more information about Christen Krumm, please access the author's website at the following address: christenkrumm.com

Published in the United States of America.
Cover Design: Sunrise Media Group, LLC

This is for anyone who never felt they belonged.

"When you pass through the waters,
I will be with you;
and when you pass through the rivers,
they will not sweep over you.
When you walk through the fire,
you will not be burned;
the flames will not set you ablaze."

ISAIAH 43:2 NIV

Jonathon Island

Meet Me on Jonathon Island (prequel novella)
Meet Me at the Grand
Meet Me on Lilac Lane
Meet Me at the Fudge Shop
Meet Me on Blueberry Hill
Meet Me at Sunset Cove
Meet Me at the Christmas Cottage

JONATHON ISLAND
N
W E
S
Jonathon Family Home
Sullivan Pumpkin Farm
Lake Shore Drive
Airport
Sunset Cove
Barrett House
State Park
Sullivan Way
MacBride Resort
Jonathon Blvd
Quinn Ranch
Sugar Maple Ln
Blueberry Hills Neighborhood
LAKE HURON
Partridge Ln
GRAND HOTEL
Dahlia Dr
Lilac Ln
Zinnia Blvd
Poppy Place
Rose Rd
Blueberry Blvd
Pinnacle Dr
Blueberry Hills Park
MAIN SREET
Downtown
Marina Way
Marina

One

Date December 15
Days until Deadline 21
Words to be written 89,973

STANDING ON THE OPEN DECK OF A ferry in near freezing temps probably wasn't the best idea, but Bronte preferred if no one overheard this conversation with her agent. Not to mention needing to escape a baby screaming its lungs out since they had boarded.

Bronte lifted her face to the sun, letting it warm her. The Jonathan Island Ferry Company boat cut through the lake on its way to the island, and she found the slight bob relaxing. Zipping the front of her coat a little higher, she shifted her phone to her opposite ear and resisted the urge to "accidentally" drop it into the water.

"Okay, run me through this again. You have how much written?"

Bronte winced, not wanting to admit just how little she had done. Maybe she could just fall over the side of the boat, but all that would probably get her was wet and freezing. "Lexi, don't make me say it."

"Are you in a wind tunnel or something? I can barely hear you. How much did you say?" Bronte's best friend and agent practically yelled in her ear.

Bronte sighed and moved out of the sun and wind to tuck herself into the alcove by the door. At least here, she'd still be able to watch their arrival to the island in relative silence. She could still hear the baby's cries, muted though they were through the door. A pang shot through her heart, but she shook thoughts of babies and families from her mind as she turned from watching the Michigan shoreline grow smaller.

"Twenty-seven. That's how much I've written." Waves lapped against the side of the boat as it cut through the glassy water. "And I'm on a ferry heading to Jonathon Island. Remember? I told you I booked a place here for Christmas."

"Twenty-seven thousand's not bad, Bront. You're at least, what? Twenty percent done?"

Oh, the faith her friend had in her.

"No, just twenty-seven. Two, seven." On the book that needed to be at least ninety thousand words.

"Does my mother know you only have 'two seven' written on this project?" Lexi choked out.

"She would if I would actually answer any of her calls. I'm not sure why I need to answer her calls anyway. You're my agent now." Bronte sank onto the bench that ran the length of the boat. She could imagine this would be a coveted seat in the summer, the perfect location to watch the island growing closer. In the winter, the wind cut through her layers like knives. Bronte didn't mind. The cold felt good, refreshing, after being in airports all day. Besides, it rivaled the winter wind whipping down the plains in good old Oklahoma, which had been her home for just a little over two years now.

Bronte's fingers gripped the bench seat as they passed under a bridge. Should she hold her breath or did the "holding your breath" rule only apply when driving through tunnels? "And you'd better not tell your mother just how far behind I am."

"First of all, I would never. Second, I'm only your agent-in-training. My mother is still technically your agent. I'm not sure ghosting her is the best choice."

Bronte snorted. "First, just because you're an agent-in-training, doesn't mean you aren't my agent. You are. Also, Margot will be fine because she'll never know how far behind I am. The newest installment of the Pike Family Saga will be on both of your desks by January fifth."

"January fifth?" Lexi squeaked. "Bronte, that's three weeks."

"Saying it's due next month sounds so much better, don't you think?"

"Bronte!"

"I know, I know." Bronte dropped her forehead into her hand. "But it's fine. Totally fine. I'm going to get it done."

"That's, like, thirty thousand words a week. Over four thousand a day."

"That's so helpful. Thank you."

"Sorry. It's just . . . a lot."

Bronte wanted to squeeze her eyes tight and pray the deadline just went away. "I know. And I've never been this behind before. But there was the press tour and movie stuff this year."

"Which you have never let get in your way before."

"It did this time." And then there had been the surgery . . .

"This is all Brad's fault."

A heavy silence followed. Bronte's chest tightened, and she blinked against the cold wind that was causing her eyes to well up. No, she wasn't going down could-have-beens. She squared her shoulders. All of that had happened ten months ago—practically a year. Brad was behind her now. She didn't care about him. She had a manuscript to write and a plan to execute.

"Okay, okay. No numbers, but I need you to hurry up and finish that book so the publishers can do their thing and we can go on tour again. You know you need your number one agent to shield you from all your raving fans."

Bronte's chest tightened. "Oh yay. Tour," she deadpanned. Why had she chosen a career that required her to fly to different cities to meet hundreds of strangers? *Calm down. A tour won't happen for at least another year.* "If they mauled me, they would never find out what happens to Theodosia, Marisol, and Vivian at the end."

"Are you going to finally give them their happy ending?"

Bronte stood and stepped back over to the railing, not

caring if Lexi couldn't hear her over the wind. She was tired of this discussion. Digging her fingers into the metal railing she replied, "You know I don't write happy books."

"I think you should. Wrap the entire series up in one big happy bow."

"And how is that going to be realistic?" Bronte pressed.

"Sometimes it's okay to give someone a happy ending," Lexi said gently.

"Happy endings don't exist." At least, not in Bronte's experience.

"Bronte—"

"Stop, it's fine. I know there are authors out there that write happy books. That's just not me. Write what you know, and what I know is not happy endings."

"All right, I get it." Lexi paused. "So, speaking of Brad—"

"We weren't speaking of Brad," Bronte interjected.

Lexi ignored her and continued. "You've been staying off social media, right?"

"Yes . . ."

Lexi huffed out a breath. "Good. Good. That's good."

"What does my staying off socials have to do with Brad?" Bronte pulled in a deep breath. In the warmer months, she'd be able to smell the verdant greenery lining the lake and enjoy the fresh breeze, but not now while her nose was frozen.

"Well . . ."

"Lex, just spit it out already," Bronte snapped, a little more sharply than she wanted. She chewed her bottom lip to keep from snapping again.

"Brad is engaged."

All the air whooshed from Bronte's lungs. "Good for him." She somehow managed to get the sentiment out. Sucking in the cold air and willing it to freeze her heart, she reminded herself she'd traveled all the way to Jonathon Island to get away from any thoughts of Brad. Dreams of holing herself up in the cutest little cottage that she had ever seen, head down, words flowing, started melting from her mind.

She would *not* give Brad anymore brain space. She imagined herself taking a broom and sweeping Brad out of every crevice in her mind. He wasn't welcome there any longer. He'd made it very clear in February that he'd decided he wanted a family. He wanted the noisy babies, and as Bronte couldn't change her mind on the matter, he didn't want to be in her life. And now he was engaged. It didn't get any clearer than that.

"Bronte? Did I lose you? Oh gosh, I shouldn't have mentioned Brad. What was I thinking?"

"I'm here, but hey, the ferry is almost to the island." They were only halfway there. "I'm going to have to let you go."

"Sure. You have a wonderful time, Bronte. Seriously call me once you get settled—"

Bronte shook her head even though Lexi couldn't see her. "I've got to write."

"Fine, send me a text. Send a carrier pigeon."

Shifting the phone to her other ear, Bronte asked, "Do those even exist anymore?"

"Just let me know you got in and settled okay."

"Yes, mother," Bronte replied sarcastically.

With well-wishes of Christmas, Bronte ended the call and dropped her phone into the pocket of her oversized black peacoat. Wind whipping at her hair, she curled her fingers tighter around the railing to keep them from doing something silly—like looking at her ex's social media accounts. She didn't need to see Brad and his fiancée. She had already swept Brad out of her mind.

But would one little peek really hurt? Once she arrived at the island, she'd put thoughts of her ex and his happiness out of her mind for good.

Ignoring the scenery she had been so looking forward to taking in, Bronte pulled her phone from her pocket and with laser focus, scrolled through the apps on her phone until she found the icon she was looking for. Fingers seemed to fly over the face of her phone as she typed Brad's username from memory. The first image contained him and Marie, with Marie flashing one of the largest rings Bronte had ever seen.

"Look at that rock."

Bronte startled, almost dropping her phone into the lake, as a girl in a camel-colored trench coat came to stand next to her. She was a bit shorter than Bronte, but then again, Bronte had always been called a giant. Five nine wasn't that tall, but that hadn't stopped boys in middle school from giving her the nickname. It wasn't her fault she'd been head and shoulders taller than them at that age.

Of course, it was better than them teasing her for being a foster kid.

The girl's blonde hair shone in the sun and was tucked perfectly into her scarf and layers. Blue eyes sparkled, and all of her features were a perfect kind of petite that Bronte had wished for her whole life. After traveling all day, Bronte had swiped the last of the mascara off her face in the airport bathroom and had to wrestle her untamed curls into a knot on top of her head—which she was pretty sure resembled a bird's nest at this point.

"Oh, sorry. I didn't mean to scare you." The girl took a step back, eyes wide. "Aubrey Jennings." She thrust her hand in Bronte's direction.

Bronte clicked her phone off and dropped it back in her pocket, taking Aubrey's offered hand. "Bronte. Parker. It's fine. I didn't need to scroll anyway."

"Right." The girl smiled and leaned against the railing next to Bronte. "Would you look at that?"

A large white building flanked in scaffolding loomed in the distance. Dirty snow glittered on the ground and covered a crane sitting quietly to the side. The Grand Hotel. Bronte remembered, after deciding to come to Jonathon Island, reading reports about the rebuilding of the hotel after it'd burned in a tragic accident years before. She wished she had been able to get a room at the hotel, but since they hadn't opened it to the public yet, she'd been compelled to find other lodgings.

"I'm so glad to see they're rebuilding the hotel. It's going to be gorgeous when they get it done." Taking a big breath, as if coming to the island was clearing her head, she turned to Bronte. "Is this your first time to the island?"

Putting her hands in her pockets, Bronte nodded. "You?"

"Oh, no. I grew up here. My grandmother still lives here."

"Back for Christmas?"

Aubrey clicked her knee-high boots as if she were Dorothy in *The Wizard of Oz*. Bronte half expected her to sigh *There's no place like home.* "Yep. Staying until New Year's."

Her heart clenched. What would it be like to have family to visit for the holidays? A grandma waiting for her on the other side of this ride. Maybe with a steaming cup of tea and the world's best snickerdoodle cookies. When she had deadlines looming, she could visit her grandma, who would insist on making sure she stayed fed while Bronte's fingers flew over her keyboard, creating characters and entire worlds. A family didn't have to be noisy and in the way. Did it?

"What brings you to Jonathon Island?"

Aubrey's question snapped Bronte from her daydream. Probably for the best. She didn't need to spiral down the what-if tunnel. She'd accepted that wasn't a life she'd ever have a long time ago. "Just visiting. I rented a cottage out for the next few weeks." *I'm on deadline. I have a book to write*, she finished silently. Five bestsellers in, and she still found it hard to tell people what she did for a living.

"You're going to love it on Jonathon Island. The Christmas season is my favorite. There are so many fun activities planned. Oh, and this year, I've heard they're bringing back the ball."

"The ball?" She vaguely remembered reading something about a ball when booking her rental, but she hadn't looked too much into it since she was here to write her book.

"Yeah, the Christmas ball. I remember going to the Christmas balls when I was a teenager, but then the hotel burned down, and there hasn't been anything like that on the island in ages. I'm so excited they're bringing it back."

On any other trip, attending a ball might have been fun. "I've never been to anything even remotely resembling a ball. Unless line dancing counts? I've done that a few times." Bronte made a face.

"Maybe not quite the same." Aubrey laughed. "Oh, and I hope they have the lights up in the town. It's so magical."

That word—*magical*. It sobered Bronte right up. There was nothing magical about Christmas. Not for her.

Not for anyone who was alone.

Bronte just nodded and tucked her chin further under her black silk scarf. She hoped the lights weren't up. Didn't matter though. She'd be hunkered down in her cottage the whole time, writing.

They fell into silence, watching the waves go by in a quick clip.

"So, what is it you do?" Aubrey asked.

Bronte hated this question. It always made her feel self-conscious. She accepted having to talk about being a writer when she went on tour, almost to a point where she enjoyed it, but in her everyday life? Nope. Why hadn't she become something simple? Like an accountant. "I'm a writer."

Hopefully there wouldn't be any more questions after that, but Bronte knew better.

Aubrey's eyes lit up. "That's great. I always wanted to write a book. What do you write?"

Bronte's second most-hated question. "Oh, just some family sagas."

"I love to read. My ex and I used to have contests to see who could read the most books every year." Her smile wavered just for the briefest moment before returning. "Are you published? Anything I might have read?"

She almost brushed off the question, but she'd just look more ridiculous when the truth came out. "The Pike Family Saga." Almost six years since her first novel had launched her career, and she still felt awkward talking about it.

"Like the movie?"

Despite herself, Bronte relaxed. Fans of the movies were easier to handle than fans of the books. "Yes. *Color of the Stars.*"

Aubrey snapped her gloved fingers. "Yes, that's it. Wow, so you're like a celebrity."

Bronte winced. "Not really."

"So, are you working on the next in the series? Are there going to be more movies?"

"I'm working on the last book in the series." Why she had been so adamant about that, she'd never know. Now that the end was here, she didn't want to say goodbye. "But there should be more movies coming out. The rights were bought for the entire series."

"That is so exciting." Aubrey continued rambling about celebrities and movies and asked something about Liam

Hemsworth, but Bronte's mind wandered. All the movie, book, and Pike family questions were always the same.

She should talk to Lexi about asking the publisher if they could extend the series. Bronte knew they would be on board with that idea. But if she wanted to ask for more books, another contract, she needed to make sure this last book was the best one so they couldn't tell her no. Maybe Vivian Pike would run from the love of her life and move to an island. Or maybe her love would be the one to leave her, and she would still go to the island, vowing to live out her days alone. She could take over the apothecary shop, just like her mother had always wanted her to. Where would the series go from there? Maybe she should throw in a secret love child.

Bronte wrinkled her nose. No. There would be no secret love children.

"Don't you think?"

Bronte snapped back to the conversation at hand. Drat. Aubrey had asked a question, and Bronte had completely missed it.

The intercom crackled. "On behalf of everyone at Jonathon Island, we'd like to welcome you to the island. We'll be docking in just a few minutes, so please remain seated until the vessel has been secured to the dock and luggage carts have been unloaded. Please take this opportunity to collect your things. And lastly, please be courteous to your fellow passengers as you exit the ferry. Thank you, and have a nice visit."

Saved by the boat.

"Well." Aubrey pushed off the railing and turned to go back inside. "I guess that's our cue."

Turning, Bronte couldn't help but sneak one more glance at the approaching island—her home for the next two weeks. Tall, bare trees peeked over the tops of the colorful buildings that dotted the shoreline.

She had studied the map of Jonathon Island for the last month, ever since she'd decided this would be where she hid away to finish her novel. She could picture the shops along Main Street and the friendly smiles of the people who lived here year-round. Jonathon Island was the perfect place to write the last Pike novel. Bronte could already feel the inspiration calling to her from the island.

Okay, right. She could do this.

Nothing would get in the way of her finishing this novel.

Bronte was ready to hunker down and start working on this book. Now she just needed to find Mia Franklin and get the keys to the cottage she'd rented.

Having secured their luggage, Bronte and Aubrey disembarked and walked down Ferry Street. The cutest row of white and gray shops—adorned with multicolored awnings, twinkle lights swaying in the slight breeze—lined both sides of Main Street, and fine, it was a little bit magical, decorated for Christmas with its lights and wreaths and ribbons.

Even with a few of the shops vacant, Bronte could tell this was the hub of the island. She had loved what she'd seen of Jonathon Island on the House to Home YouTube channel—yes, she was that person that would rather follow a YouTube series than watch anything on primetime television.

She couldn't believe she actually stood here.

"Where are you headed?"

Bronte pulled her phone out of her pocket and scrolled to her messages. "I need to find a Martha's on Main and a Mia Franklin to get the keys to the place I'm renting."

"Martha's on Main is that way." Bronte's companion lifted her hand and pointed up the street. "I'm headed this way to catch a ride to my grandma's."

Bronte looked around, expecting to spot a car or Uber. She didn't see any.

"Thanks."

"Hope you have a great time while you're here. Maybe we'll bump into each other again."

They said their goodbyes and went their separate ways.

The wheels on her suitcase complained as they rattled over the cobblestones, catching on the uneven walkway and threatening to spill. That's all Bronte needed—for her suitcase to spill open on Main Street.

Bronte's suitcase jerked her back as it got stuck on a divot in the street. She shivered as a gust of cold air blew. The sun was deceiving. It looked like it should be a nice day with no frigid air cutting through her coat to slice her bones. Deceiving or not, Bronte couldn't see how there were snowstorms predicted for later. Not even cotton-ball clouds dotted the sky.

With one more jerk, the street gave the suitcase back, sans a wheel.

Bronte groaned. "Are you kidding me?" At least it wasn't a busted zipper. Pocketing the rogue wheel, Bronte half dragged, half carried her suitcase the remaining three shops to Martha's on Main.

Warmth of the restaurant enveloped her as she pushed in from the cold, suitcase dragging behind her. The door clambered shut as all the eyes of the patrons swung in her direction, and there were many. For a random Monday a week and a half before Christmas, the place seemed packed. Two older gentlemen played what looked to be an intense game of checkers, and there was another group of five, who looked to be deep in some kind of meeting, and she recognized a few people from the ferry.

"Just find an open seat, and we'll be with you in a moment," someone from behind the bar directed.

"I just need to meet up with Mia Franklin? She has the keys and directions to my rental."

"Rental? There aren't any rentals on the island." A larger woman with gray streaking through her dark hair, piercing blue eyes, and a too-gruff voice handed a plate to a waitress, who turned on her heel to deliver it to a nearby table.

"I, uh, am renting from Holland White?" Bronte rifled through her messenger bag, looking for the rental agreement she knew she'd printed out.

"Yes, yes, Martha, you remember. Holland is renting out her place while they're in the Bahamas." A dark-haired woman, no more than twenty-five, dressed in jeans and a white sweater, came up beside Bronte. "Hi, I'm Mia Franklin. You must be Bronte."

Bronte took Mia's proffered hand.

Martha huffed. "I still don't know why the Whites had to go off to the Bahamas for Christmas. Who has heard of such a thing?"

"Sunshine, sand, and warmer than twenty degrees, Martha. Anyone could see the appeal," Mia shot back.

Martha harrumphed, turned, and pushed through swinging doors disappearing to, Bronte assumed, the kitchen.

"Don't mind her. I hope your trip here was good," Mia said, leading Bronte back over to the dark wood booth where she had papers spread over the entire surface of the table. Putting one knee on the booth seat, Mia leaned over to dig through her briefcase. "Give me one second, and I'll get you the keys. Sorry about the mess. I'm working from here today since my kids are sick and at home with my mom. Honestly, my office was just too quiet. I'd rather be where there's people. You know?"

Bronte didn't know.

Mia continued muttering to herself as she pulled her bag closer. It must be like a Mary Poppins bag with all the digging Mia was doing. Bronte shifted on her feet, not sure if she should offer to help or find a seat to sit down and wait, maybe get something to eat before heading out.

"Ah-ha!" Mia held up a set of keys on a dark-blue plastic keychain, like one you'd find at a vintage hotel. "Found them." She held them out toward Bronte. "I went over there earlier today to make sure the heat had been turned up. The Whites have been gone for a few days already and aren't scheduled to be back until after you leave. If you need groceries or anything while you're here, Doug's Market is right down that way." Mia thumbed the direction toward the grocery store. "Of course, you'll also find Good Day Coffee, Island Pizzeria, and Kelley's Bar & Grill, which, if you need something to do in the evenings, is the place to go. They generally have line dancing or trivia night or something. Always a good time. And of course, there's Martha's." Mia swept her arms out.

"Great." Bronte flashed what she hoped was a thankful smile. After talking with Lexi and confessing exactly how much she had to get done out loud, it'd started sinking in.

What had she been thinking, waiting until the very last minute? And maybe she did have twenty-seven words down, but what she hadn't told Lexi was that she'd written those months ago. She didn't even know if they were going to stay.

What was her first line again? It didn't matter. She was here now, and this book would get written.

"Is there an Uber I can call or . . ." Bronte trailed off at the amusement in Mia's eyes.

"There are no cars on Jonathon Island."

"Oh. Right." Bronte knew that from watching the show, but hadn't that been more of a reality TV stunt? "How do you get around, then?"

"Depends on the season. From Memorial Day to Labor Day, we walk or bike. The Quinns are working on getting horses back on island next season, and Asher Quinn—yes, *that* Asher Quinn—has started up a carriage tour business with the few horses still here."

She actually didn't know *that* Asher Quinn but promised herself she'd google him later. "That's so . . . interesting."

"It really is. If you just give me one minute, I can drive you over on a golf cart." Mia started gathering her papers, tapping the stacks on the tabletop before slipping them in her briefcase and donning a coat, scarf, and hat.

"Oh, I couldn't—" Bronte started.

Mia shot a pointed look at the missing wheel on Bronte's suitcase. "Of course you can. You do not need to be dragging that thing through the streets of Jonathon Island. Besides, I'm done here anyway, and the Whites' place is basically on my way home."

Bronte took a step back to let Mia finish gathering her stuff, letting her gaze shift up to the white-tiled ceiling and pendant lighting. Martha's was a cute little restaurant, and from how many tables were full, the food must be good too. Most everyone had gone back to whatever they were doing before Bronte stepped in. *Thank goodness.*

Mia straightened, pulling the strap of her bag onto her shoulder. "Ready?"

"Don't forget this." Martha thrust a plastic bag filled with takeout containers in Bronte's direction.

Bronte stared at the bag dangling from two of Martha's fingers. "I didn't order anything."

Martha jiggled the bag. "I'm sure you're tired from traveling all day. I know Mia went up earlier and made sure there were some groceries and the like, but figured a little more couldn't hurt. And I live in the big white house only a few houses down from Holland's, so if you need anything, just come by and ask."

Bronte's face warmed, not sure why Martha would care about whether or not she had enough food. "Oh, thank you." She took the bag, scents of something savory curling up with the steam. A pang shot through her stomach. Maybe she was a little hungrier than she realized.

Grabbing her suitcase by the top strap, Bronte stuck out her hip to help heave it up so she could hobble-follow Mia back out into the cold December air.

"Sorry it's so cold." Mia led them over to a blue golf cart. "And the ride over is going to be a little chilly, but luckily the Whites' house isn't too far away."

They stored the suitcase in the back, securing it with a bungee cord. Bronte sat in the front next to Mia. Holding on to the handle, Bronte shifted as far over as she could on the golf cart's seat. There wasn't much room on the bench seat, but she didn't need to be sitting in Mia's lap.

Sighing, Bronte let her head fall back on the seat rest, head lolling to the side so she could at least see where they were going. Or maybe she didn't want to know. If she didn't know, she would be less likely to want to get out and explore instead of staying put and getting the writing done. Not that that wasn't the plan to begin with.

They passed the cutest houses painted in white and dark blues. Bronte spotted a few houses' landscaping showing off, even in the winter months. After only two minutes of driving, Mia whipped the golf cart into a driveway.

The Whites' cottage looked exactly as it did in the

photos Holland shared online—white rock skirting the bottom third, giving way to dark, moody siding and black windows. Bronte couldn't wait to get inside. This place, this house, something about it put Bronte at ease, and she knew for the first time that she would get a huge chunk, if not all, of the next Pike Family Saga written here.

"Thanks for the ride." Bronte slipped out of the golf cart and unhooked her suitcase from the back.

"Anytime." Mia followed Bronte out of the golf cart and up the sidewalk to the front of the house. "There are goodies in the cabinets, but if there's anything that you need, please don't hesitate to reach out. I know you have Holland's number, but I don't think she'll be available since they're on a cruise ship."

"That's really nice of you. Thanks." Bronte clutched the bag of takeout containers while also keeping a grip on the top strap of the suitcase. The zipper could still decide to fail her.

Mia fell into silence next to Bronte, and they stood on the sidewalk. Bronte wanted nothing more than to escape inside, get settled, and start writing. *Ninety thousand words. Ninety thousand words.* The reminder beat a rhythm in her head.

"Well." Mia clapped her hands together with a slap. "I'm going to get home and make sure my mom's not going crazy. Call me if you need anything. Anything at all!" Waving, Mia got back inside the golf cart and, after backing out of the driveway, continued down the street.

Sitting back under trees and foliage, the house seemed to say *Welcome. You are going to get so much work done.*

"I hope so," Bronte mumbled to herself as she jammed the key into the lock.

The inside was just as inviting, if not more, than the outside. Even though there weren't any Christmas decorations (thank goodness), it still smelled of cinnamon and citrus.

Leaving her suitcase next to the front door, Bronte went farther into the house. The small entryway led down a short hallway to the open kitchen and living room.

The kitchen was the perfect kind of homey, with its speckled granite countertops and mossy green cabinets with gold hardware. A wall of windows in the breakfast nook showed a big backyard. A large island separated the kitchen area from the living room, and on that island, a pile of chocolate chip cookies sat on a Santa plate with a folded card sitting next to it that said, "Welcome to the White house, Bronte."

Smiling, Bronte exchanged the bag of food from Martha for a cookie and continued her exploring.

The living room was the stuff of dreams, so different from her two-bedroom apartment that she'd never quite found the time—or energy—to decorate. The mustard velvet sectional made Bronte's heart pitter-patter. She couldn't wait to sink into it with her laptop and get to work. A large, white fireplace took up most of the wall, flanked only by a dark wood piano. She plunked at two keys while leaning over and studying the various pictures of whom she could only assume was the White family that covered the top of the piano.

She could almost watch the family grow up through the frozen images. A man with sandy brown hair, the only indication he was older being the deep grooves in his face, sat next to a beautiful older woman with salt-and-pepper hair. They were surrounded by—one, two, three…Mercy, five kids, four of which were girls. That poor brother. A handful of the siblings had dark hair, with one lone blonde sister. The solitary son stood behind his parents, his smile making Bronte feel as warm as the picture looked. Another photo showed the son in military garb. The intensity of his face in the photo made Bronte do a double-take to make sure it was the same person. Serious or not, it did nothing to detract from his handsomeness. A face like that—strong jaw, defined chin, thick eyebrows sitting on top of blue eyes that sparkled with kindness—would give any Hollywood heartthrob a run for their money.

Taking her cookie, Bronte wandered up the stairs to the second floor. There were four rooms, way more than Bronte could ever need, but this house would be perfect for pulling inspiration for the last Pike family book. The room at the end of the hallway had an evergreen wreath bearing a placard with her name expertly calligraphed in gold. After retrieving her suitcase from downstairs, Bronte unpacked, setting her folded clothes into the antique dresser. She warred between tucking herself into the window seat alcove that overlooked Jonathon Island or heading back downstairs. But with the quickly setting sun, the picturesque image would soon be painted in black.

Bag unpacked and decision about where to work made, Bronte grabbed her notebook and laptop and headed back downstairs to find a cozy spot to start working.

Settling on the velvet couch, she opened her laptop,

trying to ignore the large picture windows that led to the backyard. Holland had said in the listing that this was her childhood home. What would it have been like growing up in a house like this? Having four siblings to play with. Constant activity, running in and out, sports, homework, extracurricular activities. It must have been like a dream.

She'd hoped maybe one day she'd have that. Now . . .

A prick stung the back of Bronte's eyes. She blinked furiously. She needed to stop being ridiculous and get to work. Having overactive retrospection wasn't going to help her get anything done. She let out a quick breath. Yes, work. Writing. Getting the last Pike family story down. The last one. This was it. After this she would move on to . . . to what? Did she have anything after this?

"Focus, Bronte," she told herself, ignoring how hollow and alone her voice sounded.

She stared at the blinking cursor. Fingers poised over the keyboard, Bronte closed her eyes to imagine the words she needed to write.

Her eyes flew open. She hadn't texted Lexi to let her know she'd arrived.

Toggling over to the message app on her laptop, she fired a quick text to her friend, letting her know that she'd made it and all was good.

That finished, she moved back to her open document, closed her eyes again, and tried to conjure up the first line.

Her finger *tap, tap, tapped* against the side of the keyboard.

Ugh, this wasn't working. Her brain must be too tired from all the travel.

Bronte slammed her laptop closed. No matter. She'd rest tonight and get started first thing in the morning.

She had waited this long to get started—one more night wouldn't hurt.

Two

IF YOU'RE PLANNING ON BREAKING DAD'S *heart, don't bother coming back at all.*

Jonah's older sister Amy's words came back to him. Not that they had ever left since their call two years ago. Whether or not his decision would break their father's heart was yet to be discovered. He had listened to his sister and stayed away. Until now.

"Are you sure you want me to drop you here? Ferry doesn't run until morning, if it even runs in this storm. The snow is really starting to come down." The raspy voice of his Uber driver cut through his thoughts.

As if to prove the man's point, the wind picked up, depositing snow drifts a little faster. A bit of white stuff, or the fact the ferry didn't run overnight, wasn't going to stop Jonah. He was going to get home to surprise his family.

"I'll be fine." Jonah stepped out of the car, grabbing his suitcase and backpack out of the trunk.

The Uber driver leaned across the console of his car to look at Jonah through the open window. "Are you sure you don't want me to stay, wait a few minutes, just to make sure you get off the docks?"

"I'll be fine," Jonah repeated, shrugging into his backpack and pulling his black stocking cap further over his ears.

In truth, he didn't have an entire plan yet. The original plan had him arriving nine hours earlier for the last ferry of the day, but thanks to the weather over Atlanta and employee shortages . . . he was now on the wrong side of Lake Huron, staring through the snow in the direction of Jonathon Island.

"Whatever." The Uber driver shook his head and peeled out of the parking lot, slushy snow kicking up from the tires.

Glancing at the time on his phone, Jonah grimaced. He really didn't want to have to ask for someone to pick him up. His sister Holland had mentioned she'd gotten a boat over the summer, but she would have it docked by now. Besides, he didn't want to call anyone in his family. He wanted to show up, sneak in, and surprise everyone. Mom and Dad should be there at least. Last he'd heard, they planned on parking their RV and spending all of December on island.

In theory, the surprise would make the conversation with his dad go smoother. There would be no breaking of hearts. Hopefully.

Using his teeth, Jonah took a glove off so he could scroll the contacts in his phone, landing on Hunter Barrett's name. A friend from high school he hadn't seen or talked to since his last visit, but Jonah knew he'd be there in a pinch. Before he could change his mind, Jonah shot off a quick text.

Jonah

Hey, man. Sorry this is last minute, but I'm standing on the docks and it looks like I missed the last ferry. Would you be able to come grab me?

Jonah stared at his phone, waiting for dots to appear, indicating his friend was responding.

Two minutes later, they popped up. Jonah's shoulders relaxed. Truth was, if he couldn't get a ride to the island tonight, he'd have to hike over to the Bayside Inn in Port Joseph and wait until the ferry started running in the morning. But with the snow coming down as hard as it was already, Jonah had to agree with the Uber driver—he didn't know for sure that the ferry would be an option by morning. He'd rather get there tonight.

Hunter

Ha! Just missed it. Hang tight, we'll get you here.

Jonah pushed out a breath. He could always count on Hunter.

Shaking off the snow and folding his arm across his chest, Jonah stood under the small partition at the end of the dock and waited for his ride home.

Almost an hour later, certain he was frozen to his bones, Jonah heard the chugging motor of a boat. It sounded a bit bigger than the MasterCraft he knew Hunter to have. Five minutes later, he realized why it sounded different. It wasn't Hunter's boat.

A head poked out of the captain's cabin. "Hunter said a major needed a ride home!"

"Cody? What are you doing here? Where's Hunter?" Cody Hart was closer in age to Holland's twenty-five years—and she was ten years younger than Jonah—but Jonathon Island was small enough that the families who had been here forever, like the Whites and the Harts, were friendly. "What are you doing?"

Last time Jonah had been home, Cody had been working on his dad's fishing boat. Since then, he'd lost his best friend in a tragic accident but gained a very serious girlfriend in Mia Franklin, if Holland's gossip could be believed.

"Looks like I'm your ride to the island. Hunter's at his engagement party, so he sent me to pick you up." Cody's grin could be seen from where Jonah stood on the dock.

"Engagement party? Aw, man. I'm sorry to pull you away from that." He hadn't realized Hunter and Daisy had gotten engaged. Although, the last time he'd chatted with his sister Mika Beth, she had mentioned they were getting close.

"No worries, man. I'm glad to be your ride."

"Well, in that case, permission to come aboard?" It took everything in Jonah to keep his voice from shaking. He needed to get out of the cold and somewhere warm.

"You'd better hurry before you turn into a full-out icicle. I'd have a hard time explaining that one to your mom."

"Thanks so much for doing this, Cody."

The man nodded, scratching a thumb at his stubble as

he expertly steered the boat away from the dock toward Jonathon Island. Toward home. "Of course."

Jonah dropped his suitcase to the floor with a thud and tugged his backpack from his shoulders before propping it up against the wall. The captain's cabin may have been small, but it was clean and warmed by a small space heater. Not the warmest, but it sure beat standing in a snowstorm. "How have you been? How's Mia and her kids?"

"Doing good. The kids are growing like weeds."

Jonah nodded his thanks as he accepted a cup of coffee Cody offered. "How old are they now?"

"Finn's five and Maggie's three. I think Maggie talks more than Finn." Cody smiled. "They're really great."

What Jonah wouldn't give to raise a family on Jonathon Island—just like his parents before him. That had been the plan—get through med school and ten years in the Army, then take over his dad's practice, but now . . .

"What about you?" Cody asked, and Jonah was glad for the question. "How's the Army life treating you? Keeping you busy, I guess. I haven't seen you back island side for . . ." He trailed off.

"Two and a half years." Too long. But with the extra deployments and throwing everything into not coming home and having what-if conversations, it'd just gotten away from him.

Cody let out a low whistle. "The town's sure gone through an upgrade since you were last here." He set his coffee mug down and put both hands on the wheel, ready to guide the boat into the dock slip. "Everyone will be so excited to see you. It's a little unexpected, though, yeah? Your family—"

"My family's thrilled I'm back." At least, they would be once he arrived. Until he had the conversation with his dad that Amy had said would break his heart. *Please, don't let him be too disappointed . . .*

Cody shrugged. "Cool. I'm sure it's nice to be home."

Jonah grunted in response. He was excited to see everyone—really, he was—but it had been so long. The last time he had been home, Holland, his youngest sister, had just started talking with their parents about purchasing their childhood home. George and Renee White had started dreaming about RVing around the US when his dad retired from his medical practice, which had finally happened earlier this year. Amy, Mika Beth, and Halle had just signed the papers for their wedding planning business. Yes, there had been the weekly FaceTime calls, but it wasn't the same. So much had happened in two and a half years. So much he had missed out on, and he had no one to blame except for himself.

"I'll tie her off." Jonah slipped outside, the frigid air stealing any thoughts of his family.

He sucked in a deep breath. Being back on Jonathon Island felt like being home, a feeling he hadn't realized he'd been missing. After grabbing the ropes from the dock, Jonah secured the boat.

"Man, thanks again." Back in the captain's cabin, Jonah shouldered his backpack and hefted his suitcase up and over the side of the boat. "I really appreciate you giving me a ride, especially since I pulled you away from the party." Jonah grabbed Cody's hand in a firm shake.

"Sure thing. It's nothing. Glad I could help." Cody tugged his black beanie further onto his head and walked with Jonah to the end of the dock. He hooked a thumb toward the shops downtown. "Want to come back to the party with me? I'm sure everyone would love to see you."

The snow still fell softly on the island, and he wanted to stretch his legs. See the island again at his own pace. "Nah, I'm just going to head home. Thanks, man."

They said their goodbyes, and Jonah headed down the boardwalk, taking Marina Way up to Blueberry Boulevard, the snow falling harder by the time he reached the corner of Main Street. Probably made more sense to explore the new and improved downtown in the light of day.

He hightailed it past Blueberry Hill Park and Rose Road, turning west on Poppy Place, where he finally approached home. At least, the home he'd grown up in. He supposed it wasn't his home any longer. It belonged to Holland, the youngest White and the one with the biggest house since she'd bought it from their parents a year and a half ago with the inheritance money she'd received from their grandpa. His other three sisters lived in a house they rented together on the mainland, and he still didn't understand why they didn't relocate to the island and move in with Holland. Her bills had to be through the roof. Or maybe she still had enough inheritance to cover those as well.

The house didn't look anything like it had when Jonah was growing up in it. Holland had put her mark on it in more ways than one. Gone was the dingy-brown siding that had graced the upper level of the house. Instead, a rich dark-gray siding took its place. At least she had kept the white stones surrounding the base of the home. Holland had done a fantastic job with the renovations on the outside of the house—on the inside, too, from what he had seen via their video calls. To top it all off, she'd cut the costs of the renovations because she'd done most of it herself—with their dad's help, but still. The youngest White had all the talent. It didn't matter if she worked as a freelance photographer or self-taught handywoman.

The lack of lights on inside the house did surprise Jonah, however. He'd assumed everyone would have already gathered together.

When was the last time he'd talked with anyone in his family? Only a few weeks maybe, but he could have sworn the last time they talked, they'd been raving about how everyone would be coming in the week before Christmas—Mom and Dad for the entire month. And what was with no Christmas decorations? For all her classy, upscale taste in designing, Holland had a soft spot for the tacky Christmas blow-ups on the front lawn, but she hadn't even hung Christmas lights this year.

Frowning, Jonah found the hide-a-key under a ceramic frog garden ornament thing. The only ornament in the perfectly manicured beds. Jonah would need to talk to Holland about the safety of hiding the key under the only thing that looked like a hide-a-key. It stuck out like a sore thumb.

Scents of cinnamon and citrus warmed him as he

slipped the key in the lock, letting himself in before closing the door behind him with barely a click.

He could hear a movie playing in the living room. It sounded like . . . *Star Wars*? How long had Jonah tried to talk Holland into a *Star Wars* marathon? She had insisted that particular franchise was highly overrated. Not to mention, from Thanksgiving on, Holland very adamantly listened to only Christmas music and watched only Christmas classics or Hallmark specials. Maybe she'd turned over a new leaf.

He set his bags down quietly next to the kitchen bar so as not to wake up his sister, who had fallen asleep on the couch. The TV flashed a commercial for toothpaste in the dark room. Dark, because for some reason, Holland hadn't gone all *Elf* on her house and decorated for Christmas.

And why was she asleep on the couch instead of at Daisy and Hunter's engagement party—where he assumed the rest of his family was? Was she sick? Maybe he should just make his way upstairs and be there when everyone woke up in the morning—surprise! But where was the fun in that? No, he was going for the Jonah White entrance. One that would end in screams and rolling-on-the-floor laughing. He would tackle his baby sister in a hug.

Yep. She'd kill him.

It'd be worth it to hear her scream.

In a classic Holland move, his sister had completely covered herself in blankets and pillows. This surprise awakening was her own fault. She should have fallen asleep in her own bed.

He crept toward the couch.

Three . . .

Oh, the look on Holland's face when she woke up and found him there.

Two . . .

This would be the best hello in White history. It would trump the time Holland and his sisters had driven all night to see him in Norfolk years ago for his birthday.

One . . .

Jonah sucked in a deep breath and, as loud and deep as he could make his voice, declared, "Merry Christmas, ya filthy animal!"

The person on the couch—a woman with dark-brown hair instead of his sister's blonde—sat up, took one look at him, and let out a bloodcurdling scream.

Three

SHE WAS GOING TO DIE.

Forget about dying by deadline. Bronte Parker was going to die at the hands of the man—the *very* nice-looking man—who was looming over her.

The man let out a string of expletives, only they weren't quite curse words. Instead, she heard words like "son of a nutcracker."

What axe murderer didn't know how to curse?

Okay, so maybe he wasn't here to unalive her.

"Who are you? What are you doing here?" she asked while scanning the side table next to her for something to defend herself. Not that the man in front of her would hurt her—at least, she didn't think he would. Wouldn't he have already tried something when she'd been asleep? And what murderer in their right mind would loudly shout *Home Alone* quotes before killing their mark?

"Who am I?" her would-be murderer sputtered. "Who

are you? And what are you doing in my sister's house?" He looked around as if he were waiting for someone else to jump out and yell "Gotcha!"

"I paid for this house fair and square, buddy." Unwinding herself from the blanket nest she had settled in earlier, Bronte stood and grabbed a pillow to hold in front of her as a shield. As if a down-feather throw pillow would protect her against anything.

Pounding at the front door startled both of them.

The man looked from Bronte toward the front door. "Stay here," he commanded.

"Don't tell me what to do!" Bronte shot back. Hugging the pillow to her chest, she followed him.

The pounding stopped as soon as her unwanted guest opened the door, revealing Martha from Martha's on Main. Finally, a familiar face.

"Martha?" Bronte and the man said at the same time.

The man looked to Bronte and asked, "You know her?"

At the same time, Bronte looked at Martha and asked, "Who is this?"

"Oh, good." Martha looked between them. "You've met." Pushing in, Martha gave the man's arm a pat as she passed him, shaking the snow off her coat. "I heard screaming and figured I'd come over and make sure everything was okay. And I saw Hunter leaving his engagement party. He mentioned he sent Cody to pick you up. I got the feeling you didn't know about Bronte here. Good to see you home, Jonah. Or should I be calling you Major now?"

Bronte looked from the man, Jonah, to Martha, who

had made her way to the kitchen, pots and pans banging around as she . . . What was she doing?

Jonah ran a hand over his face before motioning for Bronte to precede him into the kitchen. Stubble grew thick on his cheeks, and his dark hair was cut in the close-cropped military way. His long-sleeved black thermal and plain hunter-green T-shirt were untucked from his cargo pants. Black combat boots brought up the full effect.

She could tell he was the military man from the photos on the piano. He was even more striking in person.

"What is even happening right now?" Bronte muttered.

Martha, it turned out, wasn't actually making a three-course meal. Instead, she had rummaged around until she'd found the coffee and a kettle, which she now held in the air. "Tea or coffee?" she asked in Bronte's direction.

"Tea please." Numbly, Bronte let herself slide onto the barstool at the farthest end of the bar. Martha was so calm. What had been her plan if she'd gotten here and found Bronte really being murdered? Had she called the police? Did this island even *have* a police department?

Bronte glanced over her shoulder at the movie that had been playing on the TV hanging on the wall opposite the couch. The end credits for *The Empire Strikes Back* rolled on one half of the screen, a Christmas advertisement for a car on the other. Her computer and notebook sat forgotten on the leather ottoman in front of the yellow velvet sectional.

This had to all be some weird dream, right? A punishment for turning on a movie instead of getting to work.

She should have figured out how to work the fireplace, gotten the atmosphere all moody, and set to work.

"Martha, what's going on? Where is my family? This woman claims to have paid to stay here." Jonah had followed Bronte into the kitchen, but thankfully, not to her retreat at the far end of the counter. He laid his hands flat on the speckled granite bar top. He must have had a stocking cap on at some point, because his hair, even with his short, cropped cut, stood every which way.

"Jonah, your family, for whatever reason, decided now would be a good time to run off on a Caribbean cruise."

"What?" Jonah sputtered out.

"Yes, apparently they got a killer last-minute deal. Your mother was going on and on about how she's always wanted to do a tropical Christmas. Crazy, if you ask me." Martha pulled a mug out of the cabinet and added a tea bag before pouring hot water over it. "Anywho, Holland rented the place to Ms. Parker here until they get back." Martha nodded in Bronte's direction, and Bronte gave Jonah a limp wave. Martha set down the cup of hot tea— chamomile, from the smell of it—in front of Bronte before handing a cup of coffee to Jonah. "Good to have so many young people returning to the island. My Declan's back again, you know." She patted Jonah's cheek as she turned back to the cabinet, pulling out another mug and filling it with coffee.

"I'm just back for the holidays."

"You can't stay here," Bronte blurted.

Martha and Jonah turned their attention back to her. Jonah scratched behind his ear. "It's my family's house."

"Which I rented until the twenty-eighth. And I didn't intend to have house guests."

Raising a brow, Martha leaned back against the counter, holding the coffee up to her face, letting the steam warm her. "Hmm. Seems you're both in a bit of a pickle."

Bronte ran a finger around the rim of her mug. Ugh, she couldn't very well kick the guy out of his family's house. "Does the island have any other place I can rent for the next couple of weeks?"

"There isn't any other place to rent on the island." Martha confirmed her fear. Bronte was going to have to go back home. "With all the families visiting for the holidays, even those who generally have extra space are full up at the moment."

Bronte hated the tears pricking the backs of her eyes. She hadn't realized how much she was looking forward to being away from normal life in order to get this book written. True, she could probably find some other destination to stay at for the next few weeks, but finding a place, booking, travel—it would all take time. Time she didn't really have. Home would be the best choice. She grabbed her phone off the side table and swiped the screen. "I'll work on finding another place."

Jonah ran his hand down his face again. "No, you don't need to do that. I can figure out somewhere else to stay. Maybe the apartment over the clinic?"

"It's rented out to the traveling doctor, Dr. Nova Lake. She's a tiny thing," Martha said. "And besides, even if she was visiting somewhere else for the holidays, Dr. Nova has a cat, and unless something has changed while you've been traversing the world with that Army of yours, you don't do cats."

"Oh." Jonah blinked. "I'll figure something out. I'll call around." He pulled his phone out of his back pocket.

"Jonah Ray White, it is almost eleven thirty. You'll do no such thing." Martha batted the air like she was going to hit Jonah's phone out of his hand.

Jonah paused, finger hovering over the screen of his phone. "Oh, right." He let it fall to the counter with a clatter. "Do you have an extra bed or couch I can crash on for the night?" He flashed a hopeful smile at Martha.

"Nope. I have a lot of extended family that came in, plus all the kids. My house is stuffed fuller than a can of sardines."

Bronte's chest fell. That would have made things a lot easier.

"I guess it's too much to hope for that the Grand Hotel has a room ready?"

"Rooms won't be ready for guests for another couple of months at least."

"The Island House Inn, then," Jonah suggested.

"All booked up for the holidays." They were all silent for a beat before Martha straightened. "Well, now that you two are all settled, I'm going to make my way back home."

"You're going to leave me alone with him?" Bronte sputtered, shooting up from the stool.

Martha looked Bronte up and down before her gaze flittered over to Jonah. "You'll be fine. Jonah is a gentleman. A soldier. He knows how to respect a woman. Right, Jonah?"

"Of course, ma'am."

"Pshaw. Don't ma'am me, mister. Even if I did used to change your diapers in the Sunday school nursery way back when." With that, she shuffled out of the kitchen, taking the cup of coffee with her. Bronte wasn't sure how the woman expected to sleep after all their excitement plus adding a cup of coffee on top of that. Maybe she'd made decaf?

Bronte heard the door open and close. She looked back to her apparent roommate for the night. He looked exhausted. Bags hung under his piercing blue eyes, making Bronte wonder how long it had been since he'd had a good night's sleep.

Jonah pushed at his sleeves, revealing tattoos that snaked their way up his arm, disappearing under his shirt and making Bronte wonder how far they went. Did they stop at his elbow? Wrap their way up his arms to his chest? Arms and chest that looked very muscular, if the way his T-shirt pulled was any indication. She swallowed.

"So, Bronte, was it?"

"Yeah, and Jonah?"

Jonah nodded. "Look, I'm really sorry about this. It's all my fault. I probably should have given my family a heads-up that I was coming in for Christmas this year. It had been so long, though, and I thought surprising them would be more fun."

Now that the excitement of Jonah's ambush and Martha's visit, and the disappointment of being told "Just kidding! You can't stay here" was sinking in, Bronte found that she was exhausted.

She held a hand up, cutting off whatever Jonah was

rambling on about. "You know what? I'm tired. I think I'm just going to go to bed." She gathered her laptop and notebook, looking longingly at the yellow velvet couch, wishing she were able to stay.

"Okay. I really am sorry. We'll figure something out tomorrow."

Bronte just nodded as she passed Jonah and trudged up the stairs.

Only when she stood behind the closed bedroom door did she allow herself to breathe. She took in the blue floral bedspread, the antique dresser, the perfect alcove with a window that looked out over Jonathon Island and onto Lake Huron.

It had been perfect.

Even if she hadn't gotten started on work right away, she knew this place held the magic she didn't believe in to get her book written. Now she could feel that magic slipping through her fingers. Tomorrow she'd leave on the first ferry and find a place to stay on the mainland. She supposed it'd have to work. Magic or not.

Leaning up against the door, Bronte pushed out a breath, determined not to think about all the ways staying in a house with a complete stranger could go wrong—even if Martha had vetted him. Jonah seemed safe enough, but Bronte locked the door and wedged a chair under the handle for good measure.

After a quick shower, she fell onto the bed with a sigh and grabbed her phone off the nightstand to look for hotels on the mainland. The two closest were showing no vacancy. Did she really want to stay somewhere that wasn't here, or would it be better to just head home? She'd like to be away for Christmas, but she couldn't afford another two days of travel.

Sighing, Bronte shot off a message to Lexi, who would definitely still be up working. The woman was a workaholic.

Bronte

Looks like I'm headed back home.

Lexi

Wait, what? I'm calling.

Bronte

Don't call. I'm fine. A family member showed up at the house and didn't get the memo that the family was gone for Christmas. Since there isn't any other place to rent on the island, I'm just going to head back home to get this book done.

Lexi

Why don't you fly here? Mom and I would love to have you.

Bronte

Can't. Have too much to write. Thanks for the offer though.

She was in the middle of messaging Holland on the rental app, trying her best to explain the situation, when her phone rang.

This late, there'd only be one person who decided to forgo their text thread and call. Bronte swiped to answer. "I told you not to call. It's so late, shouldn't you be in bed already?"

"It's not even midnight in LA." Lexi brushed her off.

Right. The two-hour time zone difference.

"Are you safe with this other family member in the house?"

"Yes, I'm safe." Bronte looked over to the door to her bedroom. Jonah may have scared her, but upon closer examination from the safe distance across the full length of the bar, he had kind, tired eyes and appeared as frustrated by the situation as she was. "He looked harmless enough, and I have my door locked and a chair under the handle." The things you picked up when you bounced back and forth in foster homes your entire life. Quick people-reading and intruder safety.

The faint sounds of a keyboard clacking came through the phone. "Is there some kind of Christmas special on fish or something up there this week?"

Bronte frowned. "I don't know. Why?" She dragged her suitcase out of the closet where she'd stashed it earlier, then tossed it on the bed.

"Because I'm checking the availability of hotels in the area, and there are none. And right now, I'm showing flights being delayed."

Stalking over to the dresser, Bronte pulled out the contents of the top drawer. Surely that was a mistake. All the flights couldn't be delayed. "I think there's another airport a little farther out."

A few more taps filtered through the phone. "Nope, looks like all those are delayed as well."

"Then I'll just take the ferry back over to the mainland

and figure something out until the flights open back up." Bronte cringed.

"And if you can't get a flight?" Lexi voiced the fear dancing through Bronte's brain.

Bronte threw her hands up. "Then I'll rent a car and drive myself home."

"You hate driving."

"I know." Bronte moved back to the dresser and yanked the second drawer open. She stuffed the contents of the drawer into her suitcase a little more forcefully than necessary. Sighing, she leaned on the side of the bed. "Look, I don't know what I'm going to do. I'll just figure it out in the morning."

"Are you sure?"

"Yep." Bronte pasted on a fake smile, hoping it came across in the sound of her voice. The smile, not the fakeness.

After saying goodbye, Bronte went back to making sure she had repacked everything. Having completed the task, she let herself plop on the bed. She just needed a good night's sleep, and then she'd figure this out in the morning.

So long as her initial impression stayed true and she wasn't murdered first, that was.

All Jonah had wanted was to come home and surprise his family, say what he needed to say—with no hearts being broken—and then . . . something. He didn't have a plan after that. Joke was on him, apparently. Although, why hadn't the family told him they were planning on a cruise or resort or wherever sunny place they were? He would have loved time with his family on the beach. At least the beach would have definitely made the news he needed to tell go down a little easier. Probably.

Or maybe he should take this as a sign. A sign that he had made the wrong decision.

But his house guest—no, not his, she was Holland's *paying* house guest—had gathered her stuff and stomped upstairs before they could formulate any kind of plan. Which room was she staying in? Knowing Holland, she'd probably given Bronte *his* old room. A few minutes later, he heard a shower turn on, the location of the sound confirming that was exactly what his sister had done.

This was a mess. Jonah ran a hand over his face and back through his hair. For once in his life, he'd like something to just work out the way it was supposed to.

His phone chimed multiple times with incoming texts. The first came from his childhood friend Oliver, who was the co-owner of a small publishing house. He wondered if Oliver would be home for Christmas. It would be great to catch up with him at some point.

Oliver

Heard you made it home for Christmas. While you're there, can you vet Dani's fiancé? Let me know if he's as great as my sister says he is. Did you hear Mr. Johnson's bookstore is up for sale? Remember all the times we hid out reading comics in the summers?

So, not coming home for Christmas then. Not able to think about vetting anyone at the moment, Jonah switched to the second text.

Cody
So, Mia probably told me at some point, but apparently, I wasn't listening. I'm pretty sure your family is out of town, and someone is renting your sister's house.

Jonah snorted. "Yep. Would have been nice for you to remember that half an hour ago, Cody." He sent back a thumbs-up emoji.

Laying his phone on the counter, Jonah opened the fridge. He should be exhausted after twenty-six hours of travel, but of course his body still thought he was in Germany. Not like he would be able to sleep with a stranger in the house anyway.

His phone chirped again. Why was he so popular tonight?

Letting the fridge door close, he set down the carton of eggs and grabbed his phone, seeing an incoming text from Reeves, one of the guys back on base who was holding down the fort while Jonah was on leave. Instead of answering it, Jonah hit the Call button. It was mid-morning halfway around the world at Landstuhl Regional Medical Center.

"You get in okay?" Reeves said in lieu of a greeting. "How's the family?"

"The family is MIA. Apparently, they decided now would be a good time to go on a family cruise in the Bahamas." Or something like that.

"I mean, can you really blame them? What's the weather like there right now?"

Jonah looked over to the picture windows that led into the backyard. For the most part, he could only see his reflection, but he knew the snow had probably started coming down. "Cold and snowy."

"Right. See? Sounds awful. I'd be stealing away to the beach as well." There was a beat, and Jonah could practically see Reeves take a gulp from what he knew was piping hot coffee. He was fairly certain that his friend's esophagus had been replaced with a metal pipe. "So, what's the plan now? Are you going to spend your leave chilling at home until they return? How long are they gone for?"

"I haven't gotten that far yet. Not only are they gone, but Holland rented the house out. There's a woman here who I'm not sure is happy I showed up."

Reeves cleared his throat. "Oooh, a gorgeous woman, I hope."

Jonah thought back to the cute button nose, rosebud lips, and that hair. The curls rivaled his niece Ruby's favorite Disney princess, Merida. If only they were red instead of dark ashy-brown. Her wide eyes had quickly turned stormy gray when she'd found out she and Jonah were stuck there together for the night. "She's all right."

"There are worse ways to spend a leave." Reeves's chuckle let Jonah know he could hear through his lie.

"I am not sharing a house with a stranger for two weeks," Jonah deadpanned as he grabbed a skillet from the cabinet and put it on the stove. "I need to see if I can reach my family."

"Well, if you can't, it's a big house from what I hear. Maybe you can just avoid the hot renter until it's time to return to base."

"For two weeks? Hardly." Jonah cracked three eggs that

sizzled when he dropped them onto the hot skillet. This had to be a sign. Amy was right, and he shouldn't have come. "I don't really know what I'm going to do if I can't get ahold of them."

"Surely someone has their travel plans. What about that island busybody you told me about? The one that knows everything about everyone."

"Martha?"

"That's the one. Get with her tomorrow, see if you can get your family's itinerary and fly out to each of their ports."

Jonah's mood started to lift. Maybe Reeves was onto something. Why hadn't he thought of that when Martha was here earlier?

He glanced at the clock, tempted to call Martha and start making arrangements now, but he decided he didn't want the ten-minute lecture for calling so late—even if Jonah knew she'd still be up. Maybe he could still have his Christmas surprise after all. "That might work. As long as the snow lets up and the ferry is running." Jonah glanced back out the picture window—not that he could see much. With the lights on, the window had turned into a makeshift mirror of sorts. If the ferry wasn't working, maybe Pete, the mostly retired pilot who now flew the air taxi, would be up for flying him over to the mainland.

After Jonah ended the call, he put the phone down on the counter and dumped the eggs onto a plate. He wandered over to the couch and flicked off the TV, which was now playing *Return of the Jedi*. He didn't feel much like watching anything, so instead, he pulled a book off his sister's shelf. A blue cover, something about kisses and bodyguards. Holland had told him about this one. Something light and easy to read to help his mind wind down.

He sat down at the kitchen table, elbows framing his plate of eggs, and cracked the spine open. He lost himself in the book, and twenty minutes later, plate empty, he refilled his coffee and made his way to the couch. Holland had been right. This one was funny. Romantic comedy might not be the genre everyone expected him to read, but with four sisters, he read the same books they did so they could talk about them. They also returned the favor and read the Brandon Sanderson books he recommended— well, Holland and Amy did. It even seemed like Ruby, Amy's ten-year-old daughter, was going to like fantasy as well. Mika Beth and Halle would rather shove pencils in their eyes.

He drained the last of his coffee, then put the empty mug on the side table, nose still stuck in the book. Tomorrow he'd figure out how to meet up with the rest of his family and leave Bronte to do whatever it was she'd planned to do alone.

Once he met up with his family, he'd figure out how to have the conversation with his dad—somehow without ruining the last part of his dad's vacation.

Yep, it would all work out. It had to.

Four

Date December 16
Days until Deadline 20
Words to be written 89,973

BRONTE'S EYES FLEW OPEN.

Sunlight streamed through the window—a window that took her six point three seconds to realize wasn't in her apartment. A few seconds more, she remembered why.

Jonathon Island. The place she was going to finish the Pike Family Saga.

Except that she wasn't. She would be heading home instead because *someone* decided to show up for Christmas without telling anyone, and now she had to figure out how to get off this island and back home so she could finish her book on time.

No use delaying the inevitable. Maybe she'd get lucky and be able to sneak out without having to see Jonah.

Something about him threw her off. She'd expected him to get angry that she was here and his family wasn't. Instead, he'd let her stay and told her they'd figure it out today. But there wasn't anything to figure out. There was no way she could get work done with someone else in the house.

Last night she'd been gung-ho to make him leave, but she couldn't kick him out of his family's house. It was on her to find somewhere else to stay, and staying on island sounded impossible. Martha had said everything was already booked and put the cherry on top when she'd told Jonah he couldn't stay at the apartment over the clinic (whatever that meant) because the doctor renting it owned a cat.

After firing off a quick text to Mia asking if she could possibly get a ride back to the docks, Bronte threw on a clean pair of black leggings and an even blacker sweatshirt. She double-checked that nothing had been left in the antique dresser she'd so carefully unpacked into the day before, then she stuffed everything down into her suitcase and zipped it up. She just needed to make it back home so she could start writing.

Room packed up, Bronte stood, hands on her hips, surveying to make sure she didn't leave anything. After a quick check in the bathroom, she heaved the suitcase up to her hip and tiptoed into the hallway. She practically held her breath as she made her way down the stairs, still hoping not to wake Jonah, not exactly sure where he'd landed for the night. It wasn't until she got to the bottom step that she heard noises in the kitchen. She peered over the banister, down the hallway, and into the kitchen.

Jonah stood at the stove, dressed in gray sweatpants and a dark-blue shirt that strained against his muscles. It should be illegal to look that good in sweatpants. If Bronte wore the same outfit, she'd be labeled homeless, yet somehow on Jonah it just looked . . . right.

"Are you going to stand there all day, or are you going to come in here and get something to eat?" Jonah asked, never turning from the stove.

Bronte propped her suitcase on the wall next to the stairs so it wouldn't fall over due to the missing wheel, then followed the scent of something amazing into the kitchen. She made it all the way to stand next to Jonah before she heard something fall behind her. Both she and Jonah turned to find her suitcase in the middle of the entryway. Good for nothing piece of junk.

Jonah looked at Bronte, one eyebrow quirked up. "Going somewhere?"

"You can't expect me to stay here, and I'm not about to kick you out of your family's house. I mean, you leaving would be the polite thing to do and all, since I've paid to stay here, but seeing as apparently there isn't anywhere else on this island to rent, one of us is going to have to go. It might as well be me."

Jonah's warm laugh made her stomach dip.

"It's not funny." Panic rose in her chest at all she had to get done. "I have work to finish, and it's not going to get done with me traveling all over the place. I'm just going to head home and work from there. It wasn't the plan, but I'll just have to make it work."

"I don't think you're going anywhere."

She hadn't expected that reaction. "W-well," she stammered. "That's very nice of you. Did you find another place to stay until your family gets back?"

Jonah winced as he shook a jar of spice over the eggs and potatoes he was cooking. "About that . . ."

Bronte's stomach clenched.

After setting the wooden spoon he'd been stirring with on the ceramic spoon rest, Jonah took Bronte by the shoulders and pointed her toward the picture windows. "I got ahold of my sister this morning, and after I got a lecture on keeping up with my emails—because apparently Mom emailed me about the cruise two weeks ago, which I completely missed—we figured out it would take a small fortune for me to fly out to meet them, so they told me to just stay here for now. They'll be back stateside on the twenty-sixth. I'm planning on flying down and meeting them then. I'd get a ride back to the mainland and find a hotel there, but it looks like that's not possible for the next couple of days at least. We're a little stuck."

Snow covered everything in white. In fact, where there had once been patio furniture, now there was just one big lawn of white. It reached halfway up the picture window, and snow was still coming down.

Bronte's mouth fell open. "What do you mean we're stuck? We can't be stuck. I-I have work to do." None of which required her to go anywhere. Hadn't she just said she didn't have time to travel? Now it seemed she had all the time in the world to work.

"Guess you'll be working here, then." Jonah pulled a

plate from the cabinet and set it on the counter. "That is, if it's portable. I'm assuming it is? What do you do?"

"How long until we can get out?" Bronte asked, ignoring his questions.

"A couple days at least."

Bronte's chest tightened.

"But the fridge is well stocked, I have the faucets dripping so the pipes don't freeze, and there are generators in the garage in case the electricity goes out."

"Electricity goes out?" Bronte squeaked. There was only one way this nightmare could get even worse—and that was it.

Jonah shrugged. "I wouldn't be worried about it. I think the last time the electricity went out because of a snowstorm I was fourteen, so it's been a while."

That didn't make Bronte feel any better. This entire trip had gone to pot. Why not throw in a little power outage with a hot Army man?

Ninety thousand. Ninety thousand. Ninety thousand.

The reminder was back, chanting in her head. If she didn't get started soon, she might have a mental breakdown.

"Would you mind getting some coffee going while I finish making breakfast? I poured the last of the pot a half hour ago." Jonah held up his mug, draining what was left.

"Um, sure." Bronte's gaze flickered to the paperback that was open, pages down on the table. A rom-com. Bronte rolled her eyes. Between the book on the table and having drunk an entire pot of coffee, had Jonah slept at all? It was only seven thirty.

"Coffee filters are in that cabinet there." Jonah nodded to the cabinet next to him as he dished out the eggs onto a plate, storing the plate in the microwave to keep them warm before putting bacon in the pan.

Bronte's mouth watered. She loved bacon. But coffee. She needed to make coffee. Not that she'd ever made coffee before. She didn't drink the stuff. It tasted like burnt mud-water. Not that she'd ever had burnt mud-water, but if she had, it would've tasted like coffee. She could figure this out—she had done plenty of research on making coffee for her books, given that the Pike sisters were all obsessed with the stuff. Plus, she was a successful thirty-two-year-old woman. Making a pot of coffee should be no problem.

She opened the cabinet and stared at the assortment of mugs and carafes and bags of coffee.

"Holland likes her coffee, and she hosts Bible studies here and always has the best on hand. She has her beans shipped in from one of her favorite roasters and makes her own syrups. I prefer mine black, but I do have to say, my sister can make a mean mixed coffee drink."

Bronte nodded, finally seeing a box of paper filters. Step one down, she turned to the complicated-looking coffee setup. How had Martha done this the night before? Bronte had been standing right there when the older woman had brewed a pot, but she hadn't been paying the least bit of attention. Bronte thought she'd just have to push a button and coffee would magically start brewing, but this was unlike any coffee maker she had ever seen. This looked more like a science experiment waiting to happen.

She looked over to Jonah. "I'm . . ."

"I know it looks complicated, but you just put the filter and grounds in the top there and hit that button there. Ow!" Jonah jerked back as the bacon grease popped.

Bronte shook her head. Grounds? Right. But exactly how many grounds went into a pot of coffee? She picked up the bag and flipped it over, searching for directions. "I'm not a coffee drinker, so I don't really know . . ." She sounded ridiculous. Who couldn't make coffee?

"Oh! Sorry. Here, switch with me."

Before she could say anything, Jonah reached over, fingers curling over her hips as he moved her in front of the bacon. She stared down at the spatula in her hand, halfway wondering how it'd gotten there so quickly.

"So, if you don't drink coffee, what do you drink? Tea? Hot chocolate?" Jonah asked as he expertly moved from the grinder, pouring the grounds into the filter that was at the top of the science-equipment-looking thing.

"Tea." Bronte jumped when the bacon popped. As much as she loved bacon, she'd forgotten how much she hated cooking it. "You know, this is a lot easier when you cook it in the oven." The bacon popped again. "Less of a mess, and no casualties."

"No way." Jonah grabbed the kettle that still sat on the back of the stove from when Martha had made tea the night before and turned to fill it at the sink. "Bacon is definitely better cooked on the stovetop."

"It's like going to war for some bacon." As soon as she said it, she wished she could stuff the words back into her mouth. Hadn't Martha said Jonah was in the Army? Would he take offense to that statement? "I mean—"

"You're right, but what's a few war wounds in exchange for protein goodness?" Jonah set the kettle back on the stove and bumped Bronte's shoulder. "Speaking of, that bacon about done? It's looking a little extra crispy."

"Oh!" Bronte pulled at the paper towels, grabbing a wad and tossing it on the plate next to the stove before transferring the bacon. Jonah was right. It was extra crispy. She bit her lip. "Sorry. I hope you like your bacon crunchy."

Jonah plucked a piece off the top of the pile and popped it in his mouth with a very audible crunch. "It's perfect, but that's for you." He pointed to a wooden box on the counter. "And my sister keeps all the tea in there. If you want to pick one out, I'll get the table set and you can eat."

Deciding against digging in her luggage for her favorite tea, Bronte settled on a cinnamon teabag. "Are you not going to eat?"

Jonah set her plate at the table before picking up his book and moving to another seat. "Nah, I already ate. My body's still in a different time zone."

Bronte nodded as she finished pouring water into her mug. Her middle warmed at the realization Jonah had cooked breakfast for her. "You didn't have to . . ." She motioned to the plate of food as she sat down with her steaming mug.

"It's nothing. I was up anyway."

Bronte nodded, her eyes darting to the window. The snow was still falling, although maybe it had let up a little bit? How could something so beautiful also be so frustrating? She had wanted it to snow while she was here—in theory—but now she wasn't so sure. Would it have been better to be stuck here in the snow by herself? Would she have known about dripping the water or the generator? How did one even start a generator? Jonah had said they'd probably be stuck here for a couple of days, so as long as she kept her head down and got the words in, she should be able to still make her deadline. With three days to spare for the read-through, as long as she put in at least seven thousand words a day, give or take, she would make it.

The best Bronte had ever done in a day was four thousand, but it was fine. She wouldn't think about it. The food in front of her started making her stomach turn. She could do this.

Couldn't she?

Taking her phone out of her pocket, Bronte sent Lexi a text explaining the situation and that she'd be staying on Jonathon Island after all. She'd barely hit Send before her phone started ringing.

"You're staying? In that house? With a strange man?" Lexi fired off before Bronte could even say hello. It was five thirty in LA. How was Lexi even up at this hour?

Bronte's eyes darted up to Jonah, who was focused on the book in front of him. "It's fine, Lex. It's not like either of us has any other choice anyway. The snow is really coming down."

Lexi let out a grunt. "Put him on."

"Lexi—"

"Let me talk to him, Bronte."

Cringing, Bronte held the phone out toward Jonah. "Um, my friend would like to talk to you."

Jonah set his book face down on the table and took the phone from Bronte, eyebrows raised.

Bronte didn't know what Lexi was telling Jonah, but she had a pretty good idea. Jonah's face gave nothing away as he calmly listened and agreed to whatever Lexi told him on the other end of the line.

"Yes, ma'am."

Yes, ma'am what? Bronte would bet Lexi was having a cow at being addressed so formally, and what was he yes ma'aming her about?

"Jonah White." An amused sigh. "Jonah Ray White." A beat of silence. "I give you my solemn word."

Bronte wanted to roll her eyes. Solemn word. But more so, she wanted to know what solemn word he'd promised Lexi. Why hadn't she put Lexi on speaker instead of just handing over the phone?

"Lexi, was it?" He paused while Bronte assumed Lexi was confirming her name. "Well, Lexi, I hope that you have a wonderful day Christmas shopping with your mom."

Wait, what? Lexi had told Jonah she was going Christmas shopping? They'd talked for a whole two minutes on the phone, and they were friends all of a sudden?

Finished, he handed the phone back to Bronte and picked up his book.

"Hello?"

"Okay, I feel a little bit better about you staying with him, but I'm still running the full stalking gambit on him." Bronte could hear Lexi typing on her laptop. Full stalking gambit started with Facebook, Instagram, and then moved on to more obscure places like Google and LinkedIn. "Goodness, Bront. This man is gorgeous."

Bronte's gaze darted back to Jonah, who looked completely engrossed in his book, but from the grin on his face, she wondered if he'd heard what Lexi had said. Bronte turned in her chair, as if that would keep Jonah from overhearing their conversation. "I guess."

"There is no guessing about it. This man is as fine as any leading man. And four sisters? *And* he's military?" The more Lexi's stalking turned up, the more it sounded as if she was on Jonah's side of things.

"So, you've deemed me safe?" Her eggs were getting cold, and Bronte was ready to wrap up this conversation.

"Yes, yes. If anything turns up, I'll let you know. I've also threatened him within an inch of his life if he hurts you."

Bronte's eyes slid closed. "You did not give him the Liam Neeson speech, did you?"

"You bet I did."

Sighing, Bronte glanced toward Jonah, still reading his book, but his smile had grown even more. "I'm going to let you go." Bronte ended the call before Lexi could protest. This day had gotten off to a fabulous start.

But whatever the case, she still had ninety thousand words to write. And it looked like she was going to have to do it not in peace and quiet but in the company of a much-too-handsome distraction.

Not ideal. But when had life ever given her what was ideal?

Bronte Parker would make the best of her lemons, just like she always did.

Jonah bit the inside of his mouth to keep from smiling. He didn't know Bronte's friend Lexi, but hearing the "Liam Neeson speech" coming from the sweet but stern voice on the other end of the phone reminded him of something one of his sisters would do. Lexi didn't have anything to worry about, he'd be gone soon enough. Hopefully.

"I am so sorry about her." Bronte picked up her fork and stabbed her eggs.

"No problem at all." Jonah turned the page of the book he was reading. Or pretending to read. Since Bronte had answered her phone, Jonah had read the same paragraph three times before giving up and just turning the page. "It's good to have someone looking out for you."

"Yeah." Bronte crunched off a bit of bacon. "It's really coming down, isn't it? Any chance of it stopping soon?"

"This is nothing." Jonah lifted his cup toward the winter wonderland. "You should have been here for the snow of '08. Almost completely snowed us in. Snow up to the top of the windows."

"That's"—Bronte paused, and Jonah could visibly see her swallow—"a lot of snow."

"What? It doesn't snow where you live?" Jonah's eyebrow quirked.

"It does. Just not like this."

Jonah took another drink of his coffee, his eyes never

drifting from Bronte. When she'd come down this morning ready to leave, his heart had dropped. Not because she expected him to leave—he completely understood that. He didn't want to be trapped in a house with a stranger any more than she did, but maybe he didn't want to be trapped here all alone either.

"So, what brings you to Jonathon Island? You mentioned work?"

Bronte wrapped her hands around her mug and stared into the backyard. "I came here to write a book."

"Like a *book* book? A real book? I didn't see that one coming. Most visitors on the island are here because of Daisy's YouTube channel. Daisy Decker, she—"

"Yeah, I'm familiar with her channel." Bronte brushed him off with a wave of her hand.

"I don't actually know her, but she's dating my buddy, Hunter. Or I guess they're engaged now. Anyway, I've heard there's been an influx of visitors to the island because of Daisy's show. Well, an influx compared to the usual numbers since the Grand burned. Before the fire, Jonathon Island was a pretty big destination for families. There was talk of abandoning the island, but . . ." Jonah trailed off. He was rambling, and Bronte's eyes were getting that glazed-over look. "But a real book? Are you writing about Daisy?"

"Yes, like a real book. No, not about Daisy." He could be mistaken, but was that a blush on Bronte's cheeks?

Color him fascinated. Jonah leaned his chin into his hand. "Reading is my favorite. Tell me about it. What do you write?"

Bronte set down her tea, opting for picking at her eggs with her fork. Was she going to tell him?

After a pause, Bronte put her fork next to her plate and wrapped her hands back around her mug. "I write about messy family relationships. The series I'm working on tells the story of a single mother and her two daughters as they navigate the ups and downs of their lives and relationships."

Jonah blinked. Her series sounded . . . boring.

"It's literary fiction," she followed up when Jonah didn't say anything.

Jonah slowly nodded. "I can't say that I've read a lot of literary fiction."

"What do you generally read?"

Jonah lifted the book he was almost finished with. "I read a lot of rom-coms." Bronte's eyebrows shot up. "Seriously. When you have four sisters, it just happens, but when I'm not reading hot-pink books, I love a good fantasy. Brandon Sanderson is my favorite."

Bronte snorted.

"What?"

"Everyone likes Sanderson."

Jonah shrugged. "Be that as it may, I still enjoy his writing. He's created an epic world that you can escape to, and what is reading but a good escape?" Jonah picked up his phone, scrolling to the eReader shop app. "What did you say the first title in your series is?"

"I didn't." Bronte's eyes sparkled over her mug as she took another drink of tea. Jonah didn't think she was going to tell him, and he was going to have to search through all the "Bronte" hits the store app gave him when she finally said *Color of the Stars.*

Jonah's mouth dropped open, and he let his phone drop to the table. "You're B.L. Parker? I've read that one, and I saw the movie."

"Really? And what did you think?"

He paused. "I hated it."

"Oh." Bronte's face fell.

"Sorry, going on, like, an hour of sleep. No filter."

"It's fine. No worries."

"No, it's not fine." The way her shoulders drooped, her mouth turned down—he'd insulted her. Maybe even hurt her feelings. The last thing he'd wanted to do. "Don't get me wrong. The writing was amazing, but the story was just so . . ." Jonah trailed off, the word not coming to him.

"Long?" Bronte tried.

Her books, at over seven hundred pages each, were long. But that wasn't it. "No."

"Stupid?"

"Definitely not." He'd only known her for a few hours, but he could see the intelligence snapping behind those big gray eyes.

"Unbelievable?"

"No. Just . . . sad." It was a simple word, but it was the one that came to him. "I found the story really sad."

Bronte scoffed. "It's real life, Jonah, and most of the time, real life is sad."

What had happened to this woman that she believed *that?* "It's okay for books to not always reflect real life. In fact, I prefer them to be happy."

"Well, you read rom-com." Bronte nodded at the book face up on the table. "They say write what you know, so I did."

Had someone hurt her? A surge of protectiveness washed over him. "Bronte—"

Bronte's eyes flashed to him, and he could be mistaken, but there may have been tears in them. A blink later, they cleared. "Enough about me and my *boring, sad* books. What about you? What do you do? Martha called you Major? That's Army, right?"

"Correct. I'm a surgeon."

"Wow. I bet that's exciting. You mentioned being in a different time zone. Where are you stationed?"

"Germany. Have you ever been?"

Bronte's eyes brightened. "It's on my bucket list. The closest I've ever been to Germany is the Munich airport for a layover. I promised myself I would make it back there one day."

"You should. It's a beautiful country." But even with it being a beautiful country, it didn't compare to Jonathon Island and the life Jonah wanted to build here.

"So, how long have you been a surgeon?"

"About ten years." Jonah took a sip of his coffee, gaze drifting to the backyard. "Feels longer though."

"So, you don't enjoy it."

"What makes you say that?"

"It's written"—Bronte waved a hand—"all over you. You don't look like you enjoy your job."

Jonah shrugged. "I've been at it for a while. I guess I'm just ready for something new."

"Like what?"

Jonah paused. While Bronte seemed nice, he didn't need to burden her with his own personal dilemmas. Best to stick with the facts. "The plan has always been that I'll take over my dad's practice once I retire from the Army. He's got a temp doctor in there now—"

"The traveling doctor with the cat staying in the apartment over the clinic?" Bronte cut in.

"Right." Jonah nodded. "She's here now, but Dad's been hanging on to his share for me."

"I sense a lack of enthusiasm for that too. You don't want to move back here?"

"What? No—I mean, I've always loved the idea of raising a big family here. It's a great place."

"You don't want to take over the practice, then?"

You do this, and you'll break Dad's heart. And if you're planning on breaking Dad's heart, don't bother coming back at all.

Jonah cleared his throat, pushed back from the table, and made his way to the coffeepot for a refill. How did this woman see right through him? "Like I said. It's always been the plan. My great-grandpa started the practice. His son took over, and then my dad took over. Now it's my turn."

"Hmm." Bronte picked up her fork and started back in on her eggs. They had to be cold by now. "So how does Doctor Jonah White not know that his entire family is gone for Christmas?"

Not ready to sit back at the table, Jonah scanned through Holland's homemade syrups in the fridge. Deciding on cinnamon and vanilla, he added them to his mug with a splash of cream. "It was supposed to be a surprise."

"I think you accomplished that on all accounts."

"Indeed, I have." Jonah raised his mug in a mock salute before taking a long gulp. He blanched. Too sweet. "In my defense," he said as he dumped the sugary concoction down the drain and poured himself another cup before sitting back at the table, "no one said anything about a Christmas vacation when I talked to them last, and I never got my mother's email with the plans and invitation."

"Sounds like you need to check your email more often."

Jonah pointed a finger. "You are probably exactly right."

"You're one of those people with, like, three thousand unread emails in their inbox, aren't you?"

More like seventy-three thousand, but he wouldn't admit to that. "Something like that. So . . ." Time for a subject change. "Bronte, author of epically long, sad books, what's the plan?"

Bronte blinked up at him as if the change in subject had given her whiplash. "Plan?"

"Yes, plan. We're stuck here, and you have work to do. What does that look like?"

"Oh, well"—Bronte pushed away her plate—"I guess I'll take my suitcase back up to my room and unpack again. I have quite a bit to write over the next couple of weeks, so I guess that looks like me just sitting at my computer getting all the words out of my head and onto the blank page until I'm done."

Where did that leave him until then? What did one do with a writer?

Her suitcase was still where it had fallen in the entry-way when she'd come downstairs. The thing looked like it weighed a ton. That was something he could do. "Okay then. I'll take your suitcase back upstairs. If you want to get your computer, you can get started. I'll make sure there's hot water on the stove for more tea."

Before she could say anything, Jonah rushed out of the kitchen and grabbed Bronte's suitcase. He was right, it did weigh a ton. He hauled it upstairs, then deposited it in the room at the end of the hall that Holland had labeled with a wreath and sign.

Maybe this wasn't the Christmas vacation he had planned, but he could say that having a little extra time before he talked about his future with his dad had him . . . relieved.

Now to find something to do for the next week and a half until he could fly out and meet everyone.

Five

SHE WANTED TO SCREAM.

Three hours later, and she only had fifteen hundred words, give or take, to show for it. She backspaced her last sentence. Make that fourteen hundred eighty-nine. She ran her fingers through her hair, massaging her scalp. Her eyes landed on her empty mug. Tea. She needed more tea.

She pushed back from the table, then walked over to the stove and turned the burner on under the kettle. Jonah had been sitting for a while on the couch reading but had disappeared about half an hour ago and hadn't returned. Maybe he was taking a nap. A nap sounded nice. Maybe that's what she needed to push through.

Ninety thousand. Ninety thousand. Ninety thousand.

Nope. She definitely didn't need a nap. She needed to figure out what happened to the Pike sisters.

Bronte opened a package of her favorite tea, then

poured the hot water over the bag and slunk back to the table. The wooden chair was starting to hurt her rear end. Now that the couch was available, she would move locations. Maybe the yellow velvet couch held magical plotting powers, and if she sat there, her writing would start to flow.

She looked toward the stairs in the entryway. It didn't seem Jonah was coming back anytime soon. Besides, he'd forfeited his spot when he'd left. Gathering her laptop, notebook, pens, and fresh mug of tea, she moved to the couch.

Tucking her legs underneath her, she grabbed the cozy, white throw off the back of the couch and put it over her lap before settling her laptop in front of her. This was better.

Okay, where had she been? Oh yes, the part where the mysterious Roarke arrives on the island. Of course, he was the one who was going to crush Marisol's heart.

Her fingers hovered over the keyboard. Where did she need to go from here? Words. She needed words. The couch wasn't doing its job.

"Gaaah!" She screamed, picking up her pen and tossing it across the room.

"Aw. What did that pen ever do to you?" Jonah appeared behind her, arms full of boxes. "Having trouble?"

Bronte chose to ignore his question. Her? Having trouble? Psh. She was completely fine. Or would be as soon as she figured out where in the world this scene was supposed to go. "Where did you come from?"

"I was in the attic."

Bronte's face scrunched. "The attic? Why?"

"I was looking for these boxes. There are six more in the garage and the big one that holds the tree. I figured since we're stuck here for a bit, we might as well decorate."

"Decorate?" Bronte looked around the room. "It seems like your sister has really good decorating taste."

"Not those kinds of decorations." Jonah motioned to the boxes in his arms. "Christmas decorations."

Putting the boxes on the hearth, Jonah turned back to Bronte, hands on his hips. He'd changed from his gray sweatpants and T-shirt into a pair of black joggers and a red hoodie. His socks had little images of Santa and reindeer, and Bronte would have rolled her eyes if they didn't seem so . . . Jonah.

"Oh. Right." Bronte melted a little farther into the couch. Of course it would be Christmas decorating.

She wouldn't have any part in that.

She turned back to her computer and stared at the blinking cursor. If she didn't know any better, she'd say the cursor was mocking her.

Looking up, she saw Jonah hadn't moved, was still standing in front of her, his hands on his hips.

"What?"

"Do you want to help?" His eyebrows quirked in an unspoken challenge.

"With Christmas decorating?" Bronte scoffed. "No, thank you."

"Come on. You need a break. You've been sitting at your computer for hours."

"As one does when one is writing a book, Jonah."

Jonah bent his knees and rolled his eyes. "Come on,

Bronte. Help me for a few minutes and then get back to writing. You have to take a break at some point."

Bronte chewed on the inside of her cheek. "I don't really *do* Christmas."

"What do you mean?" Jonah frowned, standing back up. "Do you have some sort of religious objection to it?"

"No."

"Okay, then how can you not *do* it?"

"I just don't. It's never been that big of a deal for me." But if she were being honest, she'd always wanted to know what it would be like to decorate for Christmas. "Besides, my deadline always falls in January, so I've taken to renting a new place every year for the last few weeks of December and holing up to write."

"What about your family? Don't you miss spending time with them?"

"No family. Foster kid."

"Oh." Jonah scratched behind his ear. "Well, surely someone invited you to spend Christmas with them. You and Lexi seem close. Or maybe you've got a special someone in your life . . ."

"Ha. Not anymore." And even when she had, Brad hadn't invited her to his family holiday functions. Probably should have been clue number one that things weren't going to work out between them. "And yeah, Lexi invites me over every year. But like I said . . . Christmas just isn't for me."

"Well, I just find that to be unacceptable."

She lifted an eyebrow. "Excuse me?" Her hackles rose, but the big grin he flashed her lowered them again. There was just something really . . . okay, adorable about him. But adorable equaled distracting, and distracting meant no words on the page. "Ugh. Jonah, I can't. I need to write."

"Come on. This is a huge White Christmas tradition. My father's father passed it to him, who passed it to me, and one day, I'll pass it to my sons—or daughters. I don't care, as long as there's a lot of them." He cocked his head.

"A lot of kids, huh? I've never thought having kids would be all that great." At least, she didn't now that she couldn't. Bronte turned back to her computer, glancing at the dismal number she had written for the day. Apparently, her brain had declared mutiny and decided this was the year the words dried up.

"Big families are awesome. There's just something so cool about seeing yourself in someone else." Jonah glanced to Bronte and winced. "I'm sorry, that was insensitive."

"It's fine."

"No, it's not. I wasn't thinking. I'm sorry. Really."

"I promise it's okay. I figured it out and put all my focus into my career. It's the one thing I could control."

Jonah nodded. "You never did find out if you had any other family?"

Bronte sighed and slammed her computer shut. "No other family, Jonah. It was just me and my druggy mother, and then she lost custody of me when I was six and it was just me. Like I said, it's fine. I made my own family." She motioned to her closed laptop. Except, for now, it seemed that this family was holding out on her.

Jonah stepped back, hands held up in surrender, but even as he backed off, Bronte saw kindness in his eyes.

"Fine," he said, "but I'm not taking no for an answer to the Christmas decorating. You need a break, and this is the perfect way to spend it. Trying something new."

"You're Mr. Persistent, aren't you?" Bronte folded her arms across her chest, as if that would protect her from Jonah's compassion.

He just shrugged, giving her puppy-dog eyes. Ugh. As if he could get any cuter.

Well, if that was going to be the way of things, she didn't see what a few minutes helping Jonah with decorating would hurt.

"Fine." She threw her hands up. "But only for a little bit, and then I have to get back to work."

Jonah pumped the air with his fist. "Yes! Come on, I need help getting the tree from the attic." He grabbed her hand and pulled her off the couch.

Bronte frowned at the zing zipping up her arm at his touch. That had to be because she was on her fifth—no, sixth—cup of tea. It had nothing to do with finding this Army man attractive. Not that he wasn't. Him in his hoodie, joggers, and Santa socks.

Anyway.

Bronte jerked her attention back to following Jonah through the house and into the garage, where the attic ladder unfolded from the ceiling. A snowmobile sat up on a trailer, and a golf cart was next to it, a charge cord snaking from the back and plugged into the wall. Skis, sleds, and other snow-looking items leaned against the wall.

"If you want to stand here, I'll hand down the box with the tree. You'll just need to guide it down. Then we'll take care of those." Jonah pointed to boxes stacked next to the ladder before disappearing into the attic.

Three trips and half an hour later, they had moved all the boxes marked *holiday* or *Christmas* into the living room. "It looks like Macy's holiday department threw up in here."

"Yeah. The Whites don't do things halfway. Especially Christmas."

"It's going to take forever to get all of these up." And she didn't have time for that.

"It'll be fun. We just need the perfect ambiance." Jonah grabbed a remote, and with the push of a couple buttons, the fireplace flared to life. Another remote, and Christmas music started playing softly from a surround sound.

"Surround sound? That would have been nice to know when I was watching *Star Wars* the other night."

Jonah grinned. "I love that you're into *Star Wars*, by the way. Maybe later we can watch my favorite—*Rogue One*."

Bronte snorted. "I knew you had good taste, but I'm really surprised you aren't up in arms that Jyn and Cassian didn't get their kiss before the end."

"Let's be honest. Jyn and Cassian should have kissed at the end of that movie, but they gave us so much more than a kiss. Their whole love story is"—Jonah put his fingers to his lips—"chef's kiss."

She found herself shaking her head and smiling at Jonah before she caught herself. She flicked her gaze back to her computer. It wasn't exactly calling her name, but if it'd had eyes, they'd have been boring into her right about now.

She cleared her throat. "Well, if you don't need any

more help with the boxes . . ." Bronte thumbed over her shoulder toward the couch. With all the boxes everywhere, she'd need to move back to the kitchen table. "I'll just . . . yeah." She turned on her socked heel.

"Wait." Jonah's hand wrapped around Bronte's wrist. They froze, both of their gazes dropping to Jonah's hand. A second later he dropped her hand and stuck his in his pockets, as if to keep them to himself. "I mean. I thought you could . . . I thought you'd want to help set up and decorate the tree. It's the best part."

Jonah looked like a little boy who was asking for a cookie.

"I told you. I haven't ever decorated anything for Christmas." Bronte shrugged. "I'll just be in the way."

"Well, there's no time like the present to learn," Jonah pushed. "I promise you'll have fun."

"More than likely, I'll just mess it all up." She hadn't meant to say that. She'd meant to tell him that she had lots of work to get done and it was better if she left the decorating to him. There was a reason the saying went *You can't teach an old dog new tricks.* Thirty-two wasn't *old* old, but it was old enough.

Jonah scoffed. "Not a chance." He stood up a little taller. "I'm not going to force you to come decorate the tree, but I promise you'll have a lot better time than you've been having staring at that computer."

Bronte looked longingly at her computer. Jonah was correct in his assessment that she'd have more fun decorating than she would working. At this point, she'd probably have more fun getting her wisdom teeth pulled. "Writing is normally the fun thing. I'm not sure what's happening to me."

Jonah tried one more time. "Maybe you'll get some inspiration while we decorate."

If there was even a sliver of a chance she'd get some inspiration . . . "Fine. I'll help decorate the tree."

"Awesome." Jonah did a little jig that had Bronte giggling.

Giggling? Bronte didn't giggle. She bit the inside of her cheek.

"I'll start getting the tree base put together if you want to check the lights and see which ones work," Jonah said

Bronte tugged a box labeled *lights* closer to an outlet and popped the lid off. If she'd expected a nice, neat string of lights, she had another thing coming. It looked like the lights had revolted and hosted a rave while locked in the dark side of the attic. Untangling this mess was going to take her all day.

"Um, Jonah." Bronte held up a tangle of lights. "Are these supposed to be this way?"

"Holland Renee." Jonah put his hands on his hips. "I don't know how many times I've told her that she'll regret putting the lights up that way. She just never learns."

"Looks like it's just us regretting it this year. Holland is on a boat in the middle of the Caribbean without a care in the world."

"This is true." Jonah abandoned the box he was currently digging through, which Bronte was pretty sure was the IKEA version of an evergreen forest, to join in the quest to untangle the lights. How many strands were shoved in this box, anyway?

Forty-five minutes later, Bronte decided she was done with the whole Christmas decorating thing. A group of kids was singing "Jingle Bells" through the sound system speakers, and between her and Jonah, they had only untangled four strands of lights—of which only one had all the lights working. Bronte could feel a headache coming on.

Sitting back on her heels, she rolled her neck. "You said this was going to be fun and there was no way I could mess anything up."

"First of all," Jonah started, freeing another strand from the mess, then pointing inside the box, "this is not anything you messed up. This is all Holland. And second, you aren't having fun? How could you not be having any fun? This is the most fun I've had in three months, four days, thirteen hours, and fifty-four minutes." Jonah wagged his eyebrows up and down.

"Apparently you need to get out more, and I'm really questioning what it is that you did three months ago that could be as fun as this."

"Went swimming in a fountain with a beautiful German woman."

The image of Jonah with another woman tugged at Bronte's insides. Why should it matter if he had swum in a fountain with a beautiful German woman? She didn't know Jonah. She'd just met him yesterday. Still, "Oh?" was all the response she could muster.

Jonah bumped Bronte's shoulder. "She was ninety-seven years old and proving to me that she could still have fun."

Bronte pushed up from the floor to get out from under Jonah's gaze. "Ninety-seven, huh?"

"Yep, and I was only swimming in the fountain because she pushed me in first."

Bronte barked a laugh. "I think I would have paid good money to see that." She opened a box that contained old Christmas ornaments.

"I bet you would have."

Popsicle sticks turned to stars. Construction-paper frames with little puffy shapes of trees and reindeer glued on, pictures of young Jonah and his sisters stuck inside. Family memories tucked away in a box.

What would Bronte's life be like if she had a box like this from her own little ones? If instead of Bronte and Jonah, it was Bronte and her family?

Wait. Where were these thoughts coming from? She'd decided long ago she'd be better off alone instead of taking the chance she'd end up like her mother, who was very much lacking in all things maternal. Not like it mattered. Even if Bronte did change her mind, that choice had been taken from her. Plus, she'd want a good man to raise kids with, and nobody wanted someone as broken as her.

She clenched her jaw. No, a box of family memories wouldn't be in the cards for her. There was a reason her holiday tradition was just her and her made up worlds. That's the way she liked it.

"Bronte?" Jonah's hand on her arm startled her. "Are you okay?"

"What?" She sniffed. "Of course. I'm fine." She carefully placed the homemade tissue angel back into the box of ornaments and let the lid fall in place. "Really. I'm completely fine." She brushed at nonexistent tears on her face. "I need to get back to work." She pushed past Jonah, grabbed her computer, and made her way over to the table.

She didn't have time for fun. She had too many words to write to take breaks for something as silly as decorating a Christmas tree. She'd already taken enough breaks over the past year.

This was work time. Focus.

If only a certain Army surgeon would stop being so distracting. Bronte settled into the uncomfortable wooden chair and pulled her laptop close, but she couldn't help sneaking glances at Jonah as he continued untangling even more lights while humming "Jingle Bells." A flutter tickled her middle, and she knew she was in trouble.

Jonah watched as Bronte gathered everything and practically stomped up the stairs. She'd been sitting at the table for almost an hour, heaving sighs at least every ten minutes. Not that he'd been counting.

The Christmas tree was up, and he'd gotten enough strands of lights untangled and working to grace the tree with them. The rest of the unworking tangled mess he put in a cardboard box to take out with the trash. Seriously, why had Holland even kept them? They were probably left over from when they were kids. Decorating for Christmas had always been Holland's favorite, and he suspected she had another box of lights—perfectly rolled and all working—hiding somewhere in the attic.

Having put the last of the ornaments on the tree, Jonah stood back to survey his work. It would do. He put the storage boxes in one another, then stored them in the garage and went about vacuuming up the stray needles that had fallen off the tree. Whoever said a fake tree was less mess hadn't seen the twenty-year-old tree Holland White insisted on keeping. Jonah added a new tree to the list of things he'd talk Holland into purchasing.

He should have sprung for a real tree—not that he was sure how'd he get it to the house in this weather. He hadn't expected Bronte to say she'd never decorated for Christmas before.

Deciding the living room was clean enough, Jonah switched the music channel over to *Die Hard* and went about putting together soup for lunch. He fought a yawn. After lunch, he'd take a quick nap to combat this jet lag. Exhaustion had seeped into all his cracks.

While the potatoes, kale, and sausage simmered together in broth, Jonah rummaged around the kitchen for everything to make grilled cheese. Something about snow made him crave soup and grilled cheese. And a cozy nap on the couch.

"This is a good movie. I always have liked Bruce Willis."

Jonah turned at the sound of Bronte's voice. "It's one of my favorites," he agreed.

Her hair had been down earlier. It was now piled on top of her head in some sort of topknot bun, a pencil sticking from the middle of it.

"Are you always cooking?" Her hands disappeared in the sleeves of her black sweatshirt. Jonah was beginning to wonder if she had any other color in her wardrobe. Not that it mattered or was any of his business.

"What do you mean?" Jonah went from studying her to flipping over his sandwich.

"I came down this morning and you were cooking breakfast." She pointed a sweatshirt-sleeve-clad finger in his direction. "You're cooking again. Every time I come down from upstairs, I find you here cooking."

"It's happened twice."

"I've only come downstairs twice."

"Once at breakfast, and now it's lunchtime. Would you prefer that I let you cook your own meals?"

Bronte chewed on this for half a second before she said, "No, actually. I prefer my food unburnt and edible."

Jonah's eyebrows rose. "Not much of a cook?"

Bronte shrugged as she slid onto one of the barstools. "I eat a lot of takeout."

"What were you planning on doing while you were here? Walking to town for every meal?"

"Martha had given me some take-home boxes."

Jonah remembered the takeout boxes he had found in the refrigerator. There had been a burger and an order of fries. "You were going to live off a soggy burger and a box of fries?"

"I would have figured something out."

Jonah shook his head. "Do you want a grilled cheese?"

"If it's not too much of an issue."

Jonah didn't say anything. He plated the grilled cheese from the skillet and poured a ladle of soup into a bowl.

Bronte's thanks was almost a whisper.

Jonah made another sandwich and bowl of soup and sat on the stool next to her. He bowed his head and sent up a quick prayer for his food.

"Why do you do that?" Bronte looked at him, eyebrows raised.

"What?"

"Pray. For your food."

"So I don't drop dead from unblessed food."

The shocked look on Bronte's face had Jonah biting the inside of his cheek to keep from bursting out with a laugh. "I'm kidding. People don't drop dead from unblessed food."

Bronte visibly sighed.

"At least, I don't think they do." He had to keep her on her toes.

Her spoon clattered to her bowl, and she huffed, "Then why do you do it?"

"It's the simplest way to give thanks to God for providing. We could be stuck in the house without any food. We could be stuck outside. We could have both left and gotten stuck somewhere other than here."

"It doesn't really seem like it matters." Bronte picked her spoon back up and swirled it in her soup.

"I think it does. I don't think we're left to chance. God cares about each of His children."

"I have found that God doesn't seem to care what happens to me."

Jonah stilled. "I don't believe that."

"Whether you believe it or not, God and I came to the agreement a long time ago that I don't actually matter."

"Bronte—"

Bronte held up a hand, cutting him off. "No, it's fine. I've been living with this truth for a long time. Life of a foster kid. Comes with the territory."

Jonah's heart hurt for her. He opened his mouth to respond, but Bronte cut him off, changing the subject.

"This soup is really good."

He hesitated for a minute, not sure if he should steer the conversation back to the one at hand or wait for another time. "Thanks. There's just something about snow days that makes me want soup and grilled cheese."

"Did you have lots of snow days like this growing up?"

"A few." They fell into a comfortable silence, the sounds of Bruce Willis negotiating with a terrorist playing behind them.

"How's the writing coming?" Jonah finished off the last of his soup and pushed his bowl away from him.

Bronte's shoulder lifted in a shrug, but she didn't say anything, instead just dunking her grilled cheese in her soup over and over and over again.

"Oof." Jonah winced. "That bad?"

Bronte dropped the sandwich against the bowl and let her head drop into her hands. "I don't know what's wrong with me. It's like all my words have dried up and this story doesn't want to be told."

"Have you tried writing something else? I'm not a writer, but maybe if you worked on something else, it would jog your brain into gear. Maybe," Jonah added after the glare Bronte shot him. "When I was in med school and couldn't focus on studying, I'd doodle for fifteen minutes before switching back to studying. It worked for me."

"I don't have time to write anything else." Her voice quivered. "I have to get this book done. I've procrastinated long enough. It's due in three weeks, and I still have . . ." She paused, face scrunched up as if working figures in her head. ". . . around eighty-five thousand words to write."

Jonah ignored the way she clamped her mouth shut, as if maybe that was information she hadn't wanted to freely give.

And suddenly, he wanted to help her. If he couldn't hang out with his family this holiday season, at the very least, he could help someone else. And given their current predicament, maybe God had plopped Bronte right in front of him with a "Help her" sign flashing over her head.

"What do you need from me? How can I help you make sure you get your words written?"

Bronte stared blankly at him. "You can't help me write my book."

"Oh, you wouldn't want me to help you write your book, but I can . . ." Jonah looked around the kitchen for inspiration. "Keep you fed so you don't have to worry about eating burnt food. I can make sure you always have a hot cup of tea whenever you need it. And I may not be a writer, but I am a reader. If you need to brainstorm ideas, I'll give you a listening ear."

Bronte considered him with a raised eyebrow. "Just one ear?"

"Both," Jonah amended. "You can have both, if you need them, and if they will help."

"Why would you do that?"

"Well, first off, I can't go anywhere, so you lucked out there. Secondly, why wouldn't I want to help a new friend?" Besides, it'd help him keep his mind off his sister's words and why he'd come home anyway. Maybe Bronte needed him more right now. True, she was little more than a stranger, but who was Jonah if he didn't help the downtrodden? And something about Bronte struck him as the definition of downtrodden.

Bronte's eyes snapped up. "Just until the weather clears though."

Jonah shrugged. *Maybe. Maybe not.* "Sure. It'll be a couple more days at least."

Her storm-colored eyes narrowed, moving back and forth on his. Thinking. Considering. What was going through her mind?

"And," Jonah added, whipping out his cell phone, "I'm ordering the rest of the series to read, so if you do need help brainstorming, I know the characters and plot line and can help you."

"Oh, you don't have to do that," Bronte protested.

"Already done." Jonah flashed a smile.

Bronte chewed on her bottom lip. He wanted to take all her worry and apprehension onto himself, to unburden her.

"Okay, well . . . thank you." Bronte swiveled back and forth on the barstool. "I should probably get back to work."

"Me too." Jonah held up his phone. "I have a book to read."

Bronte rolled her eyes. "You enjoy that."

"I plan to. I very much plan to."

While Bronte disappeared back up the stairs, Jonah made quick work of the dishes, the sound of the start of *Recipe for the Unspoken*—book two—in his earbuds.

After adding a few more logs to the fire, Jonah poured himself another cup of coffee (if he wanted to get sleep, he should probably lay off the coffee), and settled on the couch. Leaning back, he let his eyes close as he listened to the second book in the Pike Family Saga.

As he lost himself in the world Bronte had created, Jonah wasn't sure why he'd thought the first book had been boring. He should try to read it again. Maybe there was something to knowing an author before reading their book.

Whatever the cause, he was excited to read—or listen to—more. As he drifted off to the warm cadence of the narrator's voice reading Bronte's words, he decided he would ignore the fact that, in a little over a week, after he talked with his dad about not taking over the clinic, everything could change. Either with his dad, with Amy, or both.

His day of reckoning would come, but today was not that day.

Six

Date December 18

Days until Deadline 19

Words to be written 81,255

BRONTE CHEWED ON HER THUMBNAIL as she watched Jonah finish up the last pages of *Unraveling in the Pines* on his phone. It was amazing how fast a person could read a series when they switched back and forth between listening to the audiobook and reading the Kindle ebook. He'd read book two and almost finished book three in two days. He shouldn't have told her he was almost done with the third book. She wouldn't be able to think about anything else until he'd given his critique and moved on to the fourth book. Not like it mattered though. She'd only managed to write a couple thousand words since yesterday.

Jonah smiled as he scrolled through the pages on his

phone. He didn't look like a man who hated what he was reading . . .

Laying his phone on the counter, he looked up at Bronte. Why did she worry what he would say? Hundreds of thousands of people had read the series and loved it. Why did it matter what one hunky, tattooed G.I. Joe thought of the books? He wasn't even her intended audience.

Still, she couldn't stop herself from asking. "So? What do you think?"

Jonah just stared at her.

She was starting to think she had something on her face. Maybe there was someone standing behind her? She made it all of three more seconds before she turned to look. Nope, just the Christmas tree in all its twinkly-lighted glory. And yes, she had to admit that Aubrey from the ferry had been right. Christmas lights did make things more magical. "What? Was it that bad?"

"Bronte, this is brilliant. You are amazing. I loathe the day that I ever told you this was sad."

She wasn't sure why that made her heart flutter. "Seriously? You liked it?" Why did it mean so much to her that he liked the series?

"I didn't *love* it, but that's because I prefer books with happy endings. But your writing is brilliant, and you have a way of just pulling the reader into the story and trapping them there. I still think you can write the next book giving everyone a happy ending."

And there it was. Bronte rolled her eyes. "Not real life."

"Who's to say it can't be? Why can't real life have a happy ending?"

"I told you. That just hasn't been my experience."

Bronte stacked her things.

"I know you're currently writing the last book, but can I read what you have so far? I really need to know what happens next."

Bronte's head was already shaking back and forth. "Patience," she said, and she couldn't stop a grin from spreading on her face. "You still need to read books four and five."

"Can you at least tell me what's going to happen between Theodosia and Josh?" He leaned over, resting his elbows on the counter. "They get together, right?"

She should break it to him easily, right? How was the hero and heroine getting together at the end of the book a happy ending? Maybe she could do one of those open-ended endings where it was open to the reader's interpretation.

What was she even talking about? Three days with someone, and she was deciding to change her entire plan for the end of this book? Who was she even turning into? She narrowed her eyes. "Read the next book."

"They don't, do they?" Jonah bent his knees and threw his head back, looking up toward the ceiling. "Bronte!"

Bronte threw her hands in the air. "What? I feel like it would be too much of a nice, happy bow for them to end up together at the end of the series!"

"You're killing me, Smalls."

Bronte tugged her hoodie over her head and pulled the

strings so that only her eyes peeked out. "I'm sorry, but also, I'm not sorry."

"I'm just going to have to take it upon myself, for the sake of your readers *and* for the sake of your characters, to change your mind before you get to the end."

"Ha!" Bronte pushed her hood off her head and slurped the last of her tea from her cup. The lingering scent of cardamom and vanilla warmed her bones as her lips tugged into a smile when Jonah moved to the stove to fill the teakettle with water for another cup.

"Bronte Doesn't-Believe-in-Happy-Endings Parker," Jonah declared, wielding the kettle up like a sword, "I challenge you to write a happy ending."

Bronte wasn't sure if she was supposed to giggle, bow, or respond with a salute. In the end, she shook her head. "I wish it worked that way."

"It could work that way." Putting the kettle on the stove, Jonah moved to the cabinet, pulling down a bowl, flour, and sugar and setting them on the counter before moving to the fridge, humming yet another Christmas song.

"But it doesn't work that way." She needed Jonah to hear this. Needed him to understand. Why was beyond her, but if Jonah was making it his mission to make her believe in happy endings, then she would make it her mission to get him to see that happy endings were just the stuff of fairy tales. And she did not write fairy tales. "Life isn't all sunshine and roses. Most of the time it's thorns and disappointment. Can't you see that?" All she could see of Jonah was his very nice backside sticking out of the fridge. "Jonah? Are you even listening to me? What are you doing?"

"Got it!" Jonah appeared from behind the fridge door, wielding a stick of butter. "I knew my sister had to have a stick in there somewhere."

She threw her hands up with a groan. Here she was pouring her heart out—well, as much heart pouring as she did these days—and he was focused on butter? Her point exactly. If this had been the movies . . . Never mind if this had been the movies, because what happened in movies wasn't real. They were the epitome of fairy tales. At least the rom-com, happy movies Lexi forced her to watch. That was why she preferred action movies. Still just as unbelievable, but at least the entire thing was unbelievable. Who ever heard of superheroes saving New York City from aliens from another dimension?

"I understand everything you're saying, I just don't believe it." Jonah put the butter down on the counter and faced Bronte. "And I don't think you think you know how to write it. You're scared."

Heat bloomed in Bronte's face at the same time as rage filled her middle. Who was Jonah to tell her what she knew how to do? What she was scared of? Never mind that part of her warred over whether he was right. "What?"

"I think you think that even if you wanted to, you don't know how to write a happy ending where the girl gets her guy." Jonah leaned over on the counter, making sure to look Bronte straight in the eyes. She blinked, not sure if she wanted a stare down with Jonah. His sea-blue eyes had tiny flecks of midnight that made them magnetic. "Happy endings, where the guy gets the girl, scare you. So instead of figuring it out, you just avoid it."

She blinked, trying to break the hold he had on her, but it wasn't working. Once upon a time she had thought about making the series a happy one, but then she'd remembered everything that had happened in her life, and it'd just seemed to not make sense. And ten months ago, Brad had ripped any remaining dreams of happily ever after from her mind. "Theodosia and Josh can never end up together. There's too much messy between them."

"But that's just it. Real-life romance isn't always happy and roses. Sometimes it gets messy, and the real romance is that they stick together and work it out. That's what makes a truly great romance."

"What would you know about it? You grew up with the picture-perfect family, parents who obviously loved each other and you, and siblings you actually talk to. You've probably never overheard an argument in your life, and you've probably never had a broken heart either."

"I've had my heart broken, Bronte." Jonah stilled, blinking at her. Then he looked away, swallowing hard. "Just because I don't always show it, that doesn't mean I haven't known loss." His gaze reconnected with hers, and there was sadness mixed with something else there.

"Really?"

"Yes, really." Jonah's Adam's apple bobbed. "I had someone. Once. But she decided she didn't want a family or to be married to a military man, and she wasn't willing to wait until I got out."

She could taste the guilt in the back of her throat. "Oh."

His face softened. "But I've also known hope. And it's a gift. One I wish you knew. One I wish you'd give your readers."

A flame flickered inside her. "I'll do it."

Wait. What had she just said?

That wasn't supposed to have come out of her mouth. She needed to stick to her guns. She couldn't write a happy ending, and this late in the game, the deadline wouldn't allow any room for mistakes. This was insane. She was insane. What was Jonah doing to her?

Jonah slapped the counter and pumped the air. "Yes! You are going to kill it."

"You just said that you don't think I can do it." Bronte pushed off her stool and walked around the island to pour hot water into her mug. Jonah had his back to her, putting something into the bowl he'd gotten down earlier.

"No, my dear Bronte, I said I don't think *you* think you can do it." He bopped her nose. His hands were covered in flour. Bronte was sure she resembled Rudolph after he'd been playing in the snow. "*I*, on the other hand, know for sure you can do it."

She reached up to rub her nose. Sure enough, her sleeve came away with a smudge of flour on it. "What makes you so sure?" She brushed at the spot on her sweatshirt. "You just met me three days ago. You don't know anything about me."

Jonah picked up the bowl as he was mixing, then turned to the island. "I'm a good judge of character." He plopped the stick of butter in a glass bowl and slipped it into the microwave.

"A good judge of—Would you stop moving around? What are you doing?" He was making her nervous.

Jonah peered over his shoulder, his cocky grin firmly in place. "I'm making you something sweet to see if we can't help with that sour."

Bronte froze. "You're doing what?" The microwave dinged.

"Can you pass me that butter?"

Using the sleeve of her sweatshirt as an oven mitt, Bronte pulled the bowl from the microwave and set it next to Jonah on the counter. "So, if you think the story would be so much better with a happy ending, do tell, how would you finish it?"

"I think for this last book, you need lots of romance. Throw your readers for a loop. They always say real life makes the best stories—"

Bronte shot Jonah a look. That was what she'd been trying to tell him.

"—but I say the best stories just emulate real life. Always better with a little bit of spice."

Bronte choked. "Spice? I draw the line at spice. I don't write those kinds of books."

"I was talking about the cookies." Jonah bit back a smile. "Can you grab the cinnamon? Should be in the cabinet next to the stove."

"Fine." She handed him the jar of cinnamon and plopped back down on the barstool, watching Jonah work. "And what do you mean by lots of romance? My books have romance."

"Meh." Jonah shrugged.

"What? They do!" Bronte insisted.

"Your books have a guy and a girl that kiss, maybe, but they either aren't together or don't seem happy in the end. A kiss doesn't necessarily mean you have romance." He pointed the whisk in her direction, a glob of cookie batter plopping onto the counter. "You've got to think about it like *Rogue One*. It had all the romance, all the feels, and they didn't even kiss! You need to put feeling into your scenes."

"My scenes have feeling," Bronte muttered as she tore a napkin into strips.

Fifteen minutes later, all talk of "spice" and "happy endings" had ceased as, apparently, Jonah had somehow pulled Bronte into helping him make cookies—enough for an entire army, from the looks of the kitchen.

They'd started with chocolate chip, Jonah's grandmother's famous recipe—so famous he wouldn't even let Bronte read the recipe card. After chocolate chip, they'd moved on to sugar cookies (which Jonah had promised they could decorate), and now they were making thumbprint cookies, which Bronte had decided may be her favorite.

The last batch in the oven, Bronte plopped onto the couch, a plate of fresh cookies in front of her. Jonah joined her, grabbing a cookie off the plate and turning the television on.

"So, my sister has this thing where she watches Christmas movies from Thanksgiving until New Year's."

"Shouldn't she stop at Christmas?"

Jonah gave Bronte a pointed look. "I'll let you have that conversation with my sister when you meet her."

Bronte's heart did a little flutter. *Stop it, heart. You don't flutter.* Brad had taken all the flutterings with him when he'd told her she wasn't enough. Or was too much. He had said both in the mighty speech that he'd declared had taken him days to write and hurt him more than it'd hurt her.

Hardly.

It hadn't taken him that long to move on either, it would seem. She shook thoughts of Brad from her head, instead focusing on the overwhelming scent of sugar from the plate in front of her. No, she decided, the flutterings must be guilt over not working on her book. Or thinking that she'd be stuck in this house until the rest of Jonah's family came home.

But would that be so terrible?

Yes! Yes, it would be terrible. She had a book to write. She wasn't here for fun.

"Hey. Where'd you just go?"

Bronte blinked. "What? I haven't gone anywhere. I'm right here." The way Jonah was looking at her made her stomach dip. Bronte wanted to roll her eyes at her reaction, ignoring the fact that Brad had never looked at her like that. Never once in the six years they had been together.

"You're here, sure, but your eyes did that glazing over thing where you weren't exactly *here*."

"I was just thinking that I really need to get that book written."

"You'll get it written." Jonah sounded so sure.

Bronte hated the confidence in his voice. Confidence she didn't have. Didn't feel.

"But first"—he settled back into the couch, turning the volume up on the TV—"I think you need to watch *Elf*."

"*Elf*?"

"Only the best holiday movie ever."

"I've never seen it."

"What?" Jonah's head swung in her direction, mouth agape.

"Not a fan of the actor who plays the elf." Bronte shrugged her shoulders, plucking another thumbprint cookie off the plate. "And a man running around in tights? Please."

"You gotta give it a chance."

Bronte chewed the inside of her cheek. They had spent most of the morning making cookies, and she really did need to get caught up, but maybe there was a compromise. "How about, I'll watch *Elf* while I work, but then I should probably hole away and get some serious words down."

"Deal."

Bronte had never needed to make deals with anyone before regarding her work, and she didn't need to now. She could leave and head upstairs and get to work right now. She didn't need to watch a Christmas movie—especially one that starred her least favorite actor. But what could it hurt if she sat here for just a little bit?

The credits had just started rolling when the doorbell rang.

Bronte shot a look toward Jonah, not sure if she should answer it or if he should. Technically, she was renting the house, but he lived here. Had lived? It was his sister's house.

Before she could open her mouth and ask, Jonah popped up from the couch. "I'll get it."

Bronte tried to get back into what she had been typing, but if she was totally honest, she hadn't gotten much written in the last two hours anyway. She wasn't convinced she'd call *Elf* the greatest Christmas movie ever, but she had enjoyed it.

"Look who stopped by."

Turning, Bronte found Jonah being followed by Mia carrying a pot of soup, and a man with floppy brown hair and chocolate eyes was behind her with a loaf of homemade bread. The scent of the bread hit her two seconds later, and her stomach growled.

"Hey, Bronte. We heard about the mix-up with Jonah coming home." She shot Jonah a grin. "Cody and I wanted to stop by and see how you were doing and to bring you some vegetable soup and bread."

"Oh, wow." Bronte set her laptop aside and stood to take the pot from Mia. She'd never had neighbors check on her before. She didn't know how she was supposed to feel. "Thank you."

"Why don't you guys stay for a bit? Have some soup and bread with us," Jonah said, taking the bread from Cody and putting it on a wooden cutting board.

Mia shot a look to Bronte. "My kids' grandma is watching them for a bit since they were going stir-crazy at my house, so we've got time, but only if you're sure you don't mind."

Bronte's mouth tugged into a smile—at least, she hoped it was a smile. She was still trying to place this warm, gooey feeling in her middle. "Only if you and your husband promise to take cookies with you when you leave. We baked enough for a small army, and I'm afraid I'll eat every last one of them if they're here."

"Oh, we're just dating." Mia blushed at Cody's declaration of "for now" and cheeky grin.

"I ended up over at the house this morning checking on her and the kids," Cody said, shrugging out of his coat and draping it on the back of a chair. "I needed to make sure her snowmobile was in good working order in case they needed to get out and get somewhere."

"How are the kids doing?" Jonah asked, pulling a knife from a drawer and slicing the bread while Cody pulled bowls from the cabinet and Mia got the soup ladle from a drawer and turned the oven on low. There were no strangers in Holland's kitchen except for Bronte.

Needing to do something, Bronte grabbed the spoons from the drawer she had seen Jonah get some from earlier.

"Doing good," Cody replied, setting four bowls out on the counter. "The kids got out and played in the snow this morning. We probably shouldn't have let Maggie go out, but she's convinced she can do anything Finn can do." A grin tugged on Cody's mouth. "They made a few snow angels and fed Jack—that's the town's dog," Cody explained to Bronte. "But they only lasted about five minutes before they were inside asking for a movie and hot chocolate."

Jonah slathered butter on the bread slices and put them on a cooking sheet before sliding them into the oven. "I don't blame them. It's cold."

"At least the snow seems to have stopped, and I don't think we're supposed to get any more."

The doorbell rang again, and Bronte's gaze shot to Jonah. She was beginning to feel like the White house was Grand Central Station.

"Are you getting your writing done with Jonah here?" Mia asked after Jonah disappeared to answer the door.

Bronte shrugged. "Enough."

"Martha told us that he wasn't able to meet up with his family. I wish I could offer him a place to stay, but my house is completely packed with family for Christmas."

"It's okay, really. I'm starting to get used to him being here, and this is a big house. I'm not sure what I'd do all alone." *You'd write your book*, one part of her brain told her, while the other part told her that in a big, quiet house like this, she'd be jumping at every little noise. She should never have opted for such a big house, but then again, it wasn't like she'd had a ton of options.

"We have two more for dinner!" Jonah declared, stepping back into the kitchen carrying a tray of something, two people following him. "And they brought brownies."

"And homemade eggnog," the girl following Jonah declared, holding up a bottle of white liquid.

Jonah set the brownies on the counter, and Bronte didn't think it was possible after all the cookies that afternoon, but her mouth started watering. "Bronte, this is Dani and her fiancé, Liam."

A tall, willowy woman turned to Bronte with a smile taking up most of her face, her green eyes bright. The man, Liam, shrugged out of what Bronte could tell was an expensive coat, but even if he looked like he belonged in New York City, his cheeky grin told her he would be kind and down to earth.

"It's so nice to meet you," Dani said, and before Bronte knew it, she'd been pulled into a hug.

It took her off guard. She had to remind her arms to hug Dani back. "It's good to meet you too."

"Dani, it's great to see you out!" Mia said, getting a hug from Dani as well. She turned to Bronte again. "Dani's my cousin, but I've hardly seen her lately." She gave Dani a little side elbow and a teasing smile. "She's been hard at work planning not only the Christmas stroll but also the comeback of the Jonathon Island Christmas Ball *and* her wedding."

"You sound busy." And Bronte thought writing ninety thousand words in three weeks was stressful. "I can't imagine having to plan all that."

Dani slid onto a barstool and, lifting the plastic covering the brownies, tore a corner off one and popped it into her mouth. "Busy is one word for it."

"How's everything going?" Jonah asked, pulling the bread from the oven and dropping each perfectly buttered slice into a waiting basket. Bronte's mouth started watering again, and she wiped at it to make sure she wasn't drooling all over the place.

"Oh, you're in for it now," Liam said, stepping up behind Dani and putting his hands on her shoulders.

"I finally got all the permits and the fire department's all clear for the ballroom. I could have wrung Tommy's neck for how long he took. He's the new fire chief. But honestly, the ball's next week!"

"Someone on the ferry over was telling me about it. So, it's a pretty big thing?" Bronte was really starting to feel like Jonathon Island was the setting for a Hallmark movie—which was the only place she'd ever heard of a Christmas ball happening.

"It used to happen every year, but this will be the first one in *years*," Cody replied. "I think I was still a teenager the last ball."

"Yes, and all this snow had me worried we'd have to cancel the ball and the stroll." Dani ran her hands through her hair. "The stroll is still on for Saturday, and I expect to see everyone there." She pointed down each of them, Bronte included.

Normally Bronte would be ruffled at someone she hardly knew giving her orders, but in this case, she didn't mind. "The ferry will be back running by then?" she asked.

Dani nodded. "Yes, thankfully. I paid for it to operate a few extra times on Saturday to make sure everyone can make it over here since there isn't anywhere for tourists to stay on the island right now."

"I don't mean to ask a dumb question, but what *is* a Christmas stroll?"

"Not dumb at all. It's new this year, actually. I got the idea from something Nantucket does every year. It's basically a festival of sorts, held all day the Saturday before Christmas. Tourists come over from the mainland, all the shops have fun Christmas specials, and there are gingerbread-house-making contests, a gift-wrapping station, and a snowman-building contest." Dani's eyes sparkled as she ticked off the different events on her fingers.

"That sounds like a lot of fun. I'll be there." Wait? She would? What was it about this island that made her want to do more than just hide in her hole and write? She needed to backpedal and tell them she had a book to write and couldn't come to the Christmas festival, but her mouth stayed firmly shut. It sounded fun, and there was an entire day between now and then. A lot of work could be done in that time, and she could use the Christmas festival as her reward for getting it done.

"Dinner is ready!" Jonah declared as he handed out bowls of soup and warm slices of bread wrapped in a paper towel.

"Should we watch a movie while we eat?" Dani asked, popping up from the stool and moving to the couch. "Holland has the best collection of Christmas movies."

"But of course. What were you thinking?" Jonah asked.

"Girls pick," Mia called out, ignoring the boys' protests and moving toward the cabinet under the TV, where the movies were stored. "Come on, Bronte, help us choose."

Bronte looked to Jonah. They wanted her to help?

Jonah winked at her and nodded toward the girls in encouragement. She set her bowl on the side table and kneeled next to Dani and Mia.

"Have you seen this one?" Dani handed Bronte a case

that had Sandra Bullock and Bill Pullman with a train behind them. *While You Were Sleeping*. Sounded like something Lexi would like.

"I haven't seen this one." She handed the case back to Dani.

"What?" Mia pulled it from Dani's hands and clutched it to her chest. "We're watching this one."

"We're definitely watching that one." Dani pointed both her pointer fingers in Mia's direction.

"Which movie?" Jonah asked from the couch.

Mia held up the case.

All three guys groaned. "Come on, that's not a Christmas movie." Liam's head dropped to the back of the sectional.

"It is too." Dani glanced over her shoulder and gave her fiancé a flirty grin. "And I'll have no complaints from you, Liam Stone. I happen to know you really like this one."

"You've seen this one?" Cody's mouth hung open.

Jonah just shrugged and slurped another bite of soup.

Movie selected, everyone settled into their seats. Dani and Liam snuggled on one side of the sectional, bowls cradled in their hands. Mia and Cody somehow both fit in the oversized armchair, and she and Jonah were opposite Liam and Dani—not anywhere close to snuggling. It was strange to see couples that had a much different relationship than she and Brad had ever had. They were all touchy-feely and could joke back and forth without anyone getting their feelings hurt. Maybe it had been a knee-jerk reaction when she'd sworn off love forever.

"You good?" Jonah whispered as he leaned over. In the dim lighting, the blue in his eyes deepened.

Bronte could only nod past the lump in her throat. Jonah squeezed her shoulder and moved back to his side of the couch. He would never know how many tingles he'd left shooting through her body with that one touch. Bronte chewed on the inside of her cheek. It was more than just the tingles Jonah caused. The way these people made her feel like a part of their group after having just met her . . . she'd never really had that before. Especially considering her best friend was also her agent.

Maybe she just needed to get out more . . .

Or maybe this place was special. She could see, just a little bit, why Jonah believed in happily ever afters and true romance.

Seven

Date December 19

Days until Deadline 18

Words to be written 80,759

WHY HAD BRONTE THOUGHT SHE'D be able to make up her word count from yesterday? She couldn't. Well, maybe she could if she were able to write the correct manuscript.

Dani, Liam, Cody, and Mia had left late, but since Bronte had decided to go to the Christmas stroll on Saturday, she'd stayed up to get extra words in. After making herself another cup of tea, she'd gone to her room for the night. She'd started writing just fine, but a hundred words in, another story idea had popped into her head.

She'd agreed to write the Pike book with a happy ending and had been attempting to work toward that, but instead, she hadn't been able to get a scene for a completely different project out of her mind.

This one had friends and family gathered around and eating a big meal during the Christmas season, and there was a handsome military man with all the witty banter and adorable smiles. Before she knew it, she'd had another document open, her fingers flying to get the scene out. How the keyboard hadn't caught on fire, she had no idea.

It had been well after two in the morning before she'd stopped writing and fallen into bed. She'd woken up around seven, the story still flowing out of her, and had spent the rest of the morning typing furiously.

When was the last time a story had come to her this easily? None of the Pike novels had come out like this.

The shrill tone of her cell phone startled her out of her story. Reaching over, she pulled it off the charger, only slightly disappointed to see it wasn't Jonah. Not that he'd need to call her—or even had her number.

Pushing down the unfamiliar feelings, she answered the phone a little breathlessly. "Hello?"

"Good morning to you too."

Bronte could hear the raised eyebrow in Lexi's voice.

"I'd thought I'd call and make sure you were okay after talking to you yesterday, but it sounds like you've been . . . running?"

"Ha! The only way I would be running is if zombies were chasing me, and even then, it's questionable."

"I'd probably just let them take me. One thing I've never understood is, wouldn't it just be easier if you hunkered down in a good hiding spot? Why is that never an option?"

"You might be onto something there, Lex. Next novel, I'll make sure to write a zombie chase where everyone just hides."

Lexi hummed. "Doesn't make for a very exciting story, does it?"

"Not really, but to answer your question, no, I'm not running. I've been up for a couple hours working on a story."

There was a beat before Lexi asked, "*A* story? As in something other than the Pike story?"

Rats. Caught red-handed. Lexi knew her tendency to get a new story idea in the middle of what she was working on too well.

"Yeah. *A* story." Bronte didn't take the bait. She let her gaze wander to the window, surprised to see snow falling again. Maybe it'd snow until it buried the entire island. She hoped it would stop soon and that the extra flakes wouldn't cause issues with Dani's Christmas festival plans.

"A *new* story, Bront?" Lexi pushed out a breath. "Come on, you've got to stay focused. You were contracted for the last Pike story. We're both in this business. We both know what happens when authors don't meet deadlines, especially deadlines that have been extended twice already. Your readers want the Pike Family Saga conclusion. You can't disappoint them."

Bronte sat up and hugged a pillow, both excitement and dread pooling in her belly. "I know you're right, Lexi, but this story is different. It's good. It's *so* good. It's about this guy and girl who—"

"Bronte, I'm going to stop you right there." Bronte knew Lexi would be pinching the bridge of her nose at this point. A dreaded habit picked up from her mother. "I am really glad you're excited about a new story, but you *have* to finish the Pike Family Saga. It's due in three weeks. Give me those weeks, and then you can work on whatever new story you're excited about. You're almost done."

Disappointment stuck to Bronte like a wet blanket. Lexi was right. She needed to focus. But that didn't keep her from trying one more time. "You don't even want to know what it's about?"

"Yes, I very much want to know what it's about, but in three weeks. Hold on to it until the end of this deadline, and then go crazy."

Bronte fell back on her pillow, blinking away the tears stinging the backs of her eyes. "What if I can't finish the Pike book? What if it's awful and terrible and everyone hates it?"

"Hey, you'll get it done," Lexi promised. "And if it's awful, well, that's what edits are for."

"Right." Bronte didn't feel Lexi's vote of confidence.

"How's the hunky G.I. Joe doing today?"

Bronte was glad for the change of subject, but it didn't do much to quell the dread in the pit of her stomach. "Actually, I'm not sure. I haven't been downstairs yet this morning." But she knew he was up, because she'd heard him earlier and smelled coffee and breakfast.

"Whyever not?"

"Because I'm scared of the person I might turn into when I head downstairs." Bronte blinked at the confession, realizing how true it was.

"You sound like you turn into the wicked witch or something."

"The opposite, actually. I lose all sense of work ethic, and I find myself agreeing to baking cookies and watching movies and dinner parties and . . ." Flirting with Jonah, talking to him, making deals about writing happily-ever-after books . . . but she was loath to admit *that* to Lexi.

"It sounds like fun, and let's be honest, Bronte, you could use a little of that in your life right now."

"But the book." The real reason she was on Jonathon Island.

"One thing I know about you is that you work really well under pressure. You just need to make sure that when you do sit down to work, it's on the novel that you're under contract for." A phone rang somewhere on Lexi's end of the call. "Hey, I have to get that, but really, Bronte, I know you can do this. Just stay focused on the correct story."

"Thanks, Lexi. I'll talk to you later?" But Lexi had already hung up.

Bronte set her phone back on the nightstand and pulled her laptop onto her lap. She minimized the new story and pulled open the document for the Pike story . . . and stared at the blinking cursor. Heaving a breath, Bronte blew a rogue curl from her face. Five hundred words, and then she'd go have some of that fun she and Lexi had talked about.

Whether or not she holed herself up in her bedroom

all day, staring at the blinking cursor that mocked her, five words for the Pike novel weren't coming, much less five hundred. Instead, at every little sound, she strained her ears to see if she could figure out what Jonah was doing. She had smelled coffee and breakfast hours ago. Her stomach growled, reminding her that smelling breakfast was all she had done.

Bronte groaned and closed her laptop. She wasn't getting any work done up here. Might as well go sit at the kitchen table, where she didn't have to wonder at every little sound what Jonah was up to. Not that she cared. Not that she *should* care.

Making sure she had on something decent (another pair of black leggings and a black sweatshirt—this one had "Eat, Sleep, Write, Repeat" on the front, a reminder she should heed) and that her hair wasn't trying to take over the world too much, Bronte grabbed her laptop, notebook, and phone and headed downstairs.

Which she found completely empty.

Bronte frowned. Where was Jonah? He was here, because she'd heard him banging around not ten minutes before. Maybe he'd gone back upstairs and was taking a nap? But she hadn't heard him come back up the stairs. Had she?

Whatever. She didn't care what Jonah was doing. She'd come downstairs to write at the kitchen table. For a change of scenery. That's it.

Setting herself up on the kitchen table, Bronte opened her laptop and stared at the last words she had written on the Pike manuscript. Garbage. Where had she even been going with that sentence? She hit backspace, wishing she could backspace until the entire document was erased. Not that *that* would help her situation at all.

Bronte hovered the mouse over the new story idea. Maybe she could use this as a warm-up. Hadn't Jonah said working on a different project for a little bit worked for him? Yes, she'd let herself write for fifteen minutes on this story, and then she'd get back to work on the one that was under deadline.

Determined, Bronte cracked her knuckles like an old noir writer, tapped out a beat on the kitchen table, and started writing.

"Whoa, looks like someone got her mojo back."

Bronte started at the sound of Jonah's voice and slammed her laptop shut, as if caught with her hand in the cookie jar. "I'm not doing anything." She leaned an elbow on her laptop and turned to face Jonah.

Dressed head to toe in big, fluffy, *very* blue snow gear, Jonah waddled into the kitchen. "Right. What are you working on?"

"I may or may not be writing a rom-com." Bronte shrugged her shoulders. "Whatever."

"Hey, that's great."

"You look like you got in a fight with the Cookie Monster and lost. Or maybe the Cookie Monster lost and you're now wearing him." Bronte gasped. "Did you do something with the Cookie Monster?"

Shuffling over to the table, Jonah plopped down in a chair next to her. "What if I am the Cookie Monster, and Jonah is just my disguise?"

Bronte considered him for a minute. "I think that sounds even more terrifying. So, what's all this?" She waved a hand in his direction.

"Snow gear. I thought we could go for a midday stroll into town and maybe get some lunch at Martha's." Jonah leaned over, trying to tug on a second pair of socks. Bronte bit her lip to keep from laughing.

"Wouldn't it have been smarter to put the socks on *before* you looked like the Michelin Man rolled in blue paint?"

"Har har. Of course, but I decided at the last minute that I needed a second pair, ergo, I'm the blue Michelin Man putting on socks."

Bronte watched him for another painful thirty seconds. "Do you need some help there, G.I. Joe?"

With a heaving sigh, Jonah melted back into the chair and tossed the socks on the table. "I've just decided that I'm not wearing a second pair." He pointed down at the pair he currently wore. "These are wool and should be just fine. We'll find out for sure if I have to ask you to amputate a toe or two tonight."

The blood rushed from Bronte's face. "I'm not doing that." She threw the socks back at him. "Put them on."

"I'm just kidding. I'm not going to lose any toes," Jonah teased. "I don't think. Anyway. You want to go with me?"

"Sorry, I didn't bring any gear with me." Not that she would have, even if she'd known they would be getting this much snow. Because she was here to write a book. WRITE A BOOK. Not go tramping in the snow with a beautiful man.

"Lucky for you"—Jonah reached out and bopped Bronte on the nose—"Holland is just about your size and has all the gear you need."

"Seriously?" Bronte felt like Jonah had just handed her a Christmas present all her own.

"Seriously. I mean"—Jonah looked her up and down, and dang it if she didn't feel her face flush under his gaze—"it's pink, not black. Think that'd be okay?"

"If it means getting out of here for a little bit, it's perfectly fine." Bronte hadn't realized how much it felt like she had cabin fever. Maybe that's why she was having a hard time with really getting going on the Pike family novel.

"I'd fire up the snowmobiles, but it looks like my sister might be having issues with hers. It's on the trailer in the garage."

Bronte remembered seeing it when they were getting Christmas boxes from the attic. "A walk will be good. I really need to work on the Pike novel, but I just can't get started. When I'm at home and I have this problem, I generally go for a walk around the neighborhood."

"Great. Gear is at the top of the stairs. I'll meet you here in ten minutes, and we'll get going."

Bronte gave Jonah a curt nod and pushed away from the table. Abandoning her laptop, she all but ran up the stairs to where the bright-pink snow gear was waiting for her.

A voice in the back of her mind warned her that she'd need to make the walk quick so she could get back to work. She brushed it off. She'd make up the words tonight—Lexi had said Bronte worked well under pressure.

Besides, a walk to town and back with a hot Army man was just what she needed. No, this wasn't going to be a romantic stroll in the snow. This was going to be a regular stroll in the snow so they didn't end up getting cabin fever and killing each other.

That was a thing, right? Cabin fever made a person do crazy things. Like write rom-coms instead of the literary piece of genius she was supposed to be writing.

Everything would be fine. So long as she didn't allow herself to get sucked into the romance—writing-related or otherwise—that seemed to be calling to her more every minute.

What was he doing? He'd come here to have a conversation with his family that could potentially, if his sister was to be believed, break his father's heart, but here he was, tromping through the snow with a beautiful woman instead of trying to figure out how to tell his dad he didn't want to take over the clinic. Preferably without any hearts being broken.

"I'm going to throw myself in this snowbank and wait until spring," Bronte huffed out.

Looking over his shoulder, Jonah saw Bronte standing next to a particularly fluffy-looking pile of snow on the side of the road. "Don't do that."

Bronte tried to cross her arms, but with Holland's puffy snow jacket on, her arms just bounced back to her sides. "You're going to have to give me a pretty good reason not to."

"Because if you throw yourself into a snowbank, I'll have to stay too."

Bronte's face twisted in confusion. "Why? There's no reason for both of us to suffer for my bad decisions."

"My mom taught me better than to leave a woman in a snowbank on her own." He held his hand out in Bronte's direction.

"Well, that's just silly," Bronte said, not sounding like she thought it was silly at all. She considered his offered hand for a moment, and for a breath, Jonah thought she was going to opt for the snowbank.

"Fine." She took his hand. "You win."

Jonah leaned down closer to Bronte's ear and whispered, "I can hear the hamburgers at Martha's calling your name. Bronte! Bronte! Can you hear it?"

Bronte closed her eyes and took a slow breath. Jonah's gaze flickered over her small, upturned nose and freckles that just barely kissed her cheeks, before landing on her pink lips. His breath hitched, and he pulled back before he did something rash.

Like kiss her.

He couldn't kiss Bronte. They had just met. He found her captivating, funny, smart, and gorgeous. But he *couldn't* kiss her.

He cleared his throat. He needed to stay focused.

Bronte blinked her eyes open. "I think you're delusional. I don't hear anything. Oh my goodness, aren't delusions a sign of hypothermia? I'm pretty sure I read that once in research for one of my books."

"I'm not delusional, just hungry."

"You're always hungry."

"Come on." Jonah tugged Bronte toward the restaurant. "We need to hurry in case everyone else gets the same idea and they run out of food." Taking big steps, they half stomped, half slid the rest of the way down the street.

The glow from the window in front of Martha's and the stack of cross-country skis and snowshoes at the door told Jonah that they hadn't been the only ones with the idea to get out of the house today. Two snowmobiles sat parked in front, taking up most of the road.

"I'm beginning to think it would have been better if we'd been able to ride one of those things," Bronte huffed, jutting her chin in the direction of the snowmobiles. "Remind me to inform Holland of the pros of being prepared at all times."

Jonah leaned over to remove his snowshoes. "Will do, but you have to admit the walk did us good."

"Did you good, maybe," Bronte mumbled as Jonah reached around her to open the door.

Before Jonah could point out she needed to remove her snowshoes, Bronte stumbled into the restaurant.

Scents of burgers and craft beer, scents of coming home, overwhelmed Jonah. If he broke his father's heart, would he be able to come back? Once again, he entertained the idea of not saying anything and sticking with the plan. But just thinking it caused anxiety to rise beneath the surface.

"Bronte! Jonah!" Martha, frown securely in place, called out in greeting. "Glad to see you're both still alive."

Cries of Jonah's name went up around the room as people pushed out of booths and away from tables to crowd him and welcome him back. Jonah tried to keep Bronte tucked to his side, but she'd been pushed out of the way. He looked over everyone's heads to see if he could find her and discovered her sliding onto one of the green-topped stools at the bar top, snowshoes leaning upon the dark wood bar next to her. He might not have been home in two and a half years, but little about the restaurant had changed.

"It's good to have you home, Major!" James Sullivan exclaimed, clapping him on the shoulder.

"How was the trip back?" Frank Kelley cut in, his forever scowl still carved into his face.

"What have they been feeding you?" Henrietta Hudson, the retired baker, patted his cheek. "You're too skinny."

Jonah tried to keep up with all the questions thrown his way.

Vera Graves, ever in her black Martha's on Main T-shirt and with her dark, gray-streaked hair pulled back, elbowed her way through the crowd and grabbed Jonah's arm. "All right, everyone, back to your seats!"

Arnie Chamberlin, the pastor of the small island church, stood at one of the tables, Bible open in front of him, and it looked as if everyone had been sitting around him, hanging on his every word.

"Isn't it Friday?" Jonah asked Vera as he added his coat to the already overstuffed rack by the door.

"Last time I checked." Vera glanced at her watch.

"Is Pastor Arnie holding a church service? In Martha's?" Jonah nodded to the *Check your guns, politics, and religion at the door* sign that hung over the door.

"Naaah. Everyone has been feeling a little cabin fever-ish. Pastor Arnie came in to work on his sermon for Sunday, and one thing led to another, and I think now they're all discussing the woman at the well story." Vera led Jonah over to the bar next to Bronte. "It's a good day with Jesus and deep conversation, I always say."

"Very true," Jonah agreed, sliding onto the stool next to Bronte.

"I didn't realize how famous you were." Bronte bumped his shoulder with her own, a grin playing at her lips.

"Oh, I'm not fa—"

"So, Major, how's Germany been? You have to tell me all about it." Pastor Arnie's daughter, Jordi Chamberlain, brunette hair pulled into a low pony, slid onto the stool next to him with a mock salute, already talking a mile a minute. Not much had changed with Jordi since his last visit.

Jordi thrust a hand across Jonah in Bronte's direction. "Hi, I'm Jordi. You must be Bronte, the author who's staying at Holland's house. Nice to meet you."

Bronte returned the shake, nodding a quiet hello. Not that Jordi noticed Bronte's quietness. She went right on with updating Jonah on her life, life on Jonathon Island, and asked him no less than fifteen questions.

"Jordi, would you leave Jonah and Bronte alone? I think Declan is needing a refill." Vera put a glass of iced tea in front of Jonah with a wink.

"Jordi is Holland's best friend." Jonah leaned over and whispered to Bronte when Jordi finally took a breath as she slid off the stool and moved to check on the tables she waited on. "She must have had coffee this morning. I thought everyone had agreed to keep the caffeine away from her." Jonah pulled two menus from where they were stacked and handed one to Bronte. "Coffee has done that to Jordi since I met her." Which would have been the couple of months he'd been home after he'd graduated from college and before he'd left for basic. So long ago.

Jonah swallowed down the sudden wave of regret that came with the memory. Regret for missing so much of the lives of those he loved. Shrugging, he tried to focus on the chatter of conversation around him.

"Are you two ready to order?" Jordi reappeared, notebook in hand.

Bronte ordered soup and salad while Jonah scanned the menu—it hadn't changed that much in the years since he'd been home.

"What about you, Jonah?" Jordi asked, tapping the pad with her pen.

After deciding on his typical order of hamburger and french fries, Jordi disappeared and Jonah turned to Bronte. He opened his mouth to ask her if her mind was ready to get back to work, when four more people stopped by to pat him on the back and let him know how proud they were of him. Their food arrived in front of them, but by the time Jonah got to his, it was cold, and Bronte's was already almost gone.

"Sorry about that," he said, turning to Bronte.

Bronte shrugged. "No worries. I feel like you're the long-lost big brother finally home."

A pang shot through Jonah's heart. Why hadn't he made it a point to come home sooner?

He knew the excuses he told himself, but now that he'd made it home, they seemed weak. He hated the lack of control he felt over his schedule, his life. He lived life away from every person he cared about. But if he wanted to change that, it would mean coming home from Germany and taking over his father's practice, and he didn't want that life either. Jonah cleared his throat before too much emotion could make its way up his chest. "Yeah, you're probably right. How are you feeling after our walk?"

"I'm already sore and not looking forward to the hike home, but I'm feeling good. I think I'm about ready to dive into the Pike story again." Bronte spun her glass of tea in her hands.

"We could probably see if someone can give us a ride home on a snowmobile."

Bronte seemed to consider it for a moment before finally declining the offer. "It's okay. I think the hike will do me good."

"Are you getting more ideas for your story? You had me a little worried there, looking as stressed as you were." He had been praying for the floodgates of ideas to open up for Bronte—for her to be able to finish the book.

"Oh." Bronte waved a hand in the air. "I'm fine. It's all part of the process."

"I have to admit, I'm curious to see how the Pike Family Saga ends. I'm really enjoying what I'm reading."

Bronte wagged her eyebrows up and down. "Even if it's *sad* and *boring*?"

"I'm never going to live that down, am I?" Jonah groaned, scrunching up his face.

"Nope." Bronte let the ending of the word pop. "Never."

"Okay, I don't normally do this, but today is a special occasion." Jordi appeared, two steaming mugs clutched in her hands. "I brought you both hot chocolate. It's a recipe I made up." She leaned in closer and whispered, "And don't tell anyone else, because it's not exactly on the menu."

"Thanks, Jordi." Jonah didn't know if he should be excited or nervous that the hot chocolate was from Jordi's own recipe.

Jordi put a mug of hot chocolate in front of each of them and stepped back, waiting for them to take a drink. But then, as if deciding she didn't want to hang around to find out what they thought, she spun on her heel and made her way back to the kitchen, stopping and talking to everyone on the way.

"She's fun." Bronte smiled, her eyes following Jordi as she flitted from table to table.

"Yeah, she is. She left for a little bit after high school. Moved in with her grandparents in Boston. Holland was so bummed when she moved. You should see them together." Jonah grinned just thinking about it. "Holland can be on the more reserved side, but when she and Jordi get together, especially if there's coffee involved . . . well, it's fun to watch. One time, when Jordi and Holland had just started high school, I was home on leave, and Jordi came over. Apparently, Jordi and Holland had volunteered to make items for the school bake sale. Not a big deal, they were always doing that, only this time they forgot about it until the day before they needed them. Instead of crumbling under the pressure, they rolled up their sleeves, brewed a pot of coffee, and enlisted the help of all five White siblings. It was well after midnight, but us, Jordi, a couple other friends who had the misfortune to wander in, and Mom and Dad were in the kitchen putting the finishing touches on one hundred twenty-four cookies and four dozen cinnamon rolls." Jonah paused and took a drink of his melted iced tea. "Those two are an unbeatable force."

With a break in the *Welcome home*s, Jonah picked up his cold hamburger. It was halfway to his mouth when Jordi slid onto the stool next to him.

He sighed, putting it back down. "Yes, Jordi?"

"I just wanted to see if you were going to the Jonathon Island Christmas Ball next week." Jordi grabbed a fry off Jonah's plate and popped it in her mouth. "I'm helping Dani with some behind the scenes stuff and wanted to make sure you've got your tickets."

"We haven't talked about it." Jonah looked at Bronte, eyebrow cocked. He wanted to go. The Christmas balls were always fun, and he couldn't remember the last one he'd attended, but really it had to be Bronte's call. He didn't want to volunteer her for something and take away from her writing. "What do you say, Bronte?"

Jordi leaned around Jonah, her hands clasped together. "Please? It's so much fun."

Bronte looked back and forth between Jordi and Jonah. Jonah shrugged his shoulders at her—hopefully she didn't feel pressured into anything, what with Jordi giving those puppy-dog eyes. Between his sisters and their friends,

Jonah had been the recipient to many a puppy-dog gaze. It was hard to turn down.

"I don't even have anything to wear to a ball."

"Oh, I can take care of that." Jordi brushed off her excuse.

Bronte looked as if she was going to say no, but then she shrugged her shoulders and said, "Why not? Sounds fun."

"Put us down for two tickets, Jordi."

Jordi jumped from the stool, throwing her arms around both Jonah and Bronte, tugging them into a group hug. "I'm so excited! Okay, I have to get back to work!"

"I think you might be on to something with Jordi and her coffee." Bronte laughed as they watched Jordi disappear past the swinging doors into the kitchen. "And she is definitely a force to be reckoned with."

Eight

Date December 20
Days until Deadline 17
Words to be written 79,970

SHE WAS POSITIVELY GIDDY. WHAT WAS happening to her? If she'd believed in aliens, she would think they had kidnapped her and exchanged her body for someone (something?) else. Bronte did not get giddy. Yet here she was, typing furiously at her manuscript, slaphappy smile on her face and giggles bubbling from her midsection.

"You must be working on Whatever Rom-Com," Jonah said, standing from the couch, his gray sweatpants sitting low on his hips and his dark-green Army T-shirt stretching across his broad chest.

Bronte forced her eyes back to her computer. She needed to stop ogling Jonah. No matter how much fun she was having, she wasn't here forever. After Christmas, she'd go back to Tulsa, and he'd go back to Germany. She couldn't take him home with her. Still, when he paused his trek toward the kitchen, her stomach dipped low as he leaned over and grabbed her now empty mug.

Wait. He had said something. What had he said? Oh, right. The Whatever Rom-Com. "Why would you say that?"

"Because." Jonah filled the kettle with water and set it back on the stove before leaning his hip against the counter facing Bronte. "You seem lighter when you're working on that one."

Bronte frowned, concentrating on Jonah's Santa socks—a different pair than he'd worn earlier that week. These featured floating Santa and Rudolph heads. "Is that a good thing or a bad thing?"

"I don't necessarily think it's either one." Jonah filled the mugs, his with coffee, hers with hot water. "I can only image the Pikes are a hard family to write about. Those books are heavier. But I do like to see you having so much fun with this one."

Fun. There was that word again. It seemed she was having fun both in her life and in her writing. If only it were on the book she'd come here to write.

The book she'd come here to write.

Right.

Glancing at the clock, she realized she had been working on the Whatever Rom-Com for over an hour—which was over the ten minutes she'd told herself she was going to work on it. You know, just to get the creative juices flowing. Minimizing the romantic comedy, she opened the Pike family document, stomach curling at the word count at the bottom of the screen, mocking her.

Jonah put Bronte's now-full teacup next to her. He put an arm around the back of her chair and leaned in close, his scent of sandalwood and citrus clouding all her senses. She'd almost slid her eyes closed just to get lost in his scent when she realized what he was doing.

She snapped her laptop closed. "Nope. No peeking."

Jonah stood up, taking his scent with him. "So close."

"Go back over there and finish reading your book. You still have one more to go before you're all caught up."

"Fine." Jonah trudged back over to the couch with his cup of coffee and picked up his Kindle. "It's not my fault you write such long books."

"You love it."

"Yep. I do." Jonah settled back in, and Bronte shifted her attention back to her manuscript. She told herself she would work on the Pike story for an hour and then let herself take a short break with the rom-com. If she did that, she'd make progress on both manuscripts and be able to wrap everything up before it was time to head to town with Jonah for the Christmas stroll.

An hour later, a ping from her notifications announced an incoming text. Bronte had thought she'd silenced all notifications. Too late for that now. She minimized her document and opened her messaging app.

<u>Margo</u>

How's the writing coming?

Margot. Lexi's mother and the head of Write Stuff Literary Agency.

Bronte cringed. A follow-up from Margot couldn't be a good thing. Bronte looked down at the word count. Still not where it needed to be for this late in the game. Even if Lexi had told Bronte she worked best under pressure, Bronte could feel herself testing her limits.

Bronte
Good!

Not an all-out lie. The writing was going fine. Better on the project she had promised Lexi she wouldn't be working on, but still, progress was being made.

Margot
I'll have the Pike manuscript on my desk in two weeks?

Bronte bit her lip, her gaze wandering to Jonah—or what little she could see of him stretched out on the couch. He held his Kindle above him, completely lost in the story he was reading. Jonah had been right when he'd said Bronte seemed lighter when she was working on the rom-com. She *felt* lighter. What if there was a way to work some of that magic into the last Pike family book?

If Margot knew how good she felt about this story, she would agree with her. Holding her breath, she hurriedly typed out a response to gauge Margot's thoughts.

Bronte
Yes, you'll have it in two weeks. I'm thinking about maybe adding a little more romance and comedy into this last book.

Three dots appeared, disappeared, and then reappeared.

Margot
I'm not sure that it'd be wise to change the genre of the series this late in the game, but if you can make it work and have it on my desk in two weeks . . .

Bronte could practically see Margot's thinly sculpted eyebrow rising and the upturn of her nose as she responded.

Bronte

You won't regret this.

Margot

See that I don't.

Cracking her knuckles, Bronte went back to staring at the Pike manuscript. Margot had said she could put in more romance and comedy, she just had to make it work. Taking a deep breath, she grabbed her pen and started jotting down ideas. For the first time since she'd arrived on Jonathon Island, she was looking forward to working on the Pike Family Saga.

The sun had shown up for the Christmas stroll. It had to be at least almost above freezing temps, and with the sun shining, it could almost be considered warm.

Jonah had worked up a bit of a sweat walking from the house to Main Street, where the festivities were. Bronte had been so deep in writing when it'd come time to leave that he'd almost suggested they stay home for the afternoon. But she must have had an alarm set, because at one, she'd packed everything away, bundled up in layers and her thick wool coat, and asked Jonah how come he wasn't ready yet.

"Bronte! Jonah! Over here!" Dani called.

Jonah grabbed Bronte's hand and pulled her in the direction of where Dani had set up camp under a brightly colored canopy in front of the Tourism Bureau.

"Wow. This is a great turnout," Jonah said, giving Dani a side hug.

The street was packed with tourists and community members alike, all dressed in fluffy coats and stocking caps. All the shops that hadn't closed down for the season, plus a few that had opened back up for just the stroll, had banners and signs declaring sales. A few brave vendors had canopies set up and were selling their wares farmers-market style. At least most of them had portable heaters to keep from freezing. Christmas music pumped through the speakers, and more than one person sang or hummed along.

"I know. It's better than I could have hoped for." Dani clapped her hands together. "I wasn't sure how it was going to work out with the weather, but it's almost warm today! Hey, Bronte."

Bronte smiled and lifted her hand in a wave. She had been quiet on their walk to town. Maybe she'd changed her mind about going. Jonah had noticed that Bronte didn't react like his sisters when given the opportunity to get out of the house and around large crowds. They got all chipper and excited. Bronte, it seemed, grew quiet and withdrawn.

He tugged her closer to him. "Are you doing okay?" He

leaned in close, not minding the coconut and lavender scent from her shampoo. "We don't have to stay long if you need to get more work done today."

Bronte waved him off. "It's fine. There's just more people than I expected. I'll make up the words later." She shook her head and grinned. "That seems to be becoming my mantra."

"When you're ready to go, you just give the word, and we'll go."

"Jonah White, are you trying to get out of the snowman-building contest?" Dani asked, hands on her hips.

"I wasn't aware that I was planning on entering."

"Oh yes, and she's already put you and Bronte down as a team." Liam came up behind Dani, threading his arms around her and pulling her close.

Jonah shot a glance to Bronte. Did she even want to build a snowman? He had planned on a low-key afternoon, maybe grabbing some dinner at Martha's or Kelley's Bar & Grill before the Christmas tree lighting.

Instead of apprehension, Bronte's face lit up. "Snowman-building contest?" she exclaimed, clapping her hands. "It's been forever since I've built a snowman."

"You're up for it?" Jonah asked.

"Up for it? We're going to win," Bronte said, eyes sparkling. "What's the prize?"

"First place is a dozen cinnamon rolls from Good Day Coffee, a gift card to Martha's, a pound of fudge, and a free meal at Kelley's." Dani rattled off the list.

"We are so winning."

"Okay then," Jonah agreed. "Ready to go explore?"

Nodding, Bronte took Jonah's hand. He wished he weren't wearing gloves right now.

Dani's eyebrows shot up. "Don't forget to stop by the library and vote for your favorite gingerbread house," she called after them.

They wove their way through the crowd, Jonah letting himself be pulled along wherever Bronte wanted to go. The band kids from Jonathon Island Public School were selling poinsettias and greenery, someone Jonah didn't recognize was selling handmade wooden items, but Bronte's face really lit up when they made it to the booth for the Jonathon Island Public School Art Club, selling hand-drawn cards and art. By the time they'd made their way down the street to the library, they were both sipping on hot apple cider from the Fort Jonathon sponsored booth.

"That tree is huge!" Bronte exclaimed as they came to the end of the street. The vantage point at this end of the street, slightly higher than the other end, gave them a perfect view into the park. "When did they even put it up? Was it up yesterday when we came into town?"

"It's the magic of Jonathon Island." Jonah winked at her. "It's been up since probably Thanksgiving."

"I can't believe I missed it. They will light it up tonight, right?" Bronte asked, breathless as she stared over everyone's heads toward the park and tree at the other end of Main Street.

"As soon as it gets dark."

"We have to stay for that. Can we?" She turned back to Jonah, the excitement and cold tingeing her cheeks pink.

Jonah wasn't sure he could tell her no even if he wanted to. "Of course. The tree lighting is the main event."

Bronte shivered. "I can't wait."

"Let's get you out of the cold for a little bit." He didn't want to risk Bronte getting hypothermia. While everyone had been filtering in and out of the warm shops, he and Bronte had stuck to the outdoor canopies. "Come on, the library is right over here. Let's go throw our vote in for the best gingerbread house. Then we can go hang out in Martha's until it's time to build a snowman."

Holding the door to the library open, Jonah let Bronte go in ahead of him. They said hello to the librarians, got their score cards for the gingerbread house contest, and moved to the community-room-turned-winter-gingerbread-house-wonderland. The room even smelled as if someone had just finished baking gingerbread cookies. Confirming his suspicions, Jonah spotted a table with gingerbread cookies and a carafe of hot apple cider.

"These are seriously impressive. When Dani said there was a gingerbread contest, I wasn't sure what I was expecting, but it wasn't this."

Paper snowflakes, probably made by kids during story time, hung from the ceiling, and soft Christmas music played from a hidden speaker. The room had five folding tables set up in a horseshoe shape in the middle of the room so they could see both the front and back of each gingerbread structure. Each table had four to five gingerbread houses—or coffee shops, beaches, and even one that looked like it was supposed to be Hogwarts. A tented index card with a number sat in front of each creation.

"I don't even know where to start." Bronte looked like a deer in headlights. Seeming to shake off her indecision, she moved to the first table. "Who makes them all?"

"A lot are from the school on the island," Jonah explained, following behind Bronte. "A couple weeks leading up to Christmas break, any students who want to form a team and work on a gingerbread house are allowed to. I remember creating a gingerbread house rendition of the school and football field in my day."

"Did you win?" Bronte asked, looking up from studying a log cabin made from pretzel rods.

"Ha! No. I think we came in sixth?"

"Sixth isn't too bad." Bronte wrote something down on the scorecard in her hand.

"There were only eight houses that year."

"Oof. I guess it's grown a little since then," Bronte said, motioning toward the many-more-than-eight creations on the tables.

"It would look like it."

"How am I supposed to decide which house wins, knowing that all of them were probably made by a bunch of kids?"

Jonah thought for a minute. It was always the dilemma he faced when judging these things in the past. "Look at it this way. If tomorrow something in the world changed and you had to live in one of these"—he pointed at all the houses—"which one would you choose?"

"First of all," Bronte said as she held up her finger, "that's a horrible thought, because I would end up eating my house, and then I would be three hundred pounds and homeless."

Jonah couldn't imagine Bronte being anything but cute—even at three hundred pounds.

"But I think I'd have to go with this one." Bronte pointed to the pretzel-stilted house on a vanilla-wafer-crumb beach, surrounded by blue icing water.

"It looks like a warm place."

"I think I'm cold enough here to last a lifetime." Bronte shivered. "Next writing retreat, I'm going to make sure I'm on a cruise. Your family has it right."

"Fair enough," Jonah conceded.

"What about you?" Bronte bumped his shoulder with hers. "Which one would you live in?"

"Are you kidding me? Hogwarts is on the table. I'm living at Hogwarts."

Options made, they finished filling out their score cards and dropped them in the ballot box.

Deed done, Jonah clapped his hands together. "We have about an hour and a half before the snowman-building contest. Want to walk over to Martha's for a snack?"

"That sounds amazing, and I could eat," Bronte said, wrapping her arms around her middle.

Thankfully Martha's was next door to the library. With all the people in the street, he wasn't sure they'd have time to make it anywhere else before it was time to meet at the art center for the snowman contest.

Finding the only empty booth left, they tugged off their coats and slid into their seats. Jordi stopped by and took their order for an extra-large fry and two peppermint chocolate shakes. They sat in silence until Jordi returned with their order.

"It's freezing outside, and we're drinking ice cream." Jonah shook his head in disbelief.

"It is never too cold for ice cream," Bronte shot back, taking such a big gulp from her milkshake Jonah was afraid she'd have brain freeze.

"I'll give you that one."

Bronte chewed on her bottom lip, which distracted Jonah to no end. She opened her mouth to say something, but then snapped it closed. It happened twice more before Jonah decided to put her out of her misery. Either that or he'd start laughing, and he didn't think Bronte would appreciate that.

"You might as well spit it out," he told her before his curiosity killed him.

"Spit what out?" Bronte asked.

"Whatever it is you're afraid to ask me."

"I know this isn't any of my business, but when you said you didn't want to take over the family business, you never told me what it was that you wanted to do instead."

Jonah thought for a moment, grabbing the ketchup bottle and squirting a glob onto their plate. "I haven't admitted what I really want to do to anyone. I'm not even sure myself. Before I had the inheritance from my grandfather, I'd just accepted that I'd always be a doctor. I'd always be miserable. I know I sound crazy—giving up a medical practice for . . ."

"What is it you want?" Bronte gently urged.

"I want to open a bookstore on the island." Jonah

rushed on before he lost his nerve. "Grandfather wanted us to *do* something with our inheritance money, and mine is just sitting there. Holland bought Mom and Dad's house and remodeled it, my other sisters pooled their money and started a wedding and event-planning business, but I haven't really known what to do with mine. And I got a text from my buddy not too long after I got here that the old island bookstore is up for sale." Jonah dipped his head, afraid to see disbelief in Bronte's eyes.

Who would give up being a doctor to own a brick-and-mortar bookstore? They were closing left and right thanks to sites like Amazon. He'd be crazy to give up something steady for uncertainty.

"It almost sounds like it's meant to be."

Jonah's head snapped up. Wait. Bronte *didn't* think he was crazy?

"A bookstore would be a great way to spend your inheritance." Bronte took a drink of her shake. "Look. I can't tell you what to do, and I don't know your family, but from what I've heard about them, I don't think they'd want you to be miserable for the rest of your life. You still have a lot of life left, way more than what you spent in med school. I think your family would want you to be happy."

"They may want me to be happy, but my sister Amy says if I decide not to take over the practice, my dad will be so disappointed it'll break his heart. He took it over from his father, and his father did the same. My entire life, my dad has been drilling into me how much he wants me to take over the practice, and if I don't, what will happen to it? Who will be left to run it? Jonathon Island can't just not have a clinic."

"I don't have a lot of experience with families." Bronte let out a bitter laugh. "Okay, I have no experience with family, but I think you have a good one, and I think that, yes, your dad might be disappointed for a little bit, but at the end of the day, doesn't he just want you to be happy?"

Jonah took a deep breath. "I wish you were right, but the fact is, I've already put so much into becoming a doctor. I knew after my second year of med school that I didn't want to do this long-term, but I stuck it out, not wanting to be a disappointment. And then when Amy told me I'd break my father's heart . . . I'm just not sure I can take that chance."

Bronte looked like she wanted to say more, but instead, she just took another sip of her milkshake. Jonah wanted to stop talking about this before it made him sicker than he already felt.

He grabbed a now-cold fry from the top of the plate and popped it in his mouth, more for something to do with his hands.

Everything Bronte had said made sense, and he hoped Amy was wrong and his dad's heart didn't get broken, but at the end of the day, he just didn't know, and he couldn't, *wouldn't* take that chance.

Nine

BRONTE SQUINTED AT THE SUN RE-flecting off the snow as she tried to pay attention to the snowman-building instructions Dani was shouting through her bullhorn.

"Okay! You will have forty-five minutes after the sound of the horn to build and decorate the best snowman you can!" Dani called, balancing herself as she stood on the back of a snowmobile.

A scruffy dog jumped up on the table, grabbing a bag of carrots Bronte assumed were supposed to be for noses. "Ack, Jack, no! Bad dog!"

Jack dodged Dani's attempts to grab the bag before bouncing off. "Would someone save the snowman noses from Jack? Please?"

A couple of teens volunteered before disappearing after the dog.

"Where was I again?" Dani looked down at a clipboard

Liam held up to her. "Oh, right. Your snowman must be between four and seven feet. You may use any accessories provided by the Little Stone Bible Church. Thank you, Pastor Arnie." Dani paused while everyone clapped their gratitude. "Make sure there's no funny business trying to sabotage any other teams, and keep your snowman family friendly." Dani scanned her clipboard. "Snowmen must be able to stand on their own. If it falls over after the buzzer sounds, your snowman will be disqualified—alternatively, if you touch yours or another team's snowman after the buzzer, you'll be disqualified as well. Snowmen will be judged by our wonderful mayor, Seb Jonathon." She paused again while those gathered clapped at a tall man with a kind smile and salt-and-pepper hair, who lifted his hand in a wave. "Are you all ready? Go!" Dani held up the air horn and released three short blasts.

Ten teams, ranging from two to eight members, all shot toward the sectioned-off areas for snowman building. Bronte and Jonah got the third rectangle.

"This is a great slot." Jonah slapped his hands together. "Okay, game plan. I'll start rolling the snow for the snowman's body"—he pointed to the fluffy, untouched snow before pointing at Bronte—"if you want to go raid the accessories."

"What accessories do we want?" Bronte asked as Jonah dropped to the snow to begin pushing the snow into balls.

"Let inspiration guide you. You'll know when you see it," he called over his shoulder.

Bronte ran to the canopy that had tubs of donated ties, hats, scarves, and so many other accessories. She pushed through the other team members that were also diving through everything.

Jonah's confession from earlier swam in Bronte's head. She wasn't sure how to help him. She didn't have any experience with families, but she really believed what she'd told him. His father had to only want what was best for Jonah, right? Jonah had said he'd be judged for throwing away a career he'd spent most of his twenties in school for, but he had to see he had so much life to live. Why spend it doing something he hated?

"You know my team is going to win," a redheaded girl who had to be at least seventeen taunted a man not much older than her as she grabbed a scarf and wrapped it around her neck before rummaging around the bins.

"There is no way that's happening. We're taking the win this year," the man shot back.

People really took this competition seriously. Bronte took advantage of their bickering and ducked in front of them.

"You and Jonah doing good, Bronte?" Dani appeared on the other side of the bin Bronte was digging through.

"I think so? I have no idea what in the world we're going to accessorize our snowman with." Bronte held up both a sparkly tutu and a child's fireman helmet.

"Helping a team out is cheating, Dani. You're literally one of the judges," the teen pointed out.

"I'm not helping out, Erin, I'm just chatting, and I'm not one of the judges, I'm just the emcee," Dani fired back before turning back to Bronte.

Bronte smiled at Dani. She had just found the perfect

accessories for their snowman. Waving to Dani, Bronte tucked all the items under her arm and sprinted back to Jonah.

"Back!" she declared, dropping her items on the snow in their space and scurrying over to Jonah to help him roll the middle ball onto the larger one to create their base.

"Thanks." Jonah stood back, winded, looking at the start of their snowman. He glanced over to the pile that Bronte had dropped and raised an eyebrow. "What did you decide to go with?"

Bronte grinned and picked up the mop of curly hair off the pile. She snapped the wig on Jonah's head. "We're doing a Bob Ross snowman."

"Brilliant. Come on, we have about twenty more minutes to finish off. What do you think we can use for the beard?"

Fifteen minutes later, their Bob Ross was almost finished—complete with a paint pallet with dried paint. It was almost as if someone had hoped one of the teams would create Bob Ross. Bronte wasn't sure if that was in their favor, or if it wasn't creative enough. Either way, she hadn't built a snowman in over twenty years and was having more fun than she'd had in a very long time.

"Five . . . four . . . three . . . two . . . one!" The gathered crowd counted down the last remaining seconds before Dani blasted the air horn.

Bronte and Jonah collapsed into the snow, hands up, showing they weren't anywhere close to touching their finished creation.

"Come on, let's go get some more cider." Jonah offered Bronte his hand.

"We made a pretty good team," Bronte said, taking Jonah's outstretched hand. Secretly, she hoped that he'd hang on to it even after he helped her up and was disappointed when he dropped it.

"We made the best team." Jonah stood back, admiring their snowman. "I think we have a pretty good shot at winning one of the prizes too."

Bronte looked at their snowman through squinted eyes. "You think so? He doesn't look a little wobbly to you?"

Jonah turned his head to the side as if that would help him see what Bronte was seeing. "Maybe a little bit? If we back away really slowly, maybe he'll stay standing long enough to get through the judging. Come on."

Bronte couldn't help smiling when Jonah took her hand again, this time not letting go. She shouldn't be smiling like this. After Brad, she had promised she wouldn't ever get into another relationship again, but being around Jonah made her feel like breaking that promise to herself.

She was being ridiculous. She tugged free from Jonah and tucked both of her hands in her armpits. Jonah had only come into her life five days ago, and he'd be out of it just as quick. She didn't need to be entertaining ideas of anything with him, no matter how warm and gooey she felt around him.

The snow crunched under their boots as they made their way away from the snowmen and toward a canopy handing out hot apple cider.

"So, how long will it take them to judge all the snowmen?" Bronte accepted the cup of hot cider Jonah handed her and with both hands, held it up to her face to let the scent of apple and spices warm her. She wasn't sure if she wasn't cold or was so cold she'd lost feeling in her face. She suspected the latter. Also, by keeping both hands on her cup, she kept them out of trouble—like reaching over and holding Jonah's hand again.

Turning away from Jonah with her hot drink, she watched the judging process. Dani, clipboard in hand, followed Seb, who circled each snowman, hand on his chin, studying each one before taking the board from Dani, jotting a few notes down, and handing it back. He took his judging responsibilities seriously. Bronte imagined that if Seb hadn't been wearing a stocking cap and puffy jacket, his gray hair would be perfectly combed and he'd be wearing khaki pants and a crisp button-down shirt.

"It'll take Seb about fifteen to twenty minutes to look at each snowman, make his notes, and then go back and look again." Jonah came to stand next to her, close enough she could feel the heat from his body, which was highly impossible since they both had layers on top of their layers. "If they do it the same as they've done every year, Dani will take Seb's notes and add up everyone's points and then announce the winners at four o'clock."

Bronte looked at her watch. "So we have a little over an hour to wander around. Jordi had mentioned something about a snow globe collection on display somewhere?"

"Sure, I think I saw a sign for that back at the glass shop. Let's go."

They started making their way back up the street when

Bronte felt someone tap her on the shoulder. "Excuse me, but are you B.L. Parker?"

Turning, Bronte saw a woman with short blonde hair peeking from under a pom-pom beanie, a large tote bag slung over her shoulder.

Dread pooled in Bronte's stomach. "Yes?" Why had she answered with a question? She may be a *New York Times* bestselling author five times over, but she'd never be used to fans approaching her in public. She never knew what to say. It was bad enough at events and signings, but at least at those, she had time to prep beforehand. When fans approached her in public, her chest got tight and it was hard to breathe, and she did stupid stuff like answer simple questions with questions.

"Yes, this is *the* B.L. Parker," Jonah confirmed, pulling Bronte to his side in a hug, a huge smile on his face. All Bronte wanted to do was melt into the sidewalk. She thought authors created in anonymity. Why did she have to be the one who gained national acclaim? This was why Lexi accompanied her on tours. She ran interference. Bronte had learned she couldn't even do in-person signing events. Other than a thirty-minute VIP meet and greet before an event, Bronte's interaction with fans tended to be limited. Her anxiety couldn't handle more than that.

"Oh. my. goodness. My name is Marla, and my book club is never going to believe this." Marla flapped her hands in front of her. "The Pike Family Saga is our favorite series ever. We've been to every midnight release since book two, and we were first in line at our movie theater when the movie released."

"Thanks." Wait. She should have said something different. "I'm glad." Did that make her sound pompous?

"Are you her boyfriend?" Marla asked Jonah before turning back to Bronte and wiggling her eyebrows. "Good job, B.L."

While relieved Marla didn't seem concerned by her lack of enthusiasm, Bronte would rather talk about anything but her love life. Of course, there were worse guys Marla could have mistaken for Bronte's significant other.

"No, he's . . . he's not my boyfriend," Bronte managed to get out around the panic climbing up her throat. But Marla didn't appear to be listening, nodding along and digging around in her bag.

She held up her cell phone. "Could we get a picture together?"

Bronte just stared dumbly at the woman. It was like she'd forgotten what words were.

"How about I take it for you?" Jonah offered, stepping up and taking the phone, saving Bronte the embarrassment of becoming one with the sidewalk.

"You're sweet too. Wherever did you find him?" Marla batted her hand playfully at Jonah as she moved to stand next to Bronte.

Bronte remembered to lean in and put a smile on her face—at least, she hoped it was a smile and not a grimace. Normally, Lexi was behind the camera and would clue her in if her face was too . . . scowly. Surely Jonah would have said something if her face hadn't looked right.

"I guess you could say that I just snuck up on her." Jonah winked, settling Bronte's nerves into a warm pool in her belly. "Okay! Three, two, one, smile!" Jonah's thumb pressed the face of the phone multiple times. "All done. These are great."

"Are you a celebrity?" A woman in a bright-pink coat stepped between Jonah and Bronte and her fan.

"No, I—" Bronte tried to say, but before she could get anything out, Marla cut in.

"Yes, she's the famous author B.L. Parker."

"Stan, get over here," the bright-pink-coated lady yelled. "There's some famous author over here."

"A famous author? Where?"

"Is it Jane Austen?"

"Jane Austen? She's been dead for two hundred years."

"I want to see."

"Where is she?"

Before Bronte could blink, there were twenty people pushing and shoving in front of her. "Jonah?" Bronte yelled, standing on her tiptoes to see if she could catch sight of where he'd disappeared to in the crowd.

She needed to get off the street. Away from the crowd, who didn't even know it was her they were looking for. Someone just screamed "famous author," and it was as if they'd turned into a mob.

Turning quickly before anyone realized *she* was the famous author, Bronte tried to figure out which shop was most familiar that she could duck into. Of course, at this point, she would take any shop.

To her left stood a dark, empty storefront, and to her right, the realty, which was close to the street that had led up from the ferry. Maybe if she could make it there, she could sneak around back and figure out the back way into Martha's. At least, she assumed there would be a back way in.

Mind made up, Bronte headed in the direction of the street, hoping that it wasn't too crowded since there didn't look to be any booths set up that way. She could see the light at the end of the tunnel—or rather, the opening at the end of the overpacked street. Pushing past the last throng of people, Bronte stepped into the almost-empty street.

"Bronte!"

Bronte hated the relief she felt when she heard Jonah calling from behind her, but she'd unpack that later, when she was away from the crowds of people.

She spun on her heel, but instead of seeing Jonah, her feet slipped. Her arms swung like pinwheels as she tried catch her balance. The ground came up fast, and she put her hands up to break her fall, but all that accomplished was a scraped-up palm. When her forehead hit the concrete and she saw stars, the only thing she could think of was that the old cartoons had it right. Stars really did spin around one's head if they hit it hard enough.

Everything stood still.

He heard the thunk as Bronte's head hit the street, and he urged everyone to move out of his way. It felt like it was taking him forever to reach her.

Had anyone else seen her fall? He didn't know how everyone didn't hear it. It was a sickening sound, like a watermelon hitting a hard surface. He tried not to think about what happened when a watermelon hit the ground. Prayed that it wasn't as bad as he knew it could be.

A small group of people had gathered around Bronte by the time he reached her, but Jonah let out a breath of air when he saw her sitting up. An older man Jonah didn't recognize knelt beside her, a hand on her arm, trying to brush snow from her face.

"Just take it easy," he told her. "You took quite a nasty fall."

"Bronte?" Jonah slid next to her, bending over to see her face.

She spat snow and grime from her mouth before turning her head slowly to face Jonah. She winced. "Ouch."

"You might want to get your girl to the med station," the old man said, helping to steady Bronte. "I just sent my grandson to see if he could bring someone back this way."

"I will. Thank you for helping her," Jonah said, eyes still on Bronte, not bothering to correct his assumption that Bronte was his girl.

Pulling out his phone, Jonah toggled over to the flashlight. He held the phone's light in front of Bronte's face and moved it back and forth in front of her eyes. "It doesn't seem like you have a concussion, but you have a massive goose egg."

Bronte started giggling. That couldn't be a good sign.

"What's so funny?"

"You know in the old Saturday morning cartoons, how whenever a character hit its head really hard, they'd have stars circling around their heads?" She held up a finger and made a circling motion.

Why was she talking about cartoons at a time like this? "Yeah?"

"I can confirm that is real life. Hit your head hard enough and you'll see stars."

Shaking his head, Jonah carefully lifted Bronte's beanie where it had slipped down over her forehead. A hematoma the size of a golf ball had formed on her forehead. Jonah winced, reaching up to gingerly touch it. "Our friend here is right. We need to get you to the med station."

"A really good doctor just said I didn't have a concussion," Bronte teased. "I'll be fine." She tried to catch her breath, wincing instead.

Jonah didn't like the look of the goose egg either. Just because he'd checked the dilation of her pupils didn't mean there weren't other things that needed to be checked out.

"I said it doesn't *seem* like you have a concussion, but I'd still like to get you to the clinic so we can officially rule it out. You also need an ice pack and some ibuprofen. Let's get you up."

Putting his hands under her arms, Jonah hauled her to her feet. Bronte grabbed his arms, her breathing quickening.

Jonah dipped his head, stepping closer to her to support her weight better. His heart squeezed seeing her obvious pain. "You good?"

"Just give me a minute," Bronte whispered back. Jonah laced his arms around her, clasping his hands on the small of her back.

"Do you need me to carry you to the med station?"

Bronte huffed out a laugh. "I do not want to bring any more attention to myself than I already have. At least it seems like the fan club is gone."

"Aw, come on. It could be fun. Everyone will think we're filming a Hallmark movie or something."

"Jonah White, you and I have two very different definitions of *fun*."

"Jonah? Bronte? Oh my goodness!" Jordi appeared from the crowd. "A kid came by the Tourism Bureau, where the med station's set up, and said someone fell and hit their head. I never thought it'd be you."

"You're working the med station?" Jonah asked.

"No, I just stopped by to see if Dr. Nova needed anything to eat. She's been pretty busy all day but mostly with headaches and dehydration. Nothing like this. She's on her way."

"Help me get her to the med station? We'll meet the doctor on the way." Jonah shifted, still not letting Bronte go but instead keeping an arm around her.

"You got it." Jordi spun on her heel and clapped her hands. "Okay, people, make a path. We gotta get to the med station!"

Bronte winced. "That's not exactly what I had in mind when I said I didn't want to draw any attention."

Jonah chuckled and tucked Bronte even closer into his side. "I'll hide you, and we'll make it there with no one noticing you."

They met up with Dr. Nova Lake, her thick black hair in a braid draped over her shoulder, and followed her the rest of the way to the clinic. Finally, inside the warm Tourism Bureau, where Jonathon Island Medical Clinic had set up a temporary med station, they made quick introductions and Jonah explained what had happened. Dr. Nova had Bronte sit in a folding chair while she got her an ice pack.

Dr. Nova whistled, seeing the goose egg on Bronte's forehead. "That's quite the bump you have there." Taking a penlight out, she bent only slightly to shine it in each of Bronte's eyes. "Are you dizzy at all?"

Bronte started to shake her head but stopped with a grimace. "No," she said instead.

"That's good. Did you black out at all?"

"At this point, I kind of wish I had. It would have saved me from having to experience the embarrassment."

The doctor chuckled and continued going through a full exam to make sure they didn't need to head to the hospital on the mainland. Jonah knew his dad had gotten someone to fill in at the practice until Jonah could retire from the Army and come back and take over, but he had expected someone older than him, and maybe someone a little taller. Dr. Nova barely reached his shoulder, but what she lacked in size, she made up for with presence. Her wide smile made him feel at ease, and Bronte had visibly sighed.

"Well, the good thing is, the major's assessment in the field was correct. You don't have a concussion." She handed Bronte a gel ice pack and dropped her penlight into the pocket of the white lab coat she had thrown over her jeans and sweater. "But you will have an epic headache for a little while."

"Yeah, it's already hurting pretty good."

"Let me go get you some ibuprofen from the lockbox. Just sit tight, and I'll be right back." The doctor patted Bronte on her knee and ducked out of the room.

Gingerly, Bronte pressed the ice pack to her forehead. She'd taken off her beanie, her hair, still in its braid, draped over her shoulder.

He shouldn't have let himself be pushed away from her. He should have planted his feet and gotten her out of there. Jonah ran his hand down his face.

"Now, don't go blaming yourself for this," Bronte said, her voice rough with pain.

"Who said I was blaming myself?"

Bronte motioned to him. "It's all over . . . you."

"I just—"

"Nope." Bronte held up her free hand. "It wasn't anyone's fault. I'm pretty sure that's Mr. Webster's definition of *accident*."

"I just don't like to see"—he almost said *people I care about* but was worried it would freak Bronte out, so instead changed it to—"you hurt."

"It's nothing that ice, pain meds, and rest won't cure. I'm fine. I promise. A little bummed we missed the announcement of the snowman winners, but fine."

"Jordi said we won."

"We did?" Bronte's eyebrows rose before she yanked them down in a frown, which also seemed to cause her pain, because she let her face go as neutral as possible.

"Easy there, tiger." Jonah reached over and squeezed her shoulder. "We won for most creative."

"Yes." Bronte punched the air but didn't show any emotion on her face. Jonah wanted to laugh at the concentration she was using to keep her face straight, but he didn't feel like getting punched.

"Here you are." Nova reappeared holding a small plastic cup with a couple pills inside. She handed it to Bronte with a bottle of water. Confirming that Bronte took the pills, the small woman picked up a clipboard and started writing notes before turning to Jonah. "How's Army life treating you? I heard you're stationed in Germany?" Her dark-brown eyes stayed focused on the chart in front of her.

Jonah stiffened. "That's right. It's no Jonathon Island, but it'll do for now."

Nova smiled. "Well, I'm keeping the clinic warm until you come back. I think your dad said you'd be up for retirement early next year?" She glanced up from her chart and frowned. "You know, if you decided you didn't want to take over the clinic, I could probably work something out with your father about staying more long-term."

Jonah's mouth went dry. Why would she assume he didn't want to take over the clinic? Had someone overheard his confession to Bronte and already spread rumors around? He should never have opened his mouth. "What makes you think I wouldn't want to take over the clinic?"

Nova held her hands up. "I'm just saying, if you decided you weren't ready to retire yet, I wouldn't mind staying on a little longer. I think the island is growing on me."

Jonah winced. "Sorry, that came out a little harsh. Thank you for offering."

Dr. Nova clicked her pen closed and ripped something

from the pad on her clipboard. "No worries. I didn't mean to sound like I was taking over your turf." She held the piece of paper to Bronte. "You should be good with ibuprofen for the pain, but if you need anything, here's my cell number, you can call me at any time. If you start feeling dizzy or anything is off with your vision, you tell Jonah first thing, okay? But other than that, get lots of rest, and let that bump heal."

"I will," Bronte said with a slight nod. "Can I still stay to watch the Christmas tree lighting?"

Nova looked back and forth between him and Bronte. "I don't see why you couldn't, if you're feeling up for it, but stay away from ice, and be careful not to hit your head again."

"You don't have to tell me twice," Bronte said, rising from the chair. She paused once she'd straightened, and Jonah stepped forward to help if she needed it.

"You guys have fun," Nova said, hugging the clipboard to her chest. "They did a community-only lighting at the beginning of the month, and let me tell you, it is magical."

Saying her goodbyes, Nova slipped out of the room.

"I'm not sure I'll be able to put this back on." Bronte held up her beanie.

"Here, let me help." He took the hat from her and set it toward the back of her head, tugging it over her ears. It took everything in him not to pull her to him and bury his nose in her hair. Being this close to her, her coconut–lavender scent almost overwhelmed him. "There. How's that feel?"

"It feels like I'm framing the evidence of my klutziness."

Bronte sighed. "But I'd rather that than you having to amputate my ears later because they freeze off my head."

Jonah smiled. It wasn't as bad as she thought. The way her hat sat on her head, her hair fell forward, mostly covering the large knot. "I promise it's not that bad. Are you still up for going to see the snow globes, or would you rather grab something to eat at Martha's?"

"I can't say I'm all that hungry anymore, but sitting at Martha's for a little bit sounds like a good plan."

"Well, then." Jonah offered his arm to Bronte. "Let's go, shall we?"

Bronte took his arm, and they made their way out of one of the offices-turned-exam room.

Nova stood at the front of the Tourism Bureau, handing a kid a piece of candy. She lifted her hand and waved. Jonah waved back. As he and Bronte pushed out into the frigid air to make their way to Martha's, he couldn't help but think about what Nova had said about staying on Jonathon Island longer. She thought he'd want to take up her offer because he wanted to stay in the Army longer, but would she want to stay if he didn't plan to take over at all? It didn't solve Amy's concern over their dad's disappointment, but maybe knowing another trusted doctor would be taking over would help ease the disappointment.

Jonah didn't know, but something inside felt a little better knowing that at least Dr. Nova Lake seemed to be on his side.

Ten

AFTER DONNING THEIR COATS, JONAH tucked Bronte under his arm and led them out of the Tourism Bureau. He vowed to keep an eye on Bronte the rest of the afternoon. If she showed any signs of being exhausted or in too much pain, he'd march them back home. No matter how much they both wanted to see the Christmas tree lighting.

They had just stepped out of the Tourism Bureau, heading in the direction of Martha's, when Mia stopped them. "Hey, Jonah! Bronte!"

"Hey, Mia, how's it going?" Jonah lifted the hand that wasn't currently wrapped around Bronte in a wave. Seeing the small girl on Mia's hip, he asked, "Is this Maggie?"

Smiling, Mia looked to the pink-coat-clad toddler, who had just decided to hide her face in her mom's neck. "Yes, this is Maggie. Maggie, can you say hi?"

Maggie turned her head, peeking one dark-blue eye

from her hiding place and lifting her hand quickly in a wave before burying back into her mom's neck. "I'm so sorry. She's generally very sociable, but someone skipped her nap."

"No worries. I can't believe she's so big."

"They grow like weeds, that's for sure."

He couldn't wait to have a family of his own. To have his own kids who would be growing like weeds. He hadn't been lying to Bronte when he'd said he needed to be able to provide for his family. Would a bookstore really allow him to have the big family he wanted? Or should he sacrifice a little bit of happiness and just take over the clinic as planned?

Continuing their walk toward Martha's, Mia shifted Maggie in her arms and turned to Bronte, concern lacing her features. "Bronte, I heard about your fall. How are you feeling?"

Jonah felt Bronte stiffen beside him, and he tightened his arm around her.

"I'm doing okay." Bronte leaned into him, and Jonah's pulse picked up just a tick. "Just a little headache."

Jonah knew Bronte was downplaying how "little" her headache must be, but he hoped the ibuprofen had kicked in.

"I'm so glad. Please let us know if you need anything, okay? I know you're in good hands with Jonah here." She playfully nudged Jonah with her shoulder.

Bronte smiled and ducked her head.

"Well, this is me." Mia motioned to the shop they were in front of, *Beautiful Homes Art and Realty* painted on the door. "Maggie and I are going to warm up for a bit, and I'm going to see if I can't get her to sleep for an hour before the Christmas tree lighting. You guys will be there, right?"

"We wouldn't miss it!" Jonah replied.

They said their goodbyes and dodged the few people on the sidewalk to make their way next door to Martha's.

The sun had started to set, making all the lights on Main Street brighter. Crisscrossing between one side of the shops and the other, the lights had always been one of Jonah's favorite parts about Christmas on Jonathon Island. The shops spared no expense in their decorating. Even the few shops that were still empty had a Christmas window display—including one with a very lifelike Nativity scene—upon closer examination, Jonah realized it was real people.

At one time, Martha's had been the only restaurant open on the main strip during the holiday season, and there wouldn't have been any open booths. Thankfully, with the pizzeria and the bar and grill now open, they should be able to get a spot to sit for a few minutes before the lighting.

Warm air engulfed Bronte and Jonah as they stepped into the buzzing restaurant, and Jonah could feel Bronte physically sigh at the warmth. Jonah scanned the room for an empty table, and his stomach fell when he didn't see any—there weren't even any spots at the bar.

"Jonah, Bronte, back here!" Dani lifted her mug in greeting and motioned for them to join her, Liam, Declan, and Lily in the corner booth in the back.

After taking off his gloves and shoving them in his coat

pocket, Jonah held up two fingers in Vera's direction and mouthed *hot chocolates* before weaving through the tables to the back booth. Dani motioned for Liam to move farther into the booth, leaving room for Jonah and Bronte to join them.

"Bronte, this is Lily and Declan."

Jonah nodded at the couple on the opposite side of the horseshoe booth as he slid in next to Dani. He had to admit he'd been glad when Mika Beth had mentioned in one of their monthly calls that Lily and Declan had gotten back together. Lily's fun, purple-streaked hair went perfectly with Declan's put-together MBA self. "Declan is Martha's son, and he and Lily own the fudge shop in town. Still rocking the purple hair, I see, Lily."

"They're just highlights, and it's lavender, Jonah," Lily pointed out, twisting a strand of hair in her fingers.

"Lavender, purple. Same thing, right?"

Lily's nose wrinkled. "Uh, no."

"I like them," Declan said, nuzzling Lily's hair.

Lily giggled. "It's nice to meet you, Bronte."

"Nice to meet you too," Bronte said as she slid in next to Jonah, who turned to help her out of her coat.

"Nice goose egg," Liam pointed out.

Dani playfully backhanded him. "Jordi told us what happened, Bronte. How are you doing?"

"I'm okay. My head hurts a little bit, but other than that and feeling like an idiot, I'm good." Bronte took a fry off the plate that Declan slid her way.

"I'm so glad. Oh!" Dani turned and dug through her bag sitting on the seat next to her. She held out an envelope toward Bronte and Jonah. "Congratulations on winning for most creative snowman. You guys won a gift card to Good Day Coffee."

"Thanks." Bronte smiled, accepting the envelope before folding it and putting it in her coat pocket. "How has your day been going?"

"So good. Not only is this the best Christmas stroll ever, we've already sold out for the ball on Wednesday." Dani's grin spread over her entire face.

"Were you really worried you weren't going to sell out?" Lily asked, moving plates and glasses around on the table so Vera could put down giant mugs of hot chocolate in front of both Jonah and Bronte.

"Thanks, Vera." Jonah nodded to the older woman. "Yeah, doesn't it generally sell out?"

"She's been worried about this for weeks," Liam said, putting his arm around Dani.

"It's just that it's been so long. I wasn't sure if anyone was interested, and I'm in charge this year, so I just really want to make sure that everything goes well, you know?"

"We'll be there for sure, Dani," Declan said, raising his glass in Dani's direction.

"Us too," Jonah agreed.

"Speaking of, I wanted to know if I could get all of you to help on Tuesday for the finishing touches on the ballroom."

Lily winced. "We have to work at the fudge shop, but if it's super slow, we could probably close down a little early and come help."

"I can be there." Jonah looked to Bronte. He didn't want to volunteer her, knowing she had work to get done.

Bronte just shrugged. "Sure, I'll be there. What time?"

They made plans, Liam letting them know that they would come pick them up on the snowmobiles so they wouldn't have to walk.

Dani glanced at her watch. "We've got to get going," she said to Liam.

"We need to head out too," Lily said, pushing Declan out of the booth. "See you guys over there in a little bit." The couple waved as they moved toward the swinging kitchen door.

"The Christmas tree lighting is happening in thirty minutes. Are you guys coming?" Dani stood from the booth, swinging the strap of her purse over her shoulder.

Jonah took a drink from his hot chocolate. He glanced at Bronte, eyebrow raised in question.

"I've been waiting all day for this. You're not getting me to go home now," she exclaimed.

"Pro tip." Dani leaned in, Liam's hand on her back. "Have Vera sneak you out the back so you don't get stuck fighting everyone for good seats."

"And if you want, feel free to hang out with me in the control box," Liam added. "If you don't feel like fighting the crowds."

Jonah was grateful Dani and Liam were making Bronte feel welcome and giving her an option for avoiding crowds of people after her accident. "Thanks, guys. We'll catch up with you in a bit."

When Dani and Liam left, Jonah moved across from

Bronte. He caught her with her eyes closed, head resting on the back of the booth. "You doing okay? We don't have to go to the lighting if you're feeling bad."

"Just a little tired," Bronte said, lifting her head back up, eyes fluttering open. "I really don't want to miss the lighting, but maybe we can hide in the control box with Liam? If you don't mind."

"Sure thing. Go ahead and finish up your hot chocolate, and we'll head over there."

Jonah needed to keep a close eye on her. She said she was doing okay, but the last thing he wanted was for her to overdo it. Seeing Bronte fall and then rushing her to the med station had made him realize how much he didn't want to run the clinic on the island. He'd had to be the bearer of bad news to too many families when a procedure didn't go as planned. It would only be a matter of time before the person rushed to the clinic was someone he loved, and everyone would rely on him to make sure they went home.

He had grown up on this island, so everyone was someone he loved. He didn't want that responsibility. If only he could make his father understand why he would be walking away from it all.

"I just wanted to let everyone know," Jordi called, breaking into Jonah's thoughts from where she stood on a chair in the middle of the restaurant. "It's time to head to the park. The Christmas tree lighting is happening in ten minutes!" Jordi jumped off the chair and went to help ring up customers so they could make their way to the park.

While most of the patrons in Martha's headed toward

the front of the restaurant, Jonah reached for Bronte's hand and, with a nod from Vera, tugged her toward the kitchen door, which would lead them out.

Pushing out into the night behind the shops, Jonah led Bronte up to the boardwalk. A few others had the same idea to skip the crowded street and sneak up the boardwalk to the park. Lights from the ferry glinted off the black water. The last ferry of the evening would leave a little later than normal, allowing for the tourists to enjoy the Christmas tree lighting as the grand finale of the Christmas stroll. They made it to the park, and Jonah located the control booth—or a temporary canopy tent set up over a control board for the lights and music.

"Hello, again, friends." Liam greeted them from where he stood over a nest of wires, all snaking their way to the main switch he was ready to pull at Dani's signal. "Come in and find a place. I'm just triple-checking all the connections and settings to make sure we're good to go."

Jonah and Bronte stepped to the side of the booth, out of the way and free from the wires. "Do you need help with anything?" Jonah asked, pulling Bronte toward him. She sighed and leaned her head back to rest against his shoulder. He regretted asking Liam if he needed any help, knowing he'd have to move away from her.

Liam glanced up from the wires he was checking, a knowing smirk on his face. "I got it."

Under the dim camping light Liam had set up near the control panel, Jonah studied Bronte. She had her eyes closed. Were the meds wearing off? He should have insisted they go back to the house. Bronte didn't have a concussion, but walking around with a purple knot the size of a golf ball on her forehead couldn't be comfortable. They needed to get more ice on it, although he supposed the cold air could be just as good.

Their conversation from earlier came back to him. His sister had him convinced his decision would break their father's heart. But Bronte's confidence that his family wouldn't want to see him miserable—that being what would break their hearts—had stayed with him.

Was this a situation he couldn't win no matter which way he sliced it? Would hearts be broken no matter what he did? An ache pressed behind his breastbone.

"Hey, where'd you go?" Bronte asked groggily.

Jonah shifted his arms around her to pull her closer, her presence easing the ache but at the same time replacing it with a yearning of a different kind. "How are you feeling?"

Bronte gave him a pointed look. "Don't try and change the subject." She faced him, the sudden space between them making Jonah want to shiver. If talking made her move from his arms, he'd be silent forever. "You're thinking about your dad again, aren't you?"

Could he be read that easily? "Maybe."

Bronte gave him a ghost of a smile. "Jonah, you are going to have to talk to him. You can't get out of it. You aren't going to be able to sweep this under a rug or take it all on your shoulders. I don't have a family, but one thing I know is that family is supposed to be there for each other. I'm sure after talking with your dad, you'll be able to figure something out that doesn't end in anyone's heart being broken."

Her words were balm on his tender soul. "How are you so wise, Bronte Parker?"

"Eh." Bronte shrugged a shoulder, mouth lifted in a smirk. "You learn a couple things when you get to study many different families."

"I'm sorry you don't have family, Bronte. I'm sorry you were hurt."

Bronte's breath hitched. "It's fine."

Jonah reached up and pushed a rogue curl behind her ear, being careful not to touch her forehead. "No, it's not."

Tears swam in her eyes. He hated that he had some part in putting them there, but how could Bronte not see how amazing she was?

"Almost time, guys," Liam called. Jonah saw Liam in his peripheral vision, leaning closer to the opening and listening to whatever Dani said in her bullhorn.

Jonah wiped a thumb under Bronte's eye, catching a tear. Her eyes were smoke and glitter.

"Ten . . . nine . . . eight . . ."

Dani began the countdown, shouting through the bullhorn, the crowd joining in, but Jonah's gaze locked on Bronte's, the gap between them slowly disappearing. Jonah shifted his body, now facing Bronte. He encircled her in his arms, bringing her closer. Her eyes slid closed as his lips found hers. She tasted like chocolate and peppermint but somehow sweeter than any concoction they could find at Martha's or anywhere else. Bronte turned in his arms, pulling him closer, deepening the kiss. He couldn't get enough of her. He was a man dying from thirst, and she was the water saving him.

Jonah was vaguely aware of the Christmas tree coming to life and Liam laughing while muttering something about new love and make-out sessions moments before the soundtrack for the lighting also sprang to life.

But Jonah was completely lost in the spell Bronte cast. And he was perfectly fine with that.

Eleven

Date December 21
Days until Deadline 13
Words to be written 77,533

SHE WAS FALLING FOR JONAH.

She couldn't fall for Jonah. It wasn't—practical. She needed to prevent the walls protecting her heart from completely shattering. She needed to keep herself safe and Jonah at arm's length. Jonah wanted something she couldn't give him, and look how that had turned out with Brad.

Still. One kiss from Jonah and she'd felt more than any of Brad's hundreds of kisses had ever made her feel. She should tell Lexi more than the quick update she'd just texted her, but she didn't want her friend worrying about her in another relationship after what felt like minutes since Bronte had found out about Brad's engagement.

Was that all this was? Was she trying to make herself feel better because Brad had already picked someone new?

Lexi

So let me get this straight. You slipped, hit your head, and Jonah came to your rescue? You're an idiot, but a genius romantic idiot.

Bronte

😳 Only you would think slipping and falling to be romantic. I hit my head really hard. I could be dying.

Lexi

Oh, right. Are you ok?

Bronte rolled her eyes, and then promptly winced at the pain shooting through her head.

Bronte

I'm fine, Lex.

Fine, if not a little confused. Had she really kissed Jonah last night?

Her lips still tingled, and she bit down on them to keep from smiling.

Bronte dropped her phone on the side table and stretched her arms over her head. The last thing she remembered from the night before was Jonah insisting they needed to watch an old Claymation movie with Rudolph and Frosty. They must have fallen asleep during the movie. Jonah was still asleep on the wingback, his Santa-socked feet propped on the coffee table, and his neck at a weird angle that made Bronte wince. That was going to hurt later.

Gingerly, Bronte felt the knot on her forehead. Still tender, but at least a little smaller. Scooting off the couch, she grabbed the quilt she'd been using and draped it over Jonah.

She tiptoed to the kitchen, shook two ibuprofen from the bottle, and popped them in her mouth, swallowing them dry before putting the kettle on the stove. A strong cup of tea and her laptop were what she needed. Even if what she wanted to do was curl up on the couch and go back to sleep.

Waiting for the kettle to sing, Bronte thought back to the night before. About the kiss she could still feel. She had to be crazy to be thinking about kissing Jonah. She had sworn off relationships after Brad. She was broken goods, and she'd do well to remember she was better on her own. Even if she felt different around Jonah. Felt like he actually cared. Had she felt like that when she and Brad first met? She couldn't remember, but she didn't think so.

Her phone pinged with another incoming text from Lexi. Seeing that it started with "How is your book . . ." Bronte set her phone to ignore all notifications before laying it face down on the countertop.

Lexi didn't need to know how dismal her word count still was. That would just bring up questions of what she had been doing instead of writing and who she had been spending all her time with. Which would ultimately turn into Lexi telling Bronte to forget about the fun she told her to have and to just write her book.

Bronte gazed at Jonah, sleeping on the wingback chair. He looked so peaceful, hands folded across his chest. Like an old man who had fallen asleep watching the nightly news. Bronte bit back a smile before turning back to the kettle that just started to boil. She had *just* told herself she was better on her own, and here she was ogling Jonah. Again.

Tea made, she slid in front of her laptop, which was still sitting at the table where she'd left it the day before she and Jonah had walked to town. She'd had every intention of coming back and working, but instead, she and Jonah had stayed up all night nursing her headache with eggnog, popcorn, and old Christmas movies.

Heaving in a deep breath, she toggled her mouse to the Pike Family Saga document on her laptop. Today was a new day, and she would get a massive amount of words written—hopefully on the correct book this time.

It was amazing how hard it was to get words on the page when one had a splitting headache. Anytime she thought about the plot of the Pike Family Saga and tried to add more romance into it, another pulse would shoot through her skull. So she did what any normal person trying to get a book written would do. She worked on the project that made her happy and didn't make her head feel worse.

Three hours in and she had added almost five thousand words on the wrong project. She still found it ridiculous she was writing a rom-com. She couldn't remember the last time she'd written this much in a small amount of time. Her fingers flying over the keyboard brought a smile to her lips. She loved it when a story flowed like this.

"How's it going?"

Bronte squealed.

Jonah appeared next to her, hair wet from a shower, the scent of his soap filling her senses. "I'm so sorry. I thought you saw me!" he apologized, hands up in defense.

"When did you even get up from the couch?" Bronte choked out, her hands on either side of her computer on the kitchen table, grounding her. "I didn't even see you leave the living room."

"I can tell," he said, sliding into the chair next to her. "How are you doing?"

Bronte tried to shrug but winced at the movement of her head. She hadn't realized her pain meds had worn off. Or even that she'd been sitting at the table long enough for them to. "I'm doing okay."

"Do you have a headache?"

"Maybe a little bit." She squinted. "Nothing that I can't live with."

"When was the last time you had meds?"

Bronte looked at the clock on her computer. "A few hours."

Jonah shook two ibuprofen from the bottle and slid the glass of water sitting in front of Bronte a little closer. She took the pills and washed them down. "Thank you."

Jonah ran a hand down his face. "I can't believe I slept so long. Sorry about that."

"We stayed up pretty late. I didn't have the heart to wake you. I'm surprised you're already up. It's barely lunchtime." In fact, he looked like he could use a few more hours of sleep. The bags under Jonah's eyes had bags. "And besides, I really needed to get some work done. No point in waking you up just to watch me type."

"But what if you'd needed something?"

"I'm sure it would have been fine, Jonah. It's not that big of a deal."

"Well, thank you for letting me sleep. I can't tell you the last time I slept that long. I guess jet lag and everything finally caught up with me." Jonah pushed away from the table. "Are you hungry?"

"Now that you mention it, I'm starving," Bronte said, closing her laptop. She couldn't remember the last time she'd been so wrapped up in a story that she'd lost track of time. It was a good feeling. But now that Jonah had mentioned food and she'd realized how long it had been, her stomach let her know that it had been neglected.

"I meant to get up and go to church this morning," Jonah said, pulling out tomatoes, onions, and garlic.

"Little Stone Bible Church? The one that donated all the fun snowmen accessories for the contest yesterday?" Bronte asked, moving from the table to the island bar.

"That's the one." Turning the tap on, Jonah ran the tomatoes under the water. "I grew up in that church. Do you go to church anywhere in Tulsa?"

Bronte shook her head. "I haven't been to church in ..." She thought back. When was the last time she'd been to church? "It's been a long time."

"I'm sorry." Shaking the extra water off the tomatoes, Jonah placed them on the cutting board.

Bronte shrugged. "I was in some good homes and some not so good homes." Bronte picked at something that had dried on the counter. "One family, the Martins, took me to church with them on Sunday mornings. I really enjoyed it. I felt like I belonged there. I even asked Jesus into my heart and got baptized—I did all the right things, but . . ." Bronte sucked in a shaky breath, not sure why telling this story made her emotional. She'd loved that church, but in the end, the inevitable had happened. "The Martins had planned to adopt me, but they got pregnant and my adoption fell through. I was only with them for six months before I was moved again."

Jonah was quiet for a moment before asking, "Did you get moved a lot?"

"I did." Bronte left it at that and went back to picking at the spot on the countertop. "I think that's when I decided that it was all too good to be true. All that stuff about being adopted into God's family. I guess I'm too much for God too. Or not enough. Brad told me that as well, among other things."

"Brad?" Jonah's eyebrow quirked as he glanced up from chopping tomatoes and onions.

"Yeah, Brad. He is . . . was my boyfriend." *Stop talking.* It was one thing to tell him about failed adoptions and growing up in foster care, but it was a whole other thing to tell him about Brad. "We broke up earlier this year." Or rather, he'd broken up with her. "He said a lot of things."

"I'm sure most of them weren't true."

Bronte blinked, looking Jonah in his eyes the color of the ocean, and she believed him. She believed that what Brad had told her wasn't true.

"Bronte, you're never too much for God. God can always handle your problems, and I want you to know that you're always welcome here too."

They fell quiet. Jonah reached across the bar and entwined his fingers in hers. Bronte stared at their hands. Heat burned in her middle at how right it felt to hold his hand. Jonah rubbed a thumb over her knuckles. Would he lean over and kiss her? A chill ran down her spine. She pulled her hand back and put it in her lap. Her guard was slowly coming down, but she didn't think Jonah would hurt her.

"Thank you." Her voice was husky, and she had to swallow down emotions that were best left deep. "I wish we could have gone to church too."

"I believe there's a midnight candlelight service on Christmas Eve if you want to go—we could go after the ball." Jonah had turned back to the stove, dumping in the tomatoes he'd finished chopping.

"I'd really like that." But would she? On one hand, she was excited at the possibility of going back to church. At feeling that sense of belonging she'd had as a child. But there were also nerves about what was happening to her heart. The one she'd poured concrete over and boarded up after everything that'd happened with Brad. She'd already made the decision she'd be better off alone.

Had coming to Jonathon Island been a mistake, or the *happiest* of mistakes? The more time she spent on the island and around Jonah, the more the hardness around her heart was being chipped away. And she didn't know if that was a good thing or if she was just setting herself up for more heartbreak.

Watching Jonah's strong, broad back at the stove, her

stomach twisted. If her heart broke this time, would she ever be able to recover?

Jonah tried not to laugh at the plastic souvenir currently being held up for his inspection. Wanting to give Bronte the uninterrupted time to get writing in, he'd snuck off to get a couple of things from Doug's. He'd been thinking about Christmas gift ideas for Bronte when he bumped into Cody and Finn, who were getting out of the house for a bit to give Mia a break while Maggie took a nap. When Finn had heard that Jonah couldn't figure out a good gift for Bronte, the little boy had promised he had the "perfectest idea ever" before dragging him over to a display of plastic sharks and animals.

"This is the most perfectest one." Finn held up a plastic shark with *Jonathon Island* painted on the side, a huge grin on his face at the treasure he'd found.

Jonah found it funny that Doug's Market would have plastic sharks. Sure, Jonathon Island was on the water, but as far as he knew, the lake housed no sharks. The small grocer on the island carried a handful of novelty items and souvenirs since the actual souvenir shop had closed with the season.

Kneeling down, Jonah inspected the shark Finn held up. "I'm not sure that's something Bronte would like as much as you do."

Finn's face scrunched in confusion. "Why not? This is the best shark I ever found."

"Why don't we get that one for you, buddy? We'll look

for something else for Jonah's friend," Cody said, ruffling Finn's hair.

The boy's face lit up. "Really? I can keep this one? Oh boy, wait 'til I show Maggie. She's going to love it. I need to find one for her too." The boy plopped back down on the floor in front of the bin of sharks and started digging around.

"So, what exactly are you looking for?" Cody asked after he had made sure Finn was occupied with finding his younger sister a shark of her own.

What *was* he looking for?

His and Bronte's conversation bounced around in his mind. Her having been raised in foster care made so many other things click. Like why many of the Christmas traditions were new to her and why she'd never had a real family Christmas. He wanted to make sure Bronte had the full Christmas-morning experience this year.

Jonah shrugged at his friend's question. "I don't know. Something perfect." He tried to think back to Christmas mornings at the White house and started making a mental list, but other than presents, atmosphere, and the snacks his mom always made, he came up blank. His mom and sisters were so much better at this kind of stuff than he was. What he wouldn't give to have them home helping him right now.

Cody laughed. "Thanks, that really narrows it down. Not sure I'm going to be much help."

"Bumping into you and Finn made this a lot more fun," Jonah reassured him. "It's just . . ." How could he explain what he was feeling to Cody? "I want it to be something special. I don't think she's ever had a great Christmas, so I want this to be . . ."

"Perfect," Cody supplied.

Jonah shrugged. "Yeah."

Cody slapped Jonah on the shoulder. "I know you'll be able to find the gift you're looking for and give Bronte the Christmas she deserves. She's pretty special to you, isn't she?"

"I know it's crazy because we just met, but I don't know. There's just something there." He needed to tell himself to calm down. Yes, they'd shared one kiss. One firework-inducing kiss, at least in his experience. But then they'd gone home, and she hadn't brought it up, hadn't tried to kiss him again. He wanted to talk to her about it, but he didn't want to make it awkward if she thought it had been a mistake.

Besides, if she wanted to do more kissing like that, they'd never get anything else done. It was stupid. He knew they'd go their separate ways and probably never see each other again. This wasn't one of the rom-coms his sisters recommended. Strangers didn't meet and fall in love and spend a lifetime together.

"When you just know, you know. It's a saying for a reason."

"I'm hungry." Finn came to stand next to Cody, three plastic Jonathon Island sharks clutched in his tiny hands.

"We just ate lunch an hour ago, buddy," Cody reminded him.

Finn shrugged, studying a thread on Cody's jeans, face scrunched. "Mom says I'm a growing boy, so I eat more."

Cody ruffled Finn's tawny curls. "Your mom is right there. I guess this means it's time for us to go. We'll see you Wednesday at the ball?" he asked Jonah.

"For sure. We'll be there." It wasn't lost on Jonah how he'd so easily responded in the plural. We. Jonah and Bronte. It sounded so right in his mind.

Cody and Finn walked to the front of the store. They paid for Finn's collection of sharks and, after Cody had made sure Finn had his hat and gloves in place, pushed out into the cold island afternoon.

Not finding anything more they needed from Doug's, Jonah made his final purchases and headed to the Fudge Shop on the Corner. The sweet treat might be a nice reward for Bronte after an afternoon of working.

"I thought you were leaving the island and meeting up with your family." Declan's voice greeted him from behind the fudge shop's counter.

Jonah laughed at the lack of greeting from the shop owner. "Not until the twenty-sixth."

"Oh my goodness, you're so rude." Lily, her lavender-streaked hair pulled back into a low ponytail, stared, flabbergasted, at Declan before turning to Jonah. "How's Bronte's head doing? That was quite a knot. I'm a little surprised she didn't have a concussion."

"Yes, very large bump, but no concussion. Thank God. She's doing good. I'm trying to stay away this afternoon so she can get some writing done."

"And you decided to come here?" Declan raised an eyebrow.

"Declan!" Lily slapped his chest with the back of her

hand. "I'm sorry about him, Jonah. Are you wanting some fudge?"

"Yes, please. I thought it might be a nice treat for Bronte after working hard all day." He scanned the display of different fudges. "Just give me two pounds of a mix. The best ones."

"It's all the best," Declan mumbled as he folded a box and began filling it with a variety of fudge.

"Hush, Declan," Lily said. "We'll have that ready for you in just a moment if you want to have a seat over there." She pointed to a table in a small alcove. "There's coffee at the end of the bar. You can help yourself if you'd like."

Jonah poured himself a cup of coffee and sat down at the table overlooking the main strip. The snow left on the street was more of a dirty slush pile after the events of the weekend. Even still, the storefronts with their ribbons and garland, and the lights strung back and forth across the street, gave something magical to Jonathon Island at Christmastime.

"Here you go." Lily put a box of fudge on the table in front of him.

Jonah reached for his wallet. "How much do I owe—"

Lily waved him off. "Nonsense. Put your money away and think of it as a welcome home and Merry Christmas present."

"Lil, I can't let you—" Jonah started to protest.

"Of course you can," Declan said, wrapping his arms around Lily and resting his chin on her shoulder. "I've quickly learned you do what Lily says, no questions asked."

"Thank you." Jonah took a twenty from his wallet and shoved it into the tip jar. "See you guys at the ball."

He pushed out into the cold air coming off the water and looked down Main Street, catching sight of the steeple of Little Stone Bible Church. Remembering what Bronte had said about church being a place where she had felt at home, he suddenly had an idea for a gift for her—well, numerous gifts. The first required he visit Doug's again, where he thought he remembered seeing Jonathon Island stockings. Yes, they might be a little cheesy, but they'd have to do in a pinch.

Tucking his bags close to him, he made his way back up the street to Doug's, then he planned to head to the church. He hoped Pastor Arnie was there to let him in and that there was an extra Bible he could have.

He knew just the gift to make sure Bronte had the most perfect Christmas.

Twelve

Date December 23

Days until Deadline 12

Words to be written 74,122

WHILE HELPING TO SET UP THE Christmas ball probably shouldn't have been on her list of things to do today, Bronte had to admit the break from staring at the ever-blinking cursor was nice. After writing (or staring at the aforementioned blinking cursor) for most of the morning, Jonah and Bronte had bundled up and hiked to the Grand Sullivan Hotel.

The main part of the hotel still resembled a snow-covered construction site, but at five stories high with a tall veranda and the long summer porch, the Grand Hotel really would live up to its name once it was finished. Bronte really wished it would have been possible to have stayed there. But if she had stayed there, she probably wouldn't have met Jonah or Mia or Dani or anyone else.

Speaking of Dani, she was in full boss mode and approached them, clipboard in hand, as they were stashing their coats with the pile from the other volunteers.

"Jonah, can you help Arnie finish hanging ornaments from the ceiling?" Dani asked, consulting her clipboard before turning to Bronte. "And Bronte, if you can help Mia and me finish up with the bows for the centerpieces, that would be great."

In all the charity events she had been to over the past few years, Bronte had never been to a Christmas ball, much less helped set up for one, but Dani was really outdoing herself. The pink-and-white-striped walls of the ballroom were lined with Christmas trees of all sizes.

Jordi, along with a woman who looked like an older version of her, strung white lights on each of the trees. Mia and another woman sat at a table, fingers threading through ribbons, making elaborate bows. Cody and Liam were setting up round tables in neat rows, leaving an open half-circle in the middle of the room for a dance floor.

Jonah squeezed Bronte's hand and joined the pastor, who tottered on a ladder, trying to attach another ball ornament to the ceiling.

"That's an interesting concept," Bronte said, watching as Pastor Arnie finally got the ornament attached to the ceiling and climbed down to choose another one.

"Thanks." Dani put her hands in the back pockets of her jeans as they watched Jonah climb the ladder this time, Pastor Arnie handing him one of the oversized ornaments.

"I loved the idea of covering the ceiling with Christmas balls."

"It looks great. I thought the hotel burned down though. There doesn't look to be any damage in here." Bronte motioned to the room.

"You probably can't tell from outside, but this building doesn't actually connect to the hotel, so other than a few superficial issues, it was spared from too much damage. Come on." Dani motioned Bronte with her head. "Let's get to work on the bows."

Bronte followed Dani over to the table where the two other women were quickly tying bow after bow. How would she ever be able to keep up?

"Bronte, you know Mia." Dani held a hand in Mia's direction. Mia glanced up and smiled at her, then Dani turned to the forty-something woman sitting across from Mia. "And this is Janine Dirks, she's the president of the Jonathon Island Historical Society."

"It's so nice to meet you," Janine said, nodding her hello. With her red hair and large glasses, she looked the part for a president of the historical society. Janine held up her hands, fingers tangled in ribbon. "I'd shake your hand, but I'm a little tied up at the moment."

Bronte smiled, taking the seat next to Mia. "That's okay, it's nice to meet you."

"It's really easy," Dani said, taking a seat across from Bronte and picking up a spool of ribbon. "You measure out about this much"—Dani stretched out a piece of ribbon and showed Bronte—"and then one, two, three, and four—and voilá, a bow." Dani held the velvet red bow she had somehow looped together in front of Bronte.

It looked easy enough, but after three tries, Bronte's bow still looked lopsided. "I don't think I'm being much help." Bronte held up her one sad bow.

"That looks great," Mia said, folding together two more bows and adding them to the pile.

"I agree," Janine said, plucking the bow out of Bronte's hand and adding it to the stack. "The trick is not to overthink it. Mia, you want to help me get the tablecloths on the tables? It looks like Liam and Cody are just about finished putting them up. We'll probably need to steam the tablecloths first, then we can start getting the centerpieces together."

Bronte grabbed another piece of ribbon and tried to twist it into submission as Mia and Janine pushed away from the table.

"So," Dani said once they were alone. "You and Jonah?"

"What about me and Jonah?" Bronte ducked her head to hopefully keep Dani from noticing her face turning red. She hated her body's response. "There's nothing going on between us." Why did she feel the need to add anything? Now it looked like she was trying to hide something. Which she wasn't. There wasn't anything to hide.

Her thoughts drifted back to their kiss. She had almost convinced herself it had been a figment of her imagination.

"Mm-hmm. That's not what Liam said." Bronte could feel Dani looking at her. "For what it's worth, I think you're good for Jonah. He seems happier when he's around you."

"Jonah just seems like a happy guy in general." Though she didn't hate the idea that she, of all people, made him happy.

"Oh, he is, but he's had some rough times, just like all of us at some point or other."

"Like what?"

"Jonah won't talk about it, and he'd kill me if he ever found out I told you, but seven years ago, he was engaged. Bree, a girl we grew up with."

Bronte swallowed. Jonah had mentioned having his heart broken by someone, but he hadn't mentioned they'd been engaged.

Dani glanced over her shoulder as if making sure no one was listening in before continuing.

"He and Bree were high school sweethearts, and everyone thought they'd end up together, but after dating for years, he came home on leave one month, and they just broke it off. No one really knew what happened, and between you and me, I don't think he ever really got over it. Until now." Dani wagged her eyebrows.

"Oh." Bronte wasn't sure what to do with this information, and why was Dani telling her all this? Was it some offhanded way of giving Bronte her blessing? Did she even need Dani's blessing?

No, she didn't, because nothing was happening between her and Jonah, and nothing ever could.

"All I'm saying is, if you think there might be something there, and I really think there is, you should go for it."

"I don't know." Bronte added another wonky bow to the pile. "Truth is, I've sworn off love."

"Maybe you're finished with love, but it might not be finished with you."

Bronte bit her lip. Her heart warred within her chest, beating so fast she felt like it would pop out at any moment. Jonah was so different from Brad. But did she really think she could take a chance again?

"Lights are done, Dani." Jordi slid into the seat next to Bronte, and Bronte couldn't have been more thankful for an interruption from her swirling thoughts and all this talk about love.

"Thanks, Jordi." Dani picked up her clipboard and checked something off.

"Is everyone still planning on going to your place tomorrow to get ready for the ball?" Jordi asked Dani as she picked up a stream of ribbon and tied it into a bow. Bronte grinned, seeing that Jordi's bow resembled her lopsided bows more than Dani's perfect one. "You too, Bronte."

That was right. Jordi had promised she had a dress Bronte could borrow for the ball, but Jordi sounded like she was inviting her over for a party. "I thought I'd just swing by and pick up the dress you had for me."

"Oh, no. I have so many that you should probably pick which one speaks to you the most, and we've planned a whole shindig. Besides us"—Jordi circled a finger that encompassed her, Bronte, and Dani—"it'll be Mia, Lily, and Sadie—have you met Lily and Sadie yet, Bronte? You'll love them. We're all going to meet at Dani's house to get ready. It'll be like prom all over again."

"I never went to prom."

Dani's and Jordi's mouths gaped open.

"What?" Dani said at the same time as Jordi exclaimed, "Seriously?"

Bronte nodded. "I actually grew up in foster homes, and the week before prom, I had to move homes, which also meant moving high schools, and I didn't really feel like going to a prom where I didn't know anyone."

"Then I'm really insisting," Jordi said. "You have to come."

"Yes. We're going to have so much fun," Dani chimed in. "Jordi has the best dresses. I might steal one from her stash as well. Oh, and I'll be bringing snack food from the pizzeria. So make sure not to eat before you come."

"I don't know how you stay so skinny when you live above the pizzeria, Dani." Jordi pinched her friend's side. "I'd be eating there every meal."

"You get used to it after a while." Dani batted Jordi away.

"Why do you have so many dresses lying around, Jordi?" Bronte tried to think of her wardrobe back at home and was pretty sure she only had one formal dress that Lexi had made her purchase for a big awards ceremony a couple years back. She had worn it once and wanted to donate it, but Lexi talked her into keeping it for any other formal event she may, or may not, attend in her lifetime. A lot of good it was doing her now, sitting at home in her closet.

"I used to do a lot of pageants." Jordi shrugged.

"Why'd you stop?" Bronte asked. She remembered Jordi mentioning her pageant days the morning she had met her.

"It was time. So, it's settled then." It wasn't lost on

Bronte that Jordi had skipped over giving them the real reason she no longer did pageants. "Dani's apartment. Tomorrow at noon?"

"I can't wait," Bronte said, only a little surprised to find out that it was true.

"See you tomorrow! Thanks for all your help today," Dani called as Jonah and Bronte left the Grand. Liam had offered to take them back on the snowmobiles, but Bronte had said she'd rather walk, hoping she'd be ready to sit and work for a while by the time they made it back to the Whites' house.

"You did a great job on that ceiling. All those ornaments, they look so cool," Bronte said, snow crunching under her feet, arms swinging at her sides.

"Why, I thank you." Jonah mock bowed. "By the end, your bows weren't looking quite as wonky."

"Hey." Bronte nudged his shoulder with hers. "Making bows is not as easy as it looks."

They'd just made it to the first line of stores when the Fudge Shop on the Corner came into view. She stopped. It was still open. Good. She needed ice cream sustenance before a long writing session. "I heard there's ice cream in this fudge shop."

Jonah stopped next to her and they peered inside. Lily was wiping down the countertop, moving items back into their places, bopping along to unheard music. Declan came up behind her and snuck a kiss on her cheek. Bronte's heart fluttered at the sight.

"There is, but they're probably closing up soon. You look kind of cold for ice cream. Besides, shouldn't we eat dinner first?" Jonah raised an eyebrow in her direction.

Bronte clenched her jaw to keep from shivering. "Gasp! Jonah White, I've already told you before, it is never too cold for ice cream. And it's on our way home. Let's go." Bronte pulled him into the fudge shop, ignoring his mention of ruining dinner. Psh. They were adults. They could eat dessert before dinner. Maybe Bronte would steal a kiss as second dessert before dinner. She ducked her head at the thought, praying her face didn't show how hot it felt.

They made their selections, with apologies to Lily for coming in so close to closing time, and headed back down the sidewalk.

"You know, someone else I knew used to like getting ice cream in the winter."

"Oooh, like an ex-girlfriend?" Bronte teased, wagging her eyebrows.

Jonah dipped his head. "Yeah, I've really only ever had one."

If he'd only ever had one, that meant . . . "Bree?" Bronte's stomach dipped. She shouldn't have said anything. Dani had told her Jonah would kill her if he found out she'd told Bronte about Bree. Would Jonah really be mad at Dani? Bronte wasn't good at this friend thing.

But Jonah just let out a chuckle. "I shouldn't be surprised you know. Who told you about Bree?"

"Dani." Bronte ducked her head. "Please don't hate her. She was just . . ." But Bronte didn't know why Dani had decided to tell her about Jonah's ex.

"I should have known." Jonah pushed out a chuckle and ran his hand down his face. "This town is so small, nothing gets by anyone."

Biting her lip, Bronte considered dropping the subject, but her curiosity won out. "What happened?" Why would anyone give someone like Jonah up?

"We had our whole lives planned out. We got engaged right out of high school, we were going to have six kids, all with names starting with J—"

"Oof, that's a little excessive, don't you think?"

Jonah grimaced. "Yeah, well, we were engaged forever, never really setting a date, and when I came home on a leave about seven years ago, she let me know that things had changed and she'd decided she didn't want a family. Or to be married to a military man. And she wasn't interested in waiting until I got out."

"Just like that?"

"Just like that."

"That had to be hard."

"It was for a while, but after things calmed down, I realized that we were young when we made those plans." His shoulder rose in a shrug. "Maybe I was still holding out for the six kids—not with names all starting with J—but Bree changed her mind, and that was okay. I guess we just weren't meant to be."

Even if he seemed nonchalant about it, Bronte still heard the underlying hurt in his voice. She regretted she had ever questioned that he never felt true pain as she had. "Still, I'm sorry."

"Thanks, but I'm good now."

He said that, but Bronte heard something in his voice. Regret, maybe?

Chill bit Bronte's cheeks as she tucked further into her coat. The sun started disappearing over the water. Maybe they should have taken Liam up on his offer of a ride back, but then they wouldn't have gotten ice cream, and Bronte would already be back to work. She'd enjoyed the break and wasn't ready for this day to end.

"Question." Bronte took the last bite of her ice cream and tossed the empty cup and spoon into a nearby trash can.

"Shoot," Jonah said, finishing the last of his ice cream and disposing of his trash as well.

"You said that if you weren't a surgeon, you wanted to open a bookstore on the island." Jonah stiffened next to her, so she hurried on. "So if you could put the bookstore anywhere here, where would it be?"

They paused at the end of the sidewalk. Jonah considered her for a breath before grabbing her hand. "Come here." He pulled her farther across Jonathon Boulevard and down Main Street.

Bronte squeaked in surprise but followed. They didn't stop until they'd made it to the other end of Main Street, stopping in front of an empty shop. Jonah held his hand toward the dark store. "This would be my bookstore."

Bronte narrowed her eyes at him, a grin on her face. The letters on the window that'd once spelled out *Island Bookstore* were peeling and half gone, spelling *I l nd Boo sto* instead. She pressed her face to the window and looked inside.

Empty shelves lined three of the walls. A dark chandelier hung down in the middle of the room, a broken couch under it. There looked to be a good layer of dirt and dust on the wood floors, but with a little elbow grease, they would be stunning. A wooden counter stood off to the side, and Bronte could imagine Jonah in the space, recommending books, face lit up when he talked about his favorite ones.

"Jonah, this is perfect!" Bronte jumped back from the window.

Jonah grinned. "Yes! This used to be one of my favorite shops as a kid. It started having trouble when Mr. Johnson—that's the owner—had a heart attack, and then the lack of tourism just drove it into the ground, and well—" Jonah shrugged his shoulders.

"I think this would be amazing." Something had come alive in Jonah's eyes as he'd shown her the bookshop. "I agree with you. The island needs a bookstore."

"Yeah? I've been thinking about giving Mr. Johnson a call and seeing if I could work out a deal with him. There are even a couple of little apartments over the top. It probably needs a lot of work, but it'd be cool."

"No, Jonah, it'd be amazing. I really think you should do it." Bronte clutched his arm.

"I don't know. It would be great, but I'm supposed to be the island doctor, which, let me remind you, is a very stable job. Being a business owner is tough. At least the clinic is already established. How am I supposed to support a family on a dream? I don't know if I even have the business sense to make an indie bookstore work. Maybe if I called Oliver . . ."

Bronte frowned. "Who's Oliver?"

"Oliver is Dani's brother," Jonah said as if being snapped out of his thoughts. "He's a good friend, really business savvy. He mentioned the bookstore was for sale. I think he might have some ideas on how to make a bookstore profitable."

"I think you should do it." Bronte bobbed her head in a curt nod. "Call Oliver. See what he can tell you. Besides, it might be good if you had a somewhat solid plan in place before you talk to your dad."

"You know, you might be on to something," Jonah said, turning them to head back in the direction of home, but not before looking over his shoulder one more time at the sleeping shop. Bronte could see the spark of a dream firing in his chest, and the wall that surrounded her heart started to crumble.

Thirteen

Date December 24
Days until Deadline 11
Words to be written 73,894

BRONTE WAS A FISH OUT OF WATER. She shouldn't have come. She should have said she had to write words and didn't have time to meet everyone for the "getting ready" party. Which wouldn't have been a lie. There were so many sequins and tulle in this room, it was getting hard to breathe.

"Doing okay? Completely overwhelmed yet?" Dani asked, coming to stand next to Bronte and handing her a champagne glass filled with sparkling juice.

"This is . . . a lot." Bronte had to be honest. She was pretty sure the panic was written all over her face, and if she lied, she knew Dani would call her out on it.

Dani's living room had been transformed into what

Bronte imagined one of those high-end boutiques would look like, only this one had more laughter and a lot more cheese. Pop Christmas music played low, and wood floors creaked as the group of women perused through all the dresses that had taken over every available surface in the room. Scents of yeast and oregano from the pizzeria below blended with the aroma of floral candles Dani had burning.

"We're a lot, but I promise you you'll have fun. If you're hungry, there's a couple of charcuterie boards over there and lots of pizza. And there's plenty of sparkling juice and water in the kitchen if you need it. Please make yourself at home." Dani patted Bronte on the arm, crossed the room, and browsed through a rack.

Bronte nodded, not sure if she believed Dani. Part of her wished she'd just insisted on picking up a dress from Jordi, whatever she had picked out for her, but she'd gotten excited when she'd heard about the getting ready party. Now that she was here, she was wondering why she'd thought it sounded fun.

"Come over and pick out some dresses." Mia waved Bronte across the room to two racks that could hardly contain the dresses they held. Mia pointed to a few more dresses strewn on the back of the couch. At least, Bronte thought it was the couch. She wasn't entirely sure.

"These are up for grabs as well. They just couldn't fit on the rack."

Bronte nodded, sipping her juice as she stepped back against the wall to take everything in.

Jordi had said that it was just going to be her, Dani, Mia,

Lily, and someone Bronte hadn't met yet named Sadie, but there were at least three other girls that Bronte didn't know. Introductions had been made, but it seemed as if the information had gone in one ear and out the other. Everyone had brought multiple dresses—Dani explained it was so they could all pick and choose from each other's closets. This way they felt like they were getting something new while not actually breaking the bank. Bronte felt bad she didn't have anything to contribute. Not that she would have actually had anything to contribute, even if her entire wardrobe were here—just her one sad black dress, still hanging in her closet in Oklahoma.

Jordi stood next to Bronte with a plate of pizza, grease soaking into the paper. "Isn't this just great?"

Bronte looked at Jordi over her shoulder, just to make sure she was talking to her. Bronte thought she'd done it discreetly, but Jordi grinned and kept on talking.

"I'm so glad we decided to do this this year. No one really thought this would happen again. When the hotel burned and everyone started leaving, it looked pretty dark, but now Dani has taken over with her plan and really turned everything around. Do you know which dress you want to wear yet?"

Bronte felt like she was watching a one-sided ping-pong match where one player was running between both sides of the table to hit the ball. It took her a breath to realize Jordi had asked her a question. "I haven't had a chance to look through them yet. I thought I'd let everyone else choose first."

"And get the last choice? No way. You need to get in there and pick out your dress."

"No, really, it's okay." Bronte waved her away.

"You know what? I think I saw the perfect dress for you. Here, hold this." Jordi handed Bronte her soggy plate of pizza, wiped her hands on the back of her jeans, and disappeared across the room. Bronte was curious to see what kind of dress Jordi thought was perfect for her.

She didn't have to wait long. Jordi appeared moments later, clutching a black floor-length dress with gold swirls sewn into the front. The sleeves were long and the neck high, but with the back open, it was a timeless dress.

It was perfect.

Bronte couldn't stop her grin. "I love it."

"I knew you would." Jordi's grin matched her own. "And we can pile your hair up high, which will make you look so long and elegant." Jordi squealed. "Oh my goodness, it's going to look so good!"

"So does this mean you found your dress?" Dani asked, coming up to them, a pitcher of more sparkling drink in her hands. She lifted it in question to Bronte, who shook her head.

"I picked this one out for her. Isn't it perfect?" Jordi asked, holding up the dress for Dani's inspection.

Dani gasped. "That's going to look great on you." She leaned closer to Bronte and said low, so no one else could hear, "You're going to make Jonah weak in the knees."

Grinning, Bronte reached for the dress to go try it on in the bathroom.

"Dani, did you hear that Bree's back in town? I just

found out this morning from my mom." Jordi's words stopped Bronte.

"What? She's back?" Dani hissed. "Has anyone told Jonah?"

From the level of their voices, Bronte knew she wasn't privy to their conversation, but she turned around anyway. "Bree? Like *the* Bree?" Her stomach plummeted.

Jordi and Dani looked up as if they'd been caught with their hands in the cookie jar. Jordi shifted on her feet, and Dani nodded.

Bronte swallowed. This was fine. It was okay. One kiss didn't make Jonah hers to be jealous over. Even as she reminded herself, she couldn't help the growing pit in the bottom of her stomach. Hadn't Dani said she didn't think Jonah had ever gotten over Bree?

"That's great," Bronte somehow choked out. She could already see this playing out in her head. She'd never had a chance, really, even if she had started to want one. It was the plot for every romance story. High school sweethearts have a falling out, and a few years later they bump into each other at some small-town tradition and realize they were always meant to be.

It was the perfect ending for someone like Jonah—the family man who loved rom-coms and believed in happily ever afters.

Not that she wanted to . . . Oh, who was she kidding?

She wanted to. She really, really wanted to.

"Hey." Dani bumped Bronte's shoulder with her own. "It'll be fine. I'm not even sure when she got in, but there's no way she could be here for Jonah. No one knew he was coming in. She probably won't even be at the ball tonight. Her name hasn't come up on the registry."

Bronte forced a smile. "Right. It's going to be fine." She held her dress up, shaking the hanger. "Let's see if this is going to fit."

Jordi squealed again as she shooed her in the direction of the bathroom.

"You're going to look so amazing, Jonah isn't even going to remember who Bree is."

Jordi's confidence had a sliver of Bronte believing that maybe, just maybe, a Christmas miracle could happen and the stars would align, even if Bronte had her doubts.

Fourteen

S HE WAS CINDERELLA AT THE BALL. She stood at the top of the stairs, and everyone froze and turned to look as she floated down the steps into the arms of the prince.

Okay, so it wasn't exactly like that. There were no stairs, and no one was turning to look at her, but that was fine with her.

After getting ready, the girls had made their way over to the ballroom. Dani had to be there early, so Bronte wandered, taking in the stillness before the guests arrived.

Draped in lights, the garland twinkled as it fanned out from the great chandelier. Wreaths hung on the tall windows that circled the entire room. The mini Christmas trees Jordi and her mom had wrapped in lights surrounded the room, adding the perfect amount of mood lighting and making it smell as if they were actually in a pine forest. Round tables with white tablecloths and centerpieces of mirrors and tall tapered candles were set up, leaving plenty of room for the live band and dance floor. A large Christmas tree graced the center of the stage, white lights sparkling from every branch.

Once guests started arriving, dazzling in their formal wear, Bronte checked the seating list and made her way to her table, reminding herself to breathe.

Scanning the crowd, she tried to quell the sinking in her stomach when she couldn't find Jonah. Had he already found Bree? No, Dani had said Bree hadn't bought a ticket. She wouldn't be here tonight. There were so many new faces from the tourists who'd come over from the mainland and other islanders she hadn't met. Not that she could tell the difference between the two groups. She was just as much a visitor as anyone else for tonight's event.

Smiling, she wove her way toward table number one, her assigned table. Not wanting to sit at the table by herself, she decided if there wasn't anyone there yet, she'd find Dani to see if she needed help with anything. Her heart in her throat, she finally caught sight of their table, noticing that Mia and Cody sat in their seats.

"You look absolutely stunning tonight." Jonah's breath tickled her ear.

She turned, finding Jonah behind her. Jonah dressed in a T-shirt, sweatpants, and Santa socks had been her favorite, but dressed-up Jonah was a whole other thing. His dark-blue Army dress uniform fit him perfectly, and his dark shoes had been shined to perfection. His face was clean-shaven, and she wasn't sure if she preferred Jonah without his scruff, but it didn't matter because he was there, and her insides were turning to liquid butter.

"You don't look too bad yourself." She took in the medals on his chest and wanted to ask about them, but Jonah caught her hand in his and brought it to his lips.

She couldn't breathe. She vowed to never again wash the place his lips met her skin. She internally rolled her eyes at herself. She was being ridiculous.

"You're exquisite." Jonah's eyes never left hers, pulling her back into the squishy romancy space she had told herself she wouldn't step foot in again. But Jonah made her feel as if she were the only person in the room. No one had ever made her feel that, had ever made her feel seen.

He took a step closer to her.

"Hi." Her voice breathy.

"I missed you today."

Her head told her to run away, but her heart had different ideas. "I missed you too."

"I like your hair."

He rubbed circles on the back of her hand, making it hard for Bronte to follow their conversation.

"What? Oh, yeah. This is Jordi's doing." Bronte motioned with her free hand to the coil Jordi had fashioned at the base of her neck. "Like my regular bird's nest, but lower and—"

"Fancy. I like it."

"Thank you. Should we get to our table? I'm starving."

"Lead the way." Jonah motioned Bronte ahead of him but didn't let go of her hand. "Did they not feed you this afternoon?"

"There were snacks and pizza, I just couldn't eat."

"Really?"

"I was so nervous."

Jonah's eyebrows shot up. "What's there to be nervous about?"

Of course he wouldn't understand the feeling of wanting someone, or *someones*, to like her. Of being afraid that she'd say the wrong thing. But even Bronte had to admit those nerves hadn't stuck around for long before being replaced with nerves about seeing him. Not that she'd tell him that. Instead, she just shrugged. "I guess just hanging out with new people."

Bronte led them to their table, and they'd just sat down when Mia's little boy slid off his chair and circled the table to where Jonah sat.

"You remember my shark, Jonah?" The little boy held up a plastic shark, *Jonathon Island* written on the side.

"I do remember your shark, Finn. It's a very nice shark," Jonah said, bending so he was eye to eye with the boy. "Did your sister like the shark you picked out for her?"

"Oh yeah. She had to stay with Grandma tonight, but Mom said I'm a big boy, so I get to come."

Jonah and Finn continued to chat, but Bronte felt like she had cotton in her ears. Jonah was so good with kids. He was going to make a great father one day.

A pang shot through her chest. It was the one thing she knew she couldn't give Jonah. She should have closed down her heart when he'd told her he wanted to raise a big family on Jonathon Island. Why had she ignored the warnings? Maybe Jordi and Dani thought something long-distance would work, but it wouldn't. They'd never understand because she hadn't told them the whole story. It wouldn't be fair for Bronte to hope for something to happen between them when she already knew it couldn't.

When Finn skipped back to his seat, Jonah turned to look at her. His brows dipped into a frown. "What's wrong?"

"Hmm?" Bronte's eyes rose, and she did everything in her power to smile, to put on a mask that everything was fine, even if she felt a crack starting in her heart. "I'm okay."

Eyes narrowed, Jonah studied her for a breath longer. Bronte wasn't sure if he believed her or not.

"I promise, everything is great." Breaking eye contact, she reached for her glass of water.

He pulled her chair closer to his, boxing her in with one of his arms behind her on the back of her chair and one on the table in front of her. The scent of sandalwood and citrus engulfed her. She wanted to melt into his arms, tell him everything. But she couldn't. It would just cause more confusion in her brain.

She'd had enough peopling today.

If she asked, Jonah would take her home now. She could put on her sweats and . . . write her book. She didn't have time to fall into fantasies of being swallowed by Holland's amazing couch while she snuggled with Jonah and they watched another Christmas movie.

How many words did she still need? Seventy thousand? And her deadline was getting closer, faster than she'd like to admit. Reality leaked into whatever Christmas dreams she'd started dreaming during her arrival on Jonathon Island.

She leaned her forehead on Jonah's, careful not to bump the still-tender side.

"Please tell me what's wrong," Jonah whispered.

"It's just—"

"Jonah, will you play a game of Go Fish with me? I have the cards, see?" Finn's towhead pushed between them. Bronte leaned back, scooting her chair back to its place.

"Finn, stop interrupting Jonah and come sit back down," Mia said, shooting a look of apology in their direction.

"It's okay, Mia," Jonah said. "I'll play a quick round with you while we're waiting for our dinner, okay, Finn?"

Finn nodded and pulled himself up in the empty chair next to Jonah.

What had she been about to do? She couldn't tell Jonah that she was falling for him. She couldn't tell him why it would never work between them. Not here, where there were too many people to overhear. But she had to tell him. She needed to let him go so he could make his dreams come true. She'd just hold him back.

Jonah's gaze remained on her as he played a round of Go Fish with Finn, but she refused to look at him. She couldn't. If she did, she wasn't sure she'd be able to hold herself together any longer.

The pasta Dani had catered in was the definition of perfect. It gave anything Jonah had ever had in Italy a run for its money. He'd been excited about seeing how their hard work in the ballroom looked in action—comparing it to Christmas balls past—but now his mind was fully focused on Bronte. He thought she'd been having a good time, but something had happened to change her mood.

"Are you guys enjoying your meal?" As Dani stood next to Bronte's chair, her strapless gold gown made her green eyes sparkle. Or maybe it was the excitement of seeing all her hard work come to fruition.

"This is so good, Dani," Cody said. "Good call picking the catering."

"So glad you're enjoying it. Hey." Dani smiled and put her hand on the back of Bronte's chair. "Can I steal Bronte for a moment? There's a guest who's a big fan and wanted to know if an introduction could be made." She shot a glance toward Bronte. "If you're not okay with that, I could tell them now isn't a good time."

After the fiasco that'd happened at the Christmas stroll, Jonah knew Bronte would politely decline. He hoped she'd decline, but for selfish reasons. He didn't want to share her.

He swallowed his disappointment when Bronte shrugged and said, "Sure."

Dabbing her mouth, she tossed her napkin next to her plate and pushed back from the table. She still wouldn't make eye contact with him. What had happened?

"She get that a lot?" Mia asked, wiping Finn's face. He had enjoyed the pasta as well.

Jonah shrugged. "It seems like it's happening a lot here."

"I think it's fun. So, Jonah, I heard something today and

just wanted to give you the heads-up—" Mia's phone, sitting on the table, rang, interrupting whatever she had been about to tell him. Picking it up, she said, "Excuse me, it's my mom." Cody helped pull her chair out from the table.

"What was that all about?" Jonah asked, watching as Mia disappeared into a dark corner, phone tucked to her ear.

Cody shrugged and asked, "Is Bronte okay? She seemed a little quiet at dinner." Cody settled Finn back in with a coloring book and some markers he produced from Finn's backpack, which sported different kinds of sharks.

"She seems upset." Jonah straightened his silverware next to his plate as he watched Finn coloring, tongue poked out the side of his mouth. "I'm not really sure what happened."

"You don't think Finn upset her, do you?"

"Are you talking about me?" Finn paused his coloring, round eyes looking between Cody and Jonah.

"Yes, Finny." Cody ruffled the boy's hair. "It's all right. Go back to coloring that awesome dinosaur."

"I don't think so," Jonah continued when the boy was distracted again with his artwork. "Who could be mad when Finn's around? He's the best."

Finn paused again, looking up from his coloring. "Thank you," he said before diving his head into Cody's side.

"I think she's just tired, maybe?" Jonah said, frowning in the direction Bronte had disappeared. He heaved a deep sigh. "Maybe a little overwhelmed?"

"I get that. Mia told me this afternoon was a little crazy

with all the dresses, and you know how the girls can be when they all get together," Cody said, pushing back his dessert plate.

Dessert had been a fudge mousse provided by the Fudge Shop on the Corner. It was amazing, but so rich. Jonah had only made it through half before he couldn't eat anymore.

"How's she doing since her fall?" Cody took a sip from the cup of coffee that had come with desert.

"Good. She's just been under a lot of pressure to get her book done." Jonah ran a hand down his face. "It takes a toll."

"Hello, everyone!" They both turned as Dani stood in front of the band, a spotlight shining on her. "I want to welcome everyone to this year's Jonathon Island Christmas Ball and thank you for coming. Also, can we give it up for the Maritime Band." The room erupted in cheers, and the band members stood and bowed.

Dani went on, giving updates about the renovations, but Jonah didn't really hear. He scanned the room for Bronte. She'd been gone for well over ten minutes. How long did it take to meet a fan and say hello? Shouldn't she be back by now?

". . . so get out there and dance!" Dani finished, fist pumping the air.

Now he really needed to find Bronte. He'd been thinking about dancing with her all day. Couples paired together and started dancing to a croonie version of "The Way You Look Tonight."

"What about you?" Cody asked, pulling Jonah's attention back to the table. "How have you been since you got home? Looking forward to meeting up with the family in a couple of days?"

"I'm excited, but a little disappointed to be leaving Bronte all on her own."

"She really is special to you," Cody said, waving off a waiter trying to fill his mug of coffee.

"Yeah."

They fell into an easy silence, watching couples spin around the dance floor. Jonah's gaze wandered up to where he and Pastor Arnie had wrapped the beams in twinkling lights and hung hundreds of ornaments from the ceiling. Dani had done a great job organizing everything. He'd say the first Christmas ball since the fire was a success.

"You know what? I'm going to take Finn to my mom and find Mia. It's time to get a dance in."

Bronte's laugh, loud and boisterous over the music, drew Jonah's gaze. She was talking with Dani and Jordi about something only a few tables away. She threw her head back and laughed again. Maybe whatever had happened earlier was over. He was glad to see her having a good time. Liam strolled up to the girls and offered his hand to Dani.

A burning started in Jonah's chest. He didn't know what had happened before, but he planned to ask. Maybe before the Christmas Eve service. For now, he wanted nothing more than to dance with her.

He pushed himself up from the table, not taking his eyes off Bronte. A man on a mission.

A man on a mission, who was suddenly intercepted and

tugged in the direction of the dance floor. But Bronte was still over by the wall, talking to Jordi . . .

He swiveled to whoever had his hand in their grip. He'd know that blonde hair, expertly rolled into a French twist, and that petite frame anywhere. His stomach dropped.

They made it to the dance floor, and his captor dropped his hand and turned to him.

Blue eyes that had once captivated his soul. "Bree?"

Bree raised her arms, the sequins on her red dress sparkling in the twinkle lights. "Surprise!"

"What are you doing here?"

"I wanted to surprise you." Bree fiddled with the brass buttons on his dress uniform.

His fingers gently wrapped around her wrist, and he placed her hands at her sides.

"I meant to find you earlier. I've been in town for almost a week, but Grandma got sick the day I arrived, and I've barely left her house since. I wasn't even sure I'd be able to come tonight, but I made it."

It was seven years since he'd last seen Bree. The woman he had planned, at one time, to spend the rest of his life with—until she'd called it quits instead.

He waited for the emotions to wash over him. The familiar pull of attraction that had been so strong and had about killed him when she'd told him she didn't want the life they had so carefully planned out.

"How did you know I was coming home for Christmas? I didn't even know I was coming home for Christmas until last week."

Bree shrugged. "I was coming anyway, and then I saw

Amy post about your family vacation and was afraid that I'd missed you, but you're here. Have you been staying by yourself this entire time?"

"No." Jonah looked around. He wanted Bronte here on the dance floor, not Bree. He didn't even want to talk to Bree. "If you will excuse me."

Bree reached out and clutched Jonah's arm, stopping his escape. "Well, you look really good."

Jonah frowned. "Thank you, Bree. You look good too, but I really must—"

"What happened to us, Jonah?" Bree asked, looking up through her long, obviously fake eyelashes.

Jonah sighed. Apparently, they were going to have *this* conversation, right here on the dance floor. "You said you didn't want to be married to a military guy and weren't willing to wait anymore, you didn't want a big family, and you wanted to travel the world." Jonah checked off all the reasons she had given him on his fingers. "So I let you go."

"Right. Yeah. I did." Bree nodded and licked her lips. "I've been doing a lot of thinking over the last few years, and I think I was just scared. I think I would be okay with settling down now, having our big family like we planned. I miss what we had. Really miss it, Jonah."

Jonah scanned the crowd, only half listening to what Bree was going on about. But when she got quiet, he looked back at her. He saw determination in her eyes, and his stomach clenched.

"Jonah, I want to get back together."

"Wh-what?" Jonah stammered.

"I want *us* to get back together," Bree repeated.

Jonah blinked. Nothing could have prepared him for that. Six weeks ago, he might have fallen for it. If she had told him last week, he probably would have, hook, line, and sinker, and gotten back into a relationship with Bree. But now . . .

"We were so good together, Jonah. I was young and stupid." Bree huffed out a sigh. "I'm making a mess of this. Come here."

She stood on her tiptoes and wrapped her hands around Jonah's neck, tugging his head toward hers.

Fifteen

She was avoiding Jonah, and she hated it.

Ever since she'd decided he'd be better off without her, she'd begun rebuilding the protective wall around her heart. He needed to be a father. She wanted that for him. But she couldn't give that to him.

Dani had given her the perfect out when she'd asked to introduce Bronte to a fan that had come over on the ferry. When the introductions had finished, Dani had announced the dance floor was open. As couples started pairing off and flooding the open space, Jordi had pulled Bronte and Dani aside, telling them something about one of the old men trying to drive the snowplow around town and another one chasing after him in a golf cart.

If Bronte were smart, she'd find someone to take her home. Then she'd pack her bags and get off the island before anyone else knew she was leaving.

Liam stole Dani for a dance right before a tall, dark, and handsome stranger asked Jordi for a spin, leaving Bronte alone with her thoughts. A dangerous place to be.

"What are you doing over here? Why aren't you out on the dance floor with Jonah? He's looking really sharp tonight." Martha stood beside Bronte, her hands on her hips.

"Hi, Martha. What did you think of the dinner?" Bronte asked, a limp attempt to change the subject.

"The dinner was fine." Martha brushed at her black velvet dress. "I could have done a better job, but I appreciate why Dani had everything catered in, and"—she pointed a finger a Bronte—"if you tell her I said so, I'll deny every word."

Bronte dragged two fingers over her lips as if she were zipping them tight and then threw away the invisible key. "My lips are sealed."

"But really, why are you hiding here? Why aren't you out there?" Martha motioned toward the dance floor.

Tears stung the backs of Bronte's eyes. She promised herself she wasn't going to cry about this. She had cried enough over relationships when it didn't work out with Brad. Why had she thought, hoped, anything would be different with Jonah? Heaving in a deep breath, and successfully keeping the tears at bay, Bronte responded, "I just needed a moment."

The look Martha gave her let her know she wasn't buying the excuse, but they both turned and watched everyone else pairing off and joining the others on the dance floor.

As Bronte's eyes scanned the crowd, they couldn't help

but be drawn to Jonah's tall form. Emotions twisted in her belly as she watched him talking to a girl—who, from the looks of it, couldn't keep from touching him.

She frowned. The woman looked familiar, but Bronte couldn't remember where she knew her from. She didn't think she'd seen her around on the island the past few days, but everyone here was new, so maybe she had.

"Martha, who's that with Jonah?" She shouldn't feel the pang of jealousy coursing through her. Isn't this what she wanted? Jonah with someone else.

"What? Oh, her."

The way Martha said *her* made Bronte's stomach drop. "Who is she?"

There was steel in Martha's eyes. "That is Aubrey." Martha said the name it as if it were a bad word. "Or Bree, as she's known around here."

Aubrey. The girl from the ferry. She remembered now how Aubrey had said something about coming over and spending the holidays with her grandmother. Never in a million years would Bronte have thought Aubrey from the ferry and Jonah's Bree were the same person. She wanted to hate her, but she'd been so nice on the ferry.

"Everyone always expected those two to get married," Martha went on, oblivious to Bronte's pain. "They were voted most likely to get married in high school. Then one day, after years of being engaged, they just called it off. I'm not sure what happened."

Her words echoed what Dani had told her about Bree the day before.

Martha's eyes suddenly widened. "Oh." The one word

sliced through Bronte as she turned to see what had surprised Martha.

Bree wrapped her arms around Jonah's neck and pulled him toward her. Bronte turned before she could see their lips touch. A sharp pain sliced her ribs. All the breath left her. The wall she had been rebuilding slammed into place. Fully intact. This shouldn't matter to her as much as it did.

After all, this was playing out exactly as Bronte had known it would when she'd heard about Bree. But did it have to happen with her in the room? Why had she let herself imagine anything else?

No. She curled her hands into fists. She wasn't going to get upset about something that would ultimately give Jonah everything he ever wanted.

She was the bump in the couple's relationship, the one that they would look back on over their life and laugh about. The one in the movie who was the stand-in until the girl who broke the guy's heart met back up with him years later and told him that she'd made a mistake.

This would be better for Jonah anyway, Bronte told herself one more time. Jonah wanted a big family, and Bronte would bet anything that Bree still had a uterus. She knew Jonah told her that Bree had broken it off, but it looked like she had changed her mind. Bree would be able to give Jonah the life he wanted, the one with all the kids running around on the island. Once Jonah told his dad that he no longer wanted to take over the clinic, that he wanted to open a bookstore, marry Bree, and raise babies on Jonathon Island, his dad would be thrilled. Jonah's family would be excited at his life plans, excited that he'd be coming back to the island.

Mind made up, Bronte nodded, turning to Martha. She wanted to get out of here and scrub her eyes. "I think I'm ready to go home."

Martha looked back and forth between Bronte and the PDA happening on the dance floor. "But aren't you going to . . ."

"Nope. No, I'm not, Martha, because that"—Bronte blindly pointed a finger in the direction of the happy couple, not willing to look to see if she was even pointing in the right direction—"is what Jonah White wants. He's been waiting his whole life for someone who can come alongside him in his dreams, and Bree can do that."

The older woman frowned. "But—"

Bronte held up a hand, cutting Martha off. She was suddenly tired. So, so tired. "Thanks, Martha, but I'm going to get a ride home."

Martha studied Bronte for so long that Bronte hoped she'd drop a bit of wisdom. Or tell her to go break up Jonah and Bree. In the end, Martha just nodded, and Bronte left to gather her things from where they'd stashed them earlier in a side room.

"I figured you'd be dancing the night away." Dani's voice startled Bronte. "Why aren't you dancing?"

Bronte didn't feel like talking about what happened. The faster she could gather her things and get out of there, the better.

"I just came in here to get a new battery for the walkie."

Dani seemed to just realize that Bronte had gathered her things. "Wait. Are you leaving?"

"Yeah." Bronte shrugged. "I'm getting a little tired and still need to finish up my writing for today, so I'm heading out early."

"Oh, bummer." Dani exchanged the battery on her walkie, dropping the used one back into the charger. "Hope you get your words written. Thanks for coming this afternoon, and for all the help setting up yesterday. I really appreciate it. Hope you had a good time tonight."

"I'll remember it for the rest of my life."

She'd remember her entire stay on Jonathon Island. A little over a week, and she felt like she was part of a family—even more so than when she had been with Brad and his family.

But in the end, Bronte had still ended up with nothing.

"What are you doing?" Jonah pulled back from Bree before she could kiss him, and then, feeling like there still wasn't enough space between them, took a step back.

"I'm trying to tell you that I'm sorry." Bree's eyes darted around as if making sure all eyes weren't on them. "That I made a mistake when I didn't fight for us seven years ago. I want us back, Jonah." She took a step toward him, but he held out a hand, stopping her. "I would have told you sooner, but this isn't exactly something you tell someone over FaceTime."

Bree's eyes were wide, and her lower lip trembled. Any other time, it would have been Jonah's breaking point.

A crying Bree always got what she wanted, but that had been then.

Jonah ran a hand over his face. How could something that he'd wanted for so long not stir anything inside him? He just felt . . . nothing. He chuckled.

Bree blanched. "This is funny to you?"

"I wanted this for so long. When you said you were done waiting and I wasn't ready to commit, it about broke me," Jonah said with a shake of his head. Bree's face turned from one of shock, to something hopeful. Jonah was sorry to disappoint her. "But I don't. Want this"—he motioned between them—"anymore."

Bree's face fell. "What can I do to get you back, Jonah?" She put her hands on his chest. "I need you back."

Jonah gently wrapped his hands around Bree's wrists and removed them from his chest. "Bree, we aren't good for each other—"

"Yes, we are," she interrupted, sounding desperate. "We're perfect for each other. Everyone says so!"

But at the shake of Jonah's head, Bree fell silent. "That was years ago, Bree. We're not good for each other, and maybe we stayed together for so long not because we were in love but because that's what we felt like everyone expected of us." Wasn't that what he was doing now with being a surgeon? "I think we were just together for so long that we were comfortable, but comfortable doesn't mean we were right for each other."

Panic flashed across Bree's eyes. "But if we're not perfect for each other, what am I supposed to do?"

Jonah wanted to laugh again. Bree asking him for relationship advice? He barely had any answers for himself. But he took both of Bree's hands in his. "Bree, you're a wonderful person. There's someone out there that is going to be completely head over heels in love with you, and you are going to be crazy about him."

"But you're not that person," Bree finished Jonah's unsaid statement.

"But I'm not that person."

Bree took a step back. Her face flamed, and Jonah could see the tears welling in her eyes, even in the dim ballroom lights.

"I wish you well, Jonah." She started walking backward, turning when she backed against a chair, almost falling. On instinct, Jonah lunged forward to catch her, but she righted herself before he got to her. She held her hand up. "I'm good."

Was she telling him that or talking herself into it?

Jonah didn't watch her go. Instead, he scanned the place for Bronte. She had just been with Jordi and Dani, but Jordi was currently on the dance floor with a tall black man, and he didn't see Dani or Liam.

"Jonah, how are you not on the dance floor with Bronte yet?" Jordi asked, dancing over to him. "And this is Mick. He's thinking about moving to the island. You guys should talk. You'd love him."

"Jordi." Jonah pulled Jordi over to him. "I need to find Bronte. Have you seen her?"

"I haven't." Jordi shrugged from his grasp and rose on her toes. "I saw her over by the front, like, two minutes ago, talking to Martha. Maybe ask her?"

Jonah scanned the area Jodi had mentioned. "Where's Martha?"

"If you can't find her out here, I'll bet you she's in the kitchen. I know Dani banned her from there, but honestly, do we think that's going to stop her?" She grinned cheekily up at Jonah before fluttering her eyes at Mick. "Let's go round once more?" She held her hand out, and Mick spun her away.

Jonah had to force himself to keep from jogging to the kitchen. Something felt off. Something had happened before Bronte had gotten up from the table, and now he couldn't find her. Had he said something wrong? He racked his brain as to what could have set Bronte off, but nothing stuck out in his memory. He had just been talking to Finn.

The command center room. Jonah stopped halfway to the kitchen. Hadn't Dani mentioned they had set up a command center of sorts in one of the side rooms? Changing course, Jonah headed toward where he thought it would be.

What if Bronte wasn't there? Where else could she be? Maybe the bathroom. If she wasn't in the command center, he'd get someone to check the bathroom. Although, at this point, he wasn't beyond sticking his head in the ladies' room and calling out.

Compared to the dim ballroom below, the command center was brightly lit. A folding table had been transformed into a buffet. Trays of finger foods and half-eaten pizzas from the pizzeria sat on the table, and Jonah guessed it was left over from the girls' getting-ready party. An ice chest sat on the floor at the end of the table, and another smaller table held walkie-talkies and extra batteries. Clipboards were discarded on various surfaces around the room. Along one wall, bags, purses, and coats leaned in a haphazard line. But the room lacked one thing.

The person Jonah was currently looking for.

Okay then, on to find a female to help him check the bathrooms.

Rounding the corner, Jonah ran into Dani. He reached out to steady her.

"Oh! Jonah, hey, what are you doing in here?"

"Dani, sorry. I was just looking for Bronte."

Dani's face scrunched into a frown. "She left."

"Left?"

"You didn't know?"

"No."

"I thought she would have told you. I thought you would be going with her. You really didn't know?" she asked again.

Why had she left? And left without saying goodbye. Something was definitely going on. He needed to get back home to check on her to make sure she was okay. Maybe she wasn't feeling well. "I really didn't know. Thanks, Dani. Did she get a ride or walk?"

If she had decided to walk … He shivered at the thought of her strappy heels and backless dress. She'd freeze to death between here and the house.

"I don't know. You might check with the guys giving rides to and from the ferry. Maybe one of them took her back to your house?"

Jonah dodged past Dani and headed toward the front of the ballroom.

Pushing out into the cold, he hoped to see Bronte there. Instead, he was met by nothing but the tall columns on the veranda. The sparkling lights wrapped around the columns didn't give off a lot of light, but there was enough for Jonah to tell Bronte was long gone.

"There you are, you big lug."

Jonah spun, spotting Martha in the shadow of one of the columns. "Me?" He pointed a finger to his chest, but he didn't see anyone else close that Martha could be talking to.

"Yes, I'm talking to you." Martha stepped out from behind the column.

"What are you doing out here? Aren't you cold?"

Martha snorted. "I came outside for some fresh air for a minute. And don't try and change the subject. That girl was the best thing that could have happened to you, and you go and do something so foolhardy with Bree, who isn't your round peg."

"Round peg? Martha, what are you talking about?" Jonah ran his hand over his face. He didn't have time for one of her lectures.

"She's more of a square peg to your round hole," Martha muttered.

Jonah took Martha by the shoulders and dipped down so he could look her in the eyes. "Martha, what are you talking about?"

Martha threw her hands up. "Bronte. She's perfect for

you, and you had to go and kiss that Jennings girl in front of God and everyone."

"What are you talking about? I didn't kiss—" Jonah stopped. Bree. "Are you telling me that Bronte saw Bree *try* to kiss me?"

Martha scoffed. "Didn't look like you weren't enjoying it."

Jonah ran a hand down his face. "Bree tried to kiss me. I pushed her away before she got the chance to."

Martha harrumphed, lips pursed.

"I've got to get home." Jonah turned to go back inside to get his coat from the coat check. He didn't want to take the time to get it, but it was too cold.

He handed his ticket over to the teen at the coat check with a plea for him to hurry. The boy disappeared into the coat closet. It was taking him forever. Jonah rapped his knuckles on the counter. Checked his watch. How long did it take someone to find a coat?

"Make this right, Jonah White," Martha hissed from his side. She had followed him inside.

The teen appeared, handing Jonah his coat.

Jonah grabbed it and shoved his arms into the sleeves. "I plan to."

He had to.

Sixteen

WHAT HAD SHE BEEN THINKING? She had been so stupid. An entire week and a half of work completely wasted. Bronte looked at the clock in the corner of her computer, as if staring at it would give her some time back. It only seemed to remind her of the deadline looming.

Twelve days.

Tears stung the backs of her eyes. She swiped a hand over her face and clenched her jaw. She was not going to cry over another man. She may have cried over Brad, but she'd been with him for years. She sure didn't need to cry over a guy she had only known for not even two weeks.

The way to get through this was to just get through it. She needed to focus, write the words for the original plot she'd already figured out, and turn in the book. She wouldn't have time for an edit or a read-through, so this draft was going to have to be as near to perfection as she could get it. She placed her fingers back on her keyboard and started typing.

Then she backspaced what she'd written and tried again.

Bronte let out a strangled cry. This wasn't working. She picked up her phone and turned it over to see if Jonah had tried to call or text her. Of course he hadn't—he didn't even have her number. He probably didn't even realize she wasn't at the ball anymore. She supposed this meant going to the midnight service in two hours was off. Not that she felt like going anywhere anymore. She couldn't help but picture Jonah and Bree making up for lost time on the dance floor, reminiscing of times past and planning for the future. Bronte could already see half a dozen little dark-headed Jonahs and blonde Brees running around while they sat gazing longingly into each other's eyes.

Why was she torturing herself by imagining sitting on the sidelines of life, watching Jonah's love story unfold? She had only thought she'd protected her heart against the idea of something with Jonah. Well, try though she had, she hadn't succeeded, and she'd be stuffed if she sat around while Jonah fawned over someone else.

Her heart, decidedly, wouldn't be able to take it.

Minimizing her manuscript, Bronte opened a browser and found the first flight in the morning back home. Afterward, she shot a text off to Mia to see if Cody would be able to take her across the lake early in the morning—or maybe, if she hurried, she could catch a ride tonight with the rest of the tourists. If anyone asked, Bronte would make something up about an emergency back home. The emergency being her heart was breaking and she needed to get this novel done in twelve days.

That settled, Bronte went back to her novel. Which currently resembled a dumpster fire. How was she going to finish this and make it presentable in twelve days? *Twelve days.* There was a reason she didn't focus on the length of her deadlines, and this crushing feeling of panic settling on her like a wet blanket was it.

Sucking in a deep breath and pushing away all thoughts of the looming deadline, Bronte put her fingers on the keyboard, closed her eyes, and started typing.

The front door slammed, and her eyes flew open.

"Bronte?" Her heart clenched at the panic lacing Jonah's voice.

Choosing to ignore him, Bronte went back to typing, wishing she had her earbuds in so that she'd have an extra layer of "not being able to hear Jonah." He'd probably raced home to tell her the amazing story of how he and Bree were getting back together. She didn't need to hear it. She was a writer. She knew how this story ended. She'd known as soon as she'd seen them on the dance floor.

But as soon as she thought it, she knew Jonah wouldn't be that cruel.

Jonah barreled across the room, tossing his coat on the kitchen bar as he passed it on his way to her. He reached her, tugging her up into his arms. The chair she had been sitting in fell back with a clatter.

Curse her traitorous heart for squeezing and her spine for tingling at his touch. She didn't allow her arms to snake around Jonah's back and hold him close. It took everything in her power to keep them down at her sides as she waited for him to drop the bomb that would be his admission of love. For someone else.

"I am so *so* sorry. That never should have happened."

"Are you talking about you and me? Or that Bree is back in the picture now and you can't help yourself? It's fine Jonah. I'm not going to hold it against you. The heart wants what the heart wants." She should know. It was just her heart that couldn't have what it wanted.

Pulling back, Jonah placed his hands on either side of Bronte's face. She clenched her jaw to keep from reacting to the fire she felt at his touch. She wanted to melt into him. Scream and cry and just let him hold her, but she couldn't.

Jonah leaned over, putting his forehead on Bronte's. She slid her eyes closed to keep from staring into his eyes.

"I never kissed Bree. She tried, but I pushed her away. You didn't see, but I pushed her away. I haven't seen Bree in seven years, and she decided that now was when she needed to make nice. But I don't want to make nice, Bronte. I feel nothing for Bree. She isn't who I want. It's you, Bronte. I like you a lot, and I think I might be falling for you."

Bronte stilled. Ice had been poured through her veins. She opened her eyes and stared into Jonah's intense gaze. "You can't."

"But I am."

Bronte shook her head. "No. You can't." It came out a little more forcefully than she meant it.

Jonah pulled back, but he didn't take his hands from her face. "Bronte, what's going on? What's wrong?"

The words were choking her. She didn't want to tell him, didn't want them to come out. She wanted to ignore her own admission and just let Jonah love her, but she had to tell him the truth. She had to let him know that they would never be so he could change his mind about Bree. There was still a chance he could have all his dreams come true, but it wasn't going to be with her. She felt like her insides were being ripped out. How could this hurt so bad after such a short time? She'd been with Brad for almost three years, and even his betrayal hadn't felt like this.

God why does this hurt so bad? Why do I have to say goodbye?

"Tell me that you never want to live on this island or that it's too soon or that you don't feel this spark between us, but don't tell me that you don't feel something, Bronte. I have fallen so hard and so fast. I have never felt this undone by anyone in my entire life. You undo me."

Bronte tried to suck in a breath, but instead, a choked sob escaped.

"Bronte, please tell me what's happening. Let me in that beautiful brain of yours."

"I can't give you what you want, Jonah," Bronte choked out, praying he wouldn't press her further.

"I want you, Bronte. Only you."

"I can't have kids, Jonah." The words found their way around the lump in her throat and were out before she could stop them. A hot tear rolled down her face, pooling where Jonah's hand touched her skin.

"We don't have to talk about starting a family right off if you don't want. We can wait a few years."

"No, Jonah, I struggled for years with endometriosis, and earlier this year I had to get a hysterectomy. There's not even a chance of me getting pregnant." Bronte swallowed to keep from sobbing. "Ever."

"Oh, well." Jonah's Adam's apple bobbed. "That's okay. Really, it is. There are other options. Like adoption. We could adopt to start a family."

"No, Jonah. I don't want kids at all."

Jonah jerked his hands off her face as if she'd burned him. His eyes slid closed.

Bronte felt as if she were breathing out of a straw. More than anything, she wished they could go back to this morning, when they'd been laughing and looking forward to what would come. But even going back, no matter how far, wouldn't change the fact that she'd never be able to be enough for Jonah. If she had a magic genie, she'd wish to go all the way back to when she'd decided to come to Jonathon Island. She'd make a different choice. She'd go somewhere else. Somewhere she'd never meet Jonah.

Even as she thought it, she knew it wasn't true. Even with all the pain, the feeling as if her heart were being ripped from her body, she wouldn't trade anything for these last couple weeks with Jonah. She'd take the pain over never having known him.

She wanted to pull him back to her, but she couldn't touch him. If she touched him and he pushed her away, what was left of her heart would crumble. She steadied her shaking breath and took a step back.

Jonah opened his eyes and let his hands drop to his sides. "Bronte, I—"

The front door crashed open, cutting off whatever he was going to say.

"Honey, I'm hoooooome!" someone shouted.

Neither she nor Jonah moved. Part of her brain told her she should be concerned with someone bursting into the house, but she couldn't look away from Jonah. She studied the face she didn't want to ever forget. Blue eyes that pierced her soul every time he looked at her, making her feel like she was the only person in the room. Eyes that were as kind as they were intense. The way his whole face crinkled when he smiled. The scruff that, even though he'd shaved earlier, was already making its way back onto his face. She wanted to remember the way his hands were gentle as they held her.

"Jonah?" a woman's voice called.

Surely Bree wouldn't have followed Jonah home. Would she?

Someone flung themselves at Jonah's back, arms and legs circling him in a bear hug. He bent forward, and Bronte caught sight of a girl with a puffy jacket and bright-pink beanie with a puff ball on top. More people poured in from the front hallway. An older man pulling a rolling suitcase almost as big as he was, a woman with gray streaked through her dark hair, a girl with large glasses dwarfing her face who looked like she was on the brink of being a teenager, and two women who looked so much like Jonah. Bronte had seen all these people before. She'd been living under their gazes for the past two weeks.

Jonah's family was home early.

Wiping her hand over her face, Bronte stepped back, ready to gather her stuff and let Jonah have time with his family. Even with her heart crumbling, she was glad they'd surprised him. She closed her laptop, then stacked her notebook on top, creating a neat pile.

"Oh, did we just interrupt something here?" The girl who had been on Jonah's back now stood next to them, a finger bouncing back and forth between Jonah and Bronte.

"No." Jonah denied it. "Bronte, this is Holland. Holland, Bronte."

Bronte offered her hand to the smaller, feminine version of Jonah. Blue eyes sparkling with mischief, Holland looked exactly like someone Bronte would have loved getting to know. "Nice to meet you," she said, pasting a fake smile on her face. "I thought you weren't coming back for a couple more days."

Holland winced. "I guess that means you didn't get my message that we were coming home early? I know Jonah planned on flying out to see us." She tugged off her hat and tossed it to the table. "But we couldn't wait any longer and thought we'd surprise him here. I'm so sorry about the mix-up! I hope he hasn't been too much trouble. I've already refunded your money for the stay."

"Oh." Bronte's gaze darted to Jonah, who was looking anywhere but at her. "That's not necessary. It's fine. Really."

"Of course it's necessary. Besides"—she shrugged her shoulders—"it's already done. Merry Christmas!"

Bronte didn't know what to do, so she just nodded her thanks and turned back to gather her things.

Holland exclaimed, "Oh gosh, Dad, let me help you," and turned to help the older man, who was currently hidden behind the three duffel bags in his arms.

The fist in her stomach grew bigger, and she just wanted to go back up to her room to cry and pack and try to forget this night had ever happened.

Jonah stopped Bronte with a hand on her arm. It felt as if everything melted away with his one touch. Everything fell silent. In this moment it was just her and Jonah.

"Please." His eyes moved back and forth over hers. "I can tell you want to bolt, but we need to keep talking. Stay."

There wasn't anything Bronte wanted more. She wanted to stay and meet the people who had made Jonah the person he was. But that would just make the leaving that much harder.

And she had to leave.

Someone tugged at Jonah's arm, and they were pulled apart before Bronte could say anything. She couldn't be here anymore. Seeing Jonah with his family, she understood why he wanted the big family. Why he wanted lots of kids. And no matter how much they talked about it, how much they tried to work through it, Bronte would never be able to give him that. Not only because she couldn't have children but because she wouldn't know the first thing about being a mom. About being part of a real family.

It was the truth she'd had to accept a long time ago.

One she'd fought. One she'd thought maybe she could overcome. But the truth remained.

Bronte Parker would always be alone. On the outskirts. Even when people invited her in, they'd find a way eventually to replace her. It'd happened to her too many times over her life.

It was better for her—better for *him*—if she removed herself now.

While Jonah's sisters pulled him into hug after hug, she turned, gathered her stuff, and slipped out of the kitchen.

Only when she was safely slinking up the dark staircase did she let her tears begin to fall.

Because the idea of leaving him hurt more than it should.

But the idea of staying and losing him later hurt even worse.

He needed to talk to Bronte. He hadn't slowed down long enough to process everything that had happened tonight, especially not after his family walked in as soon as Bronte dropped that bombshell. He was more than excited his family was home, but couldn't they have waited at least another thirty minutes to an hour before barging in? He'd wanted to march up to his old bedroom, pull Bronte out, and sit her down so they could talk. But maybe she needed time to process. It was well after midnight, so it had been hours since she'd disappeared upstairs. He'd give her space tonight and make a point to pull her aside tomorrow and talk. They could figure this out. His heart was in shreds. He'd never thought about a plan that didn't involve a big family. But was he really ready to say goodbye to Bronte?

"Okay, there is def something going on between you and my renter. So spill, big bro." Holland plopped next to Jonah on the couch and held out a steaming mug of some coffee concoction she'd insisted he had to try.

The rest of his family all found places to land. It was the first time in over two years that the entire family was under one roof.

Amy and her daughter, Ruby, were sharing one room, Mika Beth and Halle took what used to be the girls' room, and their parents would take the old master bedroom. Holland and Jonah had opted for the couches in the living room since Bronte was still in Jonah's old room.

"Wow. You have it bad." Holland still held the mug aloft in front of him.

"I have what bad?" Jonah took the mug, staring at the milky-brown liquid inside.

Holland grinned at him over her own coffee. At some point, she had put her ridiculous beanie back on her head. "So bad."

Jonah took a drink of whatever it was that Holland had handed him. Coffee and chocolate and spices exploded on his taste buds. "This is really good, Holland."

Holland took a sip of hers, a smug smile on her face. "I know." She frowned and pointed a finger at Jonah. "Don't change the subject."

"What were we talking about?" Jonah feigned ignorance.

Holland rolled her eyes. "Stop. Seriously. What is going on between you and Bronte?"

"Bronte?"

"Yeah, her."

He had fallen in love, that's what. Had she asked a few hours earlier, Jonah wouldn't have been able to stop talking about her, but now? Now he didn't know what. He had let himself fall too hard and too fast without having the whole story.

"I don't know that there's anything going on." He ran his hand over his face.

What else was there to say? There was actually so much more to say, but he wasn't sure he could get it out.

"Riiiiight."

She saw right through him. He sighed and plopped his head on the back of the couch. "I think I fell in love."

"With Bronte? In a week?" Holland considered him with her eyebrow quirked.

"I know."

"Why do you say you're in love with her?"

Jonah appreciated that Holland didn't tell him he was insane or that what he was feeling couldn't possibly be love this early in the game. Holland would never.

"She's amazing, Holland. She's funny and smart and a writer."

"And?"

"And she can't have kids."

"Oh." Holland knew how important it was to Jonah to have a big family. It was something he'd talked about since, well, forever. "Jonah, I'm so sorry."

Jonah stared at the twinkling lights on the Christmas tree, the only light in the room other than the stove light on in the kitchen behind them. The presents under the tree reached to almost the middle of the room. Holland and his parents had pulled them out of suitcases and closets after they'd gotten home. They planned on having a traditional White family Christmas, complete with his mom's waffles and Bing Crosby playing on Holland's vintage record player. It would be the perfect Christmas morning that he had wanted to give to Bronte.

Somewhere in the pile of paper and ribbon was the gift he had purchased for Bronte. Would he give it to her now? Would she even want it?

Holland picked up the remote and turned on the TV, flipping through the channels until she found *White Christmas* playing. Bronte's new favorite.

She muted it and turned back to Jonah. "Do you really love her?"

Did he?

Jonah let the question hang in the air between them. He'd thought so. He'd thought he'd fallen so completely in love with Bronte that nothing could have changed it, but then she'd told him she couldn't have kids. That couldn't be right. God wouldn't give him the perfect woman at the cost of his biggest dream, would He? "I thought I did."

"But that love was all contingent on what she could or couldn't give you?"

"That's not what I'm saying." Holland made him sound like a jerk.

"It sure sounds like it."

Anger burned in Jonah's chest, but he couldn't figure out if he was angry at Holland, himself, or God. He leaned more toward anger at himself. Had his love for Bronte really come with contingencies? He didn't feel like it had, but did Bronte feel like he'd cast her aside just like Brad had?

"Right. So, how's the Army life?"

"Whiplash on the subject change much, Holland?" He was grateful for the change yet wished it had been to any other topic. He'd only gone from one thing he wanted to be sick about to another.

Instead of answering, he engrossed himself in watching Bing Crosby and Danny Kaye dance across the screen, singing about sisters.

"That good, huh?"

"I'm up for reenlistment."

His sister shrugged, eyes never moving from the TV. "So, don't reenlist."

"But if I don't reenlist, I retire and take over the clinic."

Holland's gaze swung to him. "I thought that was the plan. I thought you wanted to be on Jonathon Island."

Jonah looked over his shoulder. Why did his sister have to be so loud? "I do want to be on Jonathon Island, but I don't think I'm cut out for being a doctor for the rest of my life."

Holland shrugged again and turned back to the movie. "So, you tell Dad."

"I'm just waiting for the right time."

"You're stalling."

"Holland." Jonah groaned. "This has been the plan for

me since I was born. I'm not sure I even had any options other than becoming a doctor. When I talked it over with Amy a couple years ago, she told me it'd break Dad's heart if I didn't take over the clinic."

"First of all," Holland said as she jabbed him in the side with her finger, "I can't believe you talked this over with Amy before you told me. I can't believe you've been struggling with this by yourself for so long."

Jonah held up his hands. "Sorry."

"And secondly"—Holland held up two fingers—"you went into the Army because that's what you told Mom and Dad you wanted."

Jonah opened his mouth to contradict his sister, but . . . could she be right? He'd told his parents so long ago that he wanted to join the Army after college to go to med school because that's what his grandpa had done. He thought they'd agreed because he was still on track to becoming a doctor, but could it be that they'd said yes because that was what Jonah had said he wanted?

"But I'd be throwing away years of school, and for what?"

"What's your point, Jonah?" Holland threw up her hands. "If you aren't happy, if you'll *never* be happy being a doctor, I don't think Mom and Dad will force you to keep doing it. Dad might be disappointed for a little bit, but it's not the end of the world. The end of the world would be finding out you're in a life you hate because you thought you had no other choice. That would break his heart."

Hadn't Bronte told him basically the same thing? "I don't even have a good plan of what to do if I get out."

The idea of the bookstore popped into his head. It had just been a dream when he and Bronte had walked by the store. He'd never imagined that there was a world where he could live on the island, not be a doctor, and own a bookstore. Had he been worried about nothing?

"You'll figure something out. I'm sure you have a backup plan for your backup plan somewhere in that brain of yours. Besides, if you think you can use Dad as an excuse to stay in a mind-numbing life, you are highly mistaken, mister."

"What are you talking about?"

"You're using Mom and Dad as an excuse for making a decision about your life."

"I'm not. I'm just . . . it's hard to go against the plan that's been laid out for you."

Holland reached over and punched him in the shoulder. "They want you to be happy."

"I thought it was going to make me happy. It's a solid job and can provide for a family here on island. That's what I always wanted." Jonah turned back to the TV, not believing that he was confessing this to his sister. "But I just don't know if that's what I want anymore. At least the job part of it. I still want a family. Still want to stay here. Mostly, I want a woman I can partner with. Who will make me a better man."

"And that's Bronte?"

Jonah shrugged. "If she wants the same thing."

He and Bronte still had so much to talk about. But he was determined not to let her leave without telling her that having biological kids wasn't the be all and end all for him.

"Then why are you still doing the Army thing?"

Jonah huffed out a breath. He knew she was asking a rhetorical question, because he had already answered it. Or maybe she just wanted to make the question sink in.

"I think you would be surprised at Mom and Dad's reaction if you told them you weren't planning on reenlisting and you didn't want to take over the clinic. Especially if it meant you were moving back home."

Maybe he could make this work. He would tell his dad about his idea to open the bookstore, and everything would work out. He'd settle down and start a book-loving family.

Thoughts of the dreams that his mind had conjured of him and Bronte and a huge family slammed to the forefront, and he remembered what could never be. At least, not with Bronte.

Seventeen

I'M GOING HOME, LEXI."

Bronte had sequestered herself in her bedroom— *Jonah's* childhood bedroom—for the last three hours. In that time, she had packed, cried, unpacked (thinking that maybe she should stay and talk it over with Jonah, maybe they could work this out), then repacked, remembering that, one, at the end of the day she always ended up alone, and two, Jonah deserved so much better. He deserved the big house filled with kids. The White family was a crowd of people. They filled up spaces, and it was unfair for Bronte to ask Jonah to give up that dream for her.

"Hold on. Rewind. I thought you weren't going home for another week." It was after one in the morning in Michigan, but with the time change for California, it was still an acceptable calling time. Not that that would have stopped Bronte. She was desperate. "And Merry Christmas, by the way."

Bronte pinched the bridge of her nose to keep from crying again. "I told him I couldn't have kids."

Lexi was silent for a breath. "And he didn't take it well?"

"I don't know. His family walked in."

"His family?"

"Walked in. All of them. There were, like, fifty people." Bronte paced.

"Fifty?"

Bronte threw up the hand that wasn't currently holding the phone to her ear. She needed to find her earbuds so she could free her hands. "Okay, fine. It wasn't fifty, but there were a lot of them." She dug around in her messenger bag for her missing earbuds. "He has a big family, Lex. Like four sisters, and a niece, and I've lost count of all the people on the island that consider him a big brother. His family is big, huge."

"Back up. I thought you had the place rented out until the end of the week? They can't do that. They'd better be refunding you for the last few days you paid for. If you aren't going to ask for it, you'd better believe I will." There was a fight in Lexi's voice.

Bronte smiled. Of course Lexi would be ready to throw punches for her. "No, Lex, it's fine. Apparently Holland messaged me they would be coming home early. I just didn't see it because I had my notifications silenced." Bronte didn't add that she'd silenced her notifications because she'd been ignoring Lexi. "And she already refunded me for the entire stay."

"Good. That's good." Some of the bite disappeared from

Lexi's voice. "So, what does Jonah having a big family have to do with you telling him you couldn't have kids?"

"He told me he was falling for me." Bronte gave up looking for her earbuds and flopped down on the bed. "A big family is all he wants, and I could never give him that."

"So you're going home." It wasn't a question.

"I was going home before I told him." Bronte closed her eyes, but whenever she did, she saw Jonah's lips on Bree's—it didn't matter if it hadn't actually happened. It'd be better to keep her eyes open. "An old girlfriend showed up. You know how this is going to play out."

"But he told you he was falling for you before or after she showed up?"

"It doesn't matter. After I'm out of the picture, he'll see that she's actually what he needs."

"Oh." Bronte could hear in Lexi's voice that she wanted to argue, but they had argued this point so much over the years that Lexi had to know it was no use. "Bronte, I'm so sorry."

Bronte sighed, the feeling of defeat settling on her. "Yeah."

"What time are you leaving tomorrow? Do you need me to look at flights or anything?"

"I already booked a flight. I'll leave in the morning by five. I found someone to take me to the docks and have set up a ride across the lake."

"Do you want me to meet you in Tulsa?"

"Lexi, no. It's Christmas. I know how important it is to you and your mom. I'll be fine. I just needed to tell someone."

"Okay, sweetie. I love you."

"Love you too." Bronte ended the call and let her hand drop to the mattress. She stared at the ceiling, trying to conjure the energy to get up, turn the lights out, and go to bed. Cody would be here in less than four hours to give her a ride to the mainland in his boat.

"God, why does this hurt so bad?" Bronte hadn't realized how much she wished she had been able to go to the midnight service. She needed the comfort she remembered feeling as a little girl when she'd gone to church those handful of times. She had wanted to go as an adult, but fear of possibly being rejected had always kept her from trying. "I haven't even known him for that long," she whispered toward the ceiling, but there was no answer in response. Had she expected there to be one?

How many times had she told herself that God wasn't a fairy godfather who would wave a wand and make all her pains go away? But just this once, she wished He'd make an exception.

An alarm was blaring.

Bronte jolted awake, shutting off the alarm on her phone. When had she fallen asleep? It didn't matter. It still felt as if someone had dumped an entire sandbox into each eye before running her over with a dump truck. The lamp on the side table was still on, and the window still showed a sky painted black.

The alarm started blaring again, and only then did

Bronte realize that it wasn't an alarm blaring but her phone ringing. She'd thought she had turned it off.

"Hello?"

"Hey, Bronte, I'm outside. You ready to go?" Cody greeted her, far too chipper for the time.

Bronte scanned the room quickly, making sure she wasn't leaving anything behind. "Yeah, sorry. I'll be right down."

Bronte splashed water on her face, hoping it'd help with the groggy feeling. After donning her coat and wrapping her scarf around her neck, she slung her messenger bag over her shoulder and pulled her suitcase behind her, forgetting about the broken wheel. The suitcase thumped to the side when she pulled. That was no good. She'd wake the whole house pulling it out the door. Sighing, she grabbed the handle and stuck out her hip, being careful not to hit the doorframe or any walls in the hallway on her way down the stairs.

"Oh, are you leaving so soon?"

Bronte stifled a scream, remembering, just barely, that the house was still sleeping as she dropped her suitcase to the floor and turned.

One of Jonah's sisters stood in the hallway, backlit by the kitchen lights. Her sleep pants dotted with Santas made Bronte think of Jonah's collection of Santa socks. With a pang, Bronte realized she wouldn't be seeing any more of Jonah's ridiculous socks.

"Yeah, Cody's giving me a ride to the docks and then over to the mainland. I have an early flight." Bronte moved to the door, hoping Jonah didn't appear. Or maybe she hoped he *would* appear and ask her to stay, that his dream had changed. But she knew that wasn't how this ever worked.

"I'm Amy, by the way. I don't think we got to meet last night." Amy stepped forward, one hand extended while the other pushed her dark, chin-length hair behind her ear.

Bronte couldn't tell much about her in the dim light, but Amy's eyes seemed kind, like Jonah's, and she was almost the same height as her.

"Bronte." Bronte took her offered hand, juggling the suitcase so it didn't fall over in the middle of the hallway.

"Mom?" a girl with her mom's dark-colored hair whispered, coming out into the hallway.

"This is my daughter Ruby," Amy said, tucking Ruby under her arm. Ruby was a carbon copy of her mom, just with glasses added.

"I'm sorry. Did I wake you up?"

Ruby shook her head, pushing her glasses up on her nose. "It's Christmas morning. I wanted to get up before Grandma and make the waffles. But we have to get up super early because Grandma's an early riser."

"Why don't you get the ingredients out on the counter?" Amy said, pressing a kiss to Ruby's forehead.

"Uncle Jonah and Aunt Holland are asleep on the couches though."

"They'll sleep through anything, it's fine. Go on, I'll be there in just a minute." Amy watched her disappear before turning back to Bronte. "Are you sure you can't stick around for just a little longer? I'm sure Jonah would want to say goodbye. Or I could go wake him." She moved like she was going to do just that.

"Oh, no." Bronte stopped her. "Cody's already outside waiting. Let Jonah sleep. It was great meeting you."

"You too," Amy said as Bronte turned toward the door.

She shouldn't say anything else but found herself turning back to Amy. "Could you give Jonah a message for me?"

"Of course."

"Could you tell him Merry Christmas and thanks for letting me crash. And that . . . I hope he has a lovely life here, with all of you. That he deserves that." It was all she could get out before tears started stinging the backs of her eyes. She didn't want to cry anymore.

In the dim light, Amy frowned, but she nodded. "Okay, I'll tell him."

Bronte turned back to the door, blinking rapidly against tears.

"Bronte." Amy's voice stopped her one more time and Bronte turned. "Merry Christmas."

"Merry Christmas to you too." Flinging the door open, Bronte gasped when the cold air hit her, making her forget for a moment that she was about to cry.

If all it took for her to forget was almost-below-freezing temps, maybe she should just walk to the docks. Letting the door click shut behind her, Bronte squared her shoulders and dragged her suitcase to Cody and the waiting golf cart, feeling as if there was something she was forgetting. She refused to believe it was her heart.

Eighteen

Date December 28
Days until Deadline 8
Words to be written 40,435

POUNDING ON THE DOOR PULLED Bronte from her thoughts.

Pushing up from the couch that she had barely moved from in the three days since she'd been home, she made her way to the door. Only when she got there did she remember she was wearing three-day-old sweatpants, a T-shirt that hadn't been washed since—well, she couldn't remember when, and an old ratty house robe that she had bought with her first royalty check. She lifted her shirt and sniffed. Cringe. She smelled like onion rings. At least she had a bra on. Hopefully her guest wouldn't look down on her lack of hygiene.

Who was she kidding? She looked down on herself

for the lack of hygiene. Or maybe, if she were lucky, it'd scare them off.

But when she flung the door open, her best friend stood on the other side. "Lexi?"

Lexi, red hair flowing from under a cream-colored beret that would do nothing to keep her ears warm, pushed past Bronte, arms loaded down with a suitcase, a canvas messenger bag, and shopping bags. It looked as if she'd hit up the shops in Utica Square.

"By all means, come in."

Dropping the bags, Lexi turned and pinned Bronte with a look. "You don't answer your phone for three days. That in itself was nerve-racking, although I knew you were still alive because I saw you active on Instagram. Fine, you were ghosting me, whatever. But I fly all the way out here, with presents"—she motioned to the shopping bags at her feet—"and you leave me banging on your front door for five minutes? I'm pretty sure your neighbors were going to call the cops on me. And why didn't you tell me you had a hot neighbor? He literally looks like Ryan Reynolds. I almost had a heart attack when I saw him in the elevator."

"He has a girlfriend."

Lexi's face screwed up. "Is it serious?"

Bronte shrugged. "What are you doing here?"

"I was worried about you." Lexi's shoulders lifted.

"But not so worried you couldn't take a shopping spree first?" Bronte pointed at the bags at Lexi's feet.

Lexi looked down as if she just realized all the bags were there. "I got off the plane and didn't want to come empty-handed."

"Empty-handed? Lexi, you just flew a thousand miles. You are gift enough." Bronte pulled Lexi into a hug. She hadn't realized how much she'd needed to see her friend. Bronte was already starting to feel better. Something that had felt dull inside her was coming back to life.

Lexi pushed back from their hug. "Okay. Who are you, and what have you done with my friend?"

Bronte's mouth lifted in half a smile. "I'm just really glad you're here."

"That's fine and all, but you've never given me a hug the entire time I've known you."

Bronte frowned. "That can't be right." She bent over to help Lexi pick up her scattered bags. Her suitcase had to weigh a hundred pounds. "Are you planning on moving in?"

Lexi chewed on her lips. "I wasn't sure how long you would need me."

"Need you?" Bronte motioned to Lexi to follow her down the hall, toward her spare bedroom.

"You sounded upset on the phone when you left Jonathon Island, and I know you have this book you're trying to finish . . ." Lexi trailed off.

"Did your mother send you to keep an eye on me to make sure I get this book done?"

Lexi rolled her green eyes. "Of course not." She leaned in closer as if to tell a secret, even though there wasn't anyone else around. "I didn't actually tell her you haven't finished yet."

"I'm almost done," Bronte promised, opening the door to her spare bedroom and depositing Lexi's suitcase in the middle of the bed. "I only have around forty thousand words left, and then I'm going to do a really fast read-through and then—" Bronte choked on her words. She was supposed to have finished this book on Jonathon Island. Try as she might, she couldn't stop thinking of the reason she hadn't finished yet. Tears stung her eyes as she blinked rapidly to keep them from falling.

"Are you okay?" Lexi's whisper came from the hallway, almost as if she was too afraid to step into the bedroom.

Bronte sighed, teeth working her bottom lip. Staring at the blank wall of her guest bedroom, she couldn't help but remember the warmth of Holland's home.

"Do you want to talk about what happened?" Lexi stepped into the room.

"I think I fell in love with him." A warm tear trickled a path down Bronte's cheek. She swiped it away, giving Lexi a watery smile. "But it's fine. I know I'm meant to be alone, and Jonah's meant to be with someone that can give him lots of babies."

"No, Bronte."

Bronte shook her head. She thought she'd cried all her tears. She didn't have time for this. She needed to get that book done, and if she let herself start up again, she wasn't sure she'd stop. "I've never hated my lack of uterus more."

"Oh, honey." Lexi crossed the room in three steps and pulled Bronte into a hug.

Sobs racked Bronte's body. "I promised myself I was done crying over a man," she blubbered. "And I've been crying too much already. At least I made it to the plane before I fell apart the first time. The flight attendant felt bad for me and bumped me up to first class." Bronte let out a groan. "I'm so sick and tired of crying. Oh my goodness, I'm slobbering all over you."

"Who cares?" Lexi said, hugging her tighter.

"For so long I didn't think I had anyone," Bronte shuddered out. "And then I had Brad for years, but after spending two weeks with Jonah, I'm pretty sure what I had with Brad was never love."

"Well, thank goodness you've realized that." Lexi huffed a sigh of relief.

Bronte choke-laughed and wiped a hand across her face. "I just wanted a place to belong for so long, but how did I completely miss that you're my person, Lexi? I mean, who else would get on a plane and fly halfway across the country because she didn't feel like talking on the phone?"

Lexi's simple "That's not why I came" had Bronte choking up again.

"Thank you for coming all this way," she mumbled into Lexi's shoulder, finally feeling the tears subside.

"Of course." With one more squeeze, Lexi released her and took a step back. "Now. I'm not sure about you, but I'm starving. I know you have a book to write, but why don't we go get something to eat?"

Bronte's stomach grumbled as if it were agreeing with Lexi. Now that Bronte thought about it, she wasn't sure when she'd last had real food. The sour gummies and microwaved popcorn had maybe kept something in her belly, but it hadn't been enough. A pain shot through her heart as she remembered Jonah making sure she ate while she worked. She nodded to answer Lexi, but also to try and shake the memories away.

Lexi scrunched her face. "You should probably take a shower first."

Bronte laughed. "You're a good friend, Lexi."

"Of course I am. Now, go shower so we can get out of here and you can get back to work as a human. I'm going to unpack."

Bronte allowed herself to be pushed toward her own room, a smile on her face. She hadn't realized the heaviness she'd felt on her chest at the weight of her unconfessed love. But being able to tell Lexi—and Lexi not thinking she had lost her mind—made Bronte feel lighter. Maybe she would be able to salvage some of her broken heart after all.

Lexi had been right. Bronte did feel more like a human after having a shower and eating real food. Bronte had taken Lexi to Hideaway, her favorite pizza place on Cherry Street.

Turned out, when there was food in her belly and a friend by her side, she could write a lot faster. Bronte generally didn't like writing at night, but due to the looming deadline, she forced herself to. At least she found it easier to write the sad depressing book she had originally planned. She'd been delusional to ever think she could write a rom-com.

"Ready for some more tea?" Lexi held out a fresh cup of steaming chai.

Bronte set her laptop aside and stretched her arms over her head, accepting the cup and letting the scent of ginger and cinnamon warm her insides. "Thanks."

"How's it going?"

"At this rate, I might finish a little ahead of what I thought." Maybe there was something to writing while she wasn't depressed.

Lexi turned and plopped down in Bronte's wingback chair, then grabbed a manuscript she'd brought with her. How she didn't slosh hot tea all over her was an art form. "When can I read it?"

Bronte chewed on her bottom lip. At least this time, thinking of Jonah hadn't brought tears to her eyes. When would this stop being so hard?

"Uh-oh. What's that look for?"

Bronte shook her head.

"You're thinking about him again." Lexi reached over and squeezed Bronte's hand. "Aren't you?"

Bronte cringed. "Is it that obvious?"

"Your face looked like someone just burned your only copy of a manuscript. While you watched."

"I can't get him out of my mind, Lex. He was supposed to be my first read."

Lexi feigned being shocked. "I thought I was always your first read."

"I know, and it would be so much simpler if I'd just kept it that way. I can't stop thinking about him. I only knew him for ten days, Lexi. He shouldn't be so ingrained into my marrow." Bronte traced a finger around the top of her teacup. "I should have booked it out of there as soon as he walked through the door."

"If I recall right, there was a massive snowstorm and there wouldn't have been anywhere for you to go."

"Well, then I should have locked myself in my room until he left. This all could have been avoided if I'd insisted that we not stay together."

Lexi studied Bronte over her mug. "I don't know, Bront. It seems like maybe you were supposed to meet."

"I don't believe in fate or destiny or meet-cutes or anything that you're going to try to talk me into." Bronte sealed her statement with a gulp of tea. It was scalding, but she bit her tongue to keep from showing the pain.

Lexi waved a hand. "I'm not talking about any of those things. Maybe God wanted you to meet Jonah."

"Why would He want me to do that? Just to break my heart and laugh all over again?" Another sip of scalding hot tea. Maybe it'd burn the pain away.

"I don't think God is laughing, and maybe this whole thing with Jonah isn't over yet."

Bronte sighed. "Maybe God brought me into Jonah's life for a reason, but it was probably just to make him realize what had been right in front of him."

"Mm. Maybe." Lexi picked up her mug and slurped her tea.

"What's that supposed to mean?" Bronte pushed away her laptop. "Why are you taking his side?"

"I'm on your side, Bronte. Always have been, always will be. But I just feel like there's more here. Did he say anything to you before you left?"

Bronte bit her lip. "Not really. I left the ball and started working as soon as I got back to the house. Then by the time he showed up, we had two minutes before his family surprised him."

She tried to think back to the two minutes before his family had arrived. Had there been something there? She hadn't really let him talk or explain or say anything, sure he was just going to tell her what they had was a mistake and that he and Bree really loved each other. But it didn't seem as if that was what he'd been going to say.

"And you didn't say goodbye, did you? You just snuck out."

"I said goodbye to Cody, and Jonah's sister Amy."

"And did neither of them say anything about this whole thing?"

"Cody took me to the docks. And told me . . ." Actually, she had been too upset and focused on keeping it all together when Cody told her bye. "I don't remember what he told me."

"I think you need to talk this over with Jonah."

But Bronte's head already shook back and forth. "I can't, Lex."

"What? Why not? You need to get your man. It's your turn."

"He's not my man. He just happened to come home on the same night I arrived. We had an amazing week, and then it wasn't. Maybe I just need to face the fact that I'll always be the stand-in until the right thing comes along."

"You can't mean that."

"Of course I mean it. It happened to me over and over

in foster care. The Martins only wanted to adopt me until they got pregnant with their own child, and then Brad, and now Jonah . . ." Bronte shook her head. "This is real life, Lexi. People don't run after their long-lost loves. Sometimes things just happen, and all they are meant to be is a blip in this thing called life."

"No, about always being the stand-in."

"It's happened all my life, Lexi. What else am I supposed to be?"

"We live in a very broken world, Bronte. Maybe you do feel like you're just standing in for someone else until the 'real prize' arrives, but I happen to know that God thinks you're the real prize, and you'll never be a stand-in for Him. You'll always belong, Bronte."

Bronte shrugged, emotion thick in her throat. Hadn't Jonah said something similar? She pulled her laptop back onto her lap but didn't open it yet. She didn't want to talk about this anymore, but she was feeling the tug of depressing thoughts. If she gave in to them, she'd spiral again, and she'd never get this book done on time.

She opened her laptop. Time to get back to work.

Jonah listened as Reeves gave him the update about Sgt. Collins, the soldier Jonah had operated on before his leave. He'd asked to be kept in the loop on his care, and the sergeant had been doing so well he was being released early. The operation had had a few minor complications, so Jonah was relieved that post-op had gone smoothly.

"Sounds good, Reeves." Jonah pushed the button to end the call.

"Whoa, big bro, sounds like someone just sprinkled dirt on your waffles." Holland, blonde hair piled on top of her head much like Bronte wore hers when she was working, came up beside him, holding a mug of coffee out in his direction. He couldn't help but think of the scent of the vanilla caramel Bronte preferred. She'd left a tin of it on the counter.

Jonah nodded his thanks before taking a sip of coffee. "Just work stuff. A patient I had been caring for was released."

Holland studied him over the rim of her mug. "I think it's about time to have that talk with Mom and Dad."

"Mm." Jonah set his coffee down on the counter and moved to the fridge.

"Jonah, I'm serious. You've been moping around since we all got back." She paused. "Since Bronte left."

Jonah was finished looking in the fridge, but he didn't close the door. He stayed hidden, letting his eyes slide closed at the mention of her. He had somehow made it through the past three days, and yes, maybe he had been a bit quieter than normal, but if he wasn't thinking about Bronte, he was thinking about how to talk to his dad about not being a doctor anymore. He was trading one torture for another. Amy, Mika Beth, and Halle had left the day after Christmas, headed back to the mainland where they shared a house.

"If you don't tell them, I will."

Jonah snapped the fridge door closed, eyes darting to

where his parents sat on the couch watching a movie, and hissed, "You wouldn't dare."

Holland regarded him with her eyebrows raised. She snagged an apple from the fruit bowl on the counter and walked backward toward the living room, not taking her eyes off him. She wasn't kidding.

"What are you two whispering about in there?" His dad stood up from the couch, coffee mug in hand, and walked into the kitchen. George White wasn't a small man, but he still stood a little shorter than Jonah. Was he a bit shorter than the last time Jonah had been home? His hair, once blond like Holland's, was now gray. His eyes, a mirror of Jonah's own, looked rested, and his cheeks were tinged with pink from his Caribbean vacation.

"Nothing much. How's retirement and the RV life treating you?"

Holland turned where she sat on the couch, pointed two fingers at her eyes and then to Jonah in the *I'm watching you* sign. Jonah rolled his eyes and turned his back to her.

"RV life is great." Setting his mug on the counter, his dad poured himself another cup and sprinkled cinnamon on top. "Your mom and I are thinking about heading down to Florida. Escaping somewhere warm."

Jonah nodded. "Somewhere warm would be nice."

"Was that a work call I heard you on?"

Jonah shot a look over to Holland, who seemed very interested in the commercials on the TV while she bit into her apple.

"It wasn't anything important. Just Reeves calling about a patient who recently got discharged."

"Everything okay?" His eyes were sharp, as if he knew Jonah had something to tell him. Jonah never could keep anything from his dad for very long.

"Yeah, everything's good." Jonah picked an apple from the fruit bowl and twisted the stem off.

His dad hummed.

"So, Jonah, how long is your leave for?" his mom asked, joining them in the kitchen, her feet clad in a mismatched pair of Santa socks. She had her silver hair pulled back in a ponytail, her face glowing tan from the cruise.

"I have to report back on base by the seventh." The blood rushed in Jonah's ears.

"Oh, we were hoping you'd get to stay through January." His mom refilled her coffee, adding in some of Holland's homemade syrup. "It's so long since you've been home."

"Aren't you up for reenlistment soon?" His dad took a drink of his coffee. "We should talk about plans. If you want to continue on in the Army, or if you're interested in coming back here and taking over the clinic."

Wait. *If* he was interested in coming back and taking over the clinic? That sounded like he had a choice. Had he always had a choice?

He put the apple back into the fruit bowl. "I don't want to be a doctor anymore."

That had been the worst confession in the history of all confessions. Jonah looked back and forth between his parents, waiting for the pain and disappointment to appear on their faces.

But instead of heart-wrenching sadness, his parents' expressions were thoughtful. Tears shimmered in his mom's eyes. Were they happy tears?

"Do you know what you want to do instead?" his mom asked, a hopeful tilt to her voice.

Jonah's heart started to calm. His parents hadn't freaked out over him not wanting to practice medicine any longer, but would they feel the same when they heard what he wanted to do instead? That he wanted to trade a secure livelihood for one that had more risks than guarantees?

"I want to move home and reopen the old bookstore."

He glanced at his mom and dad.

His mom squealed, clapping her hands together.

"You're not mad?" Jonah frowned. This reaction was unexpected. Better than he could have hoped for, but still unexpected.

"We've been waiting for this day for years!" his dad said, clapping him on his back.

Coffee sloshed over the side of Jonah's mug, landing with a splash on the floor. He set it on the counter and washed his hands in the sink.

"Why would we be mad?" his mother asked, clutching his arm.

"Because I don't want to take over the clinic from Dad." He reached for a towel and dried his hands before tossing it next to the sink. "Because I spent so much time in med school and years in the Army, and I want to throw it all away. And if I don't take over the clinic, it'll break Dad's heart."

"First of all," his dad said as he put an arm on Jonah's

shoulder, "you've taken a lot of this on yourself. I wish you would have come and talked to me sooner. It wasn't the plan, but Nova Lake's doing an exceptional job, and everyone loves her. I can see if she'd be interested in buying me out."

Jonah's mom patted his hand. "It doesn't sound like you're really happy practicing anymore, honey. We've thought this for a while. You always sound so tired when we FaceTime, but you've never said anything."

Jonah's head snapped to Holland, who may have been sitting across the room on the couch but would be hearing every word. She held her hands up as if to say *I didn't tell them anything.* Or maybe it was more of an *I told you so.*

"I've been doing it because I thought that was the plan for my life. I thought that's what you guys wanted, and I went into the Army because that's what Grandpa did, and it seemed like the easiest way to get through med school without a ton of debt."

"You've been in the Army for thirteen years, and you're *just now* telling everyone that it isn't what you want?" Holland yelled across the room.

"Holland, stop it," his dad reprimanded. "Jonah, we apologize that you ever felt pressured into this." His dad rubbed a hand over the two-day-old scruff on his face. "We only wanted to support your dreams, and we thought this was what you wanted. In my fifty-seven years of life, I've learned that a man's plan rarely succeeds unless it's blessed by the Lord. You need to pray about this, son, and if you feel peace about a particular path, you shouldn't let anyone talk you out of it."

"So, I guess that solves that problem. You're not re-enlisting, and you're coming home, and you're going to support all of our book habits because you're going to open a bookstore." Holland perched on the arm of the wingback chair.

"Holland!" His mother shot a look in Holland's direction, but from the smile covering her face, Jonah knew his mom liked his sister's idea.

Holland just shrugged. "What? That's what Jesus just told me Jonah needs to do."

Jonah laughed. "Well, I might open a bookstore. Oliver mentioned it was for sale, and I saw it last week, still sitting vacant, and it just clicked that it's what I want to do. I'm not even sure of any of the logistics." He felt lighter than he had in days. The overwhelming urge to find Bronte and tell her about his decision almost made him pop up from his seat to go find her, but then he remembered she'd gone back to Tulsa.

"I'm so excited I feel like I'm about to burst." His mom put her coffee mug on the counter and grabbed his dad's sleeve. "George, let's call Bob and Lucinda and see what we can find out about the old bookstore. I don't think they sold it when they left." After a hug, his mom dashed out of the room, his dad following close behind.

And Jonah was left by himself in the kitchen. He shuffled to the couch and sat next to Holland. He stared at the carnage of Christmas, still left after three days. Jonah was really surprised Holland and his mom hadn't gone feral on the mess and cleaned it up.

Holland opened her mouth to say something, but Jonah cut her off. "Do not say 'I told you so.'"

"I wasn't going to even mention that," Holland said. Her bottom lip stuck out in a pout before curling up in a wicked smile. "I want to talk about the other thing that's bothering you."

"I don't know what you're talking about."

"Mm. A certain gorgeous writer who mysteriously snuck out a few days ago?" Holland took a drink of her coffee, and Jonah realized he'd left his on the kitchen table. He should get up and get it. "Drink mine." Holland, as if reading his thoughts, pushed her mug toward him. "You aren't getting out of this conversation, big bro."

"There isn't anything to talk about."

Holland rolled her eyes. "Heard that one before, and it was a lie the first time you said it too. Jonah, you fell in love. Are you just going to let that get away?"

"What do you want me to say? That I met the love of my life and somehow completely screwed it up?" Jonah would throw up his hands, but then Holland's coffee would fly everywhere, and she'd lecture him not only about making a mess but also wasting perfectly good coffee.

"You're full of mess-ups today, aren't you?" Holland patted his leg, taking her cup of coffee back and lifting it to drink.

"Haha, Holland." Jonah wasn't laughing.

Holland shrugged. "I'm just pointing out the obvious."

"Thanks for that." Jonah let his head fall onto the back of the couch. "I know Bronte and I didn't know each other for long but, Holland, she was amazing. Funny—"

"Yeah, yeah, you've already told me all this, but the fact still remains that she can't have kids."

"Right." But the hole in Jonah's heart was Bronte-shaped, and while not having a big family hurt, he was beginning to realize that not having her in his life hurt even more.

"Aaaaand?" Holland drew out the word.

"Did I say that out loud?"

Holland just looked at him with her eyebrows raised, waiting on his answer.

Like it mattered. It still didn't change the fact that Bronte had left. "And nothing. She left."

Holland reached over and smacked the back of her brother's head. Hard.

"Ouch." Jonah rubbed at the spot, sure there was a red Holland-hand-sized mark. "What was that for?"

"Because you're being an idiot." Holland jumped up and started pacing. "Seriously. I thought Amy, Mika Beth, Halle, and I raised you better than this."

"What?"

Holland stopped pacing and turned to face her brother. "It is time, dear brother, for the grand gesture."

"The what?"

Holland rolled her eyes so hard, Jonah was afraid they'd get stuck in the back of her head. "Have you learned nothing from all those romance novels we forced you to read?"

"I guess not?" Maybe Jonah should have just gone with it, because Holland seriously looked like she was about to smack him over the head again.

Instead, she groaned and threw up her hands. "Must

I do everything for you?" She pulled her cell phone out of her back pocket, fingers flying over the keyboard. "My clueless brother, she left because she loves you too."

"That doesn't make any sense. Why would she leave if she loves me?" He should probably take his sister's phone from her. He didn't like the mischievous look she had in her eyes.

"Because," Holland responded, attention never leaving her phone, "she thinks she can't give you your greatest dream."

Jonah's heart sank. "I should have gone after her. I should have forced her to talk it out. I—What are you doing?" He leaned toward her on the couch and tried to look over her shoulder, but Holland just moved out of the way.

"Done."

"What did you just do?" Jonah was a little afraid of the answer.

Holland held her phone face out to Jonah. "I booked us on the next flight to Tulsa."

"You what?" Jonah didn't know if he wanted to hug or strangle his sister.

"Don't chicken out on me now. You were just talking about how you should have gone after her. It took you long enough, but you came to the same conclusion I did. You can thank me later." Holland turned her phone back to herself. "Now, you'd better hurry. Pack a bag or something. I'm getting you out on the next ferry. Let's go get your girl."

Jonah couldn't move fast enough.

Nineteen

Date December 30

Days until Deadline 6

Words to be written 15,743

BRONTE HAD ALWAYS THOUGHT SHE wouldn't enjoy having a roommate, but since Lexi had practically moved in two days ago, Bronte couldn't remember her reasons for not having one.

Pulling late nights and early mornings to get the book done meant it was nice to have someone there to make sure she ate real food, at least every once in a while.

The manuscript was in the homestretch now. She only had the last fifteen thousand words to write and then a quick read-through before she turned it in on the fifth. This was the closest she had ever cut a deadline, and she could feel the anxiety building. All the same fears. Would she finish in time? Would her editor like it? Would her readers like it? Would this be the book to tank her career?

Shaking the useless thoughts from her head, she rolled her neck and stared at her empty teacup. She needed more tea to get through the final words. Lexi had left earlier, deciding she needed to hit up more after-Christmas sales. One thing about her new roommate was for sure—she liked to shop.

It was a little after noon, and Bronte thought about making some lunch but didn't want to slow down long enough to eat. The tea would do just fine, and maybe some popcorn. She had gone to bed around three a.m. and woken up at six to get back to work. The sleepless nights were paying off. She was going to finish today. Maybe.

Using the sleeve of her sweatshirt, she swiped at the sleep in her eyes and winced. The first thing she needed to do once she finished this draft was take a long, hot shower. Maybe Lexi's shopping habit had more to do with the smell of her roommate than actually enjoying shopping.

She should text Lexi to pick up a couple of extra candles. Anthropologie was having a sale on her favorite scent. She shot a text off to Lexi while she waited for the water to boil.

Someone knocked at the door.

Or maybe Lexi was already home.

"Lexi, what happened to your key? Did you already lose—"

Bronte opened the door to . . . NOT Lexi.

Blue eyes that haunted her dreams stared back at her. Blue eyes and dark hair that, even though it was cropped short, looked like fingers had been run through it more than once. He wore dark jeans, and his plaid button-up under his black coat was rumpled. He twisted a black cap in his hands, standing outside her door, chewing on his lip.

"Jonah?" Her heart threatened to beat out of her chest. Traitor.

"You left." His eyes were haunted, as if having her leave had almost undone him. He shoved his hands in his pockets, but Bronte wished he would pull her into his arms.

She needed to stop this. She was being ridiculous.

"I know I left." She couldn't breathe. Couldn't feel her toes. What was happening to her? "I had to." She wanted to reach out and touch him, pull *him* into her arms, but she was afraid that he wasn't actually there. What if this was just a figment of the little sleep she was getting, compounded by stress of the deadline?

"But we didn't get the chance to talk about what you told me."

"There was nothing to talk about, Jonah. No amount of talking can change it." The teakettle whistled, and Bronte let go of the door handle and turned to walk to the kitchen.

Against her better judgment, she waved Jonah in over her shoulder. Maybe he would come in, or, more likely, he'd just turn into a wisp and disappear, just a wish. She glanced over her shoulder and saw Jonah push through the door. Her heart leaped.

Maybe this wasn't a dream. She pinched her arm. Ouch. Nope. Still awake.

"Are you pinching your arm?"

"What are you doing here?" Bronte asked. "And how did you even find me?"

"My sister had your address from the rental paperwork."

"Oh."

This was a terrible idea. There was nothing to talk about. Bronte had said all she was going to say on the matter.

"I told you we needed to talk," Jonah said, making his way toward Bronte, slowly taking in her apartment.

Thank God Lexi had tidied up before she'd left this morning. Bronte turned to take in the mess of takeout boxes still littering the coffee table, the throw blanket tossed half-heartedly over the back of the couch, and random balls of paper that were strewn about that Bronte had wadded up when, in desperation, she'd switched from typing on her computer to writing scenes out.

Okay, so maybe she'd only *thought* Lexi had cleaned up. Bronte turned back to her tea so she didn't have to look at Jonah. *Keep your eyes off Jonah, and maybe you'll get out of here with your heart intact.*

"Do you want some tea? Or Lexi might have some coffee around here somewhere." Bronte opened the cabinet, looking for the coffee she knew Lexi had already finished. She froze when she felt him behind her.

She turned into Jonah's firm chest and took a step back, bumping into the kitchen counter. Jonah leaned a hand on either side of her, trapping her in the circle of his arms. He leaned down so they were eye to eye.

"You left."

Bronte focused her gaze to the ceiling, refusing to look

at Jonah. *Keep your eyes off him, Bronte.* "I said all I needed to say."

"I didn't."

Her eyes flashed to his. Mistake. "I can't give you ki-kids. I can't gi-give you the big family you deserve."

"I only want you."

Bronte's laugh was bitter. "You don't mean that."

"I want you, Bronte, and if that means we can't have kids, then we can't have kids."

"You *can't* mean that," Bronte whispered. "I know how this plays out."

"No, Bronte, you don't. I've just had the worst six days of my life."

Bronte snorted. "I can't be the reason you don't get your dream. You might be okay now, but what about in five years, ten? You'll hate me."

"You are my dream, Bronte. A life with you. Seeing where this goes and where God takes us. We can make all the plans in the world, but if they aren't God's plans, they are nothing. He sent you straight to me—or maybe me to you, that's up for debate, but who are we to question Him?"

If looking into Jonah's eyes was a mistake, letting him talk was an even bigger one, his words a soothing balm to her weary soul.

"I'm going to kiss you now." Jonah put a hand on either side of Bronte's face. Hot tears pooled where his hands met her skin.

Using his thumb, Jonah wiped at her tears. "Don't cry, Bronte."

He leaned in ever so slowly. Bronte wanted to throw her arms around his neck and pull him close and never let him go again.

The front door crashed open just before their lips met.

One voice screamed, "Yes!" while another yelled, "I told you so!"

Jonah groaned and dropped his forehead to Bronte's shoulder. "Holland," he growled as Holland and Lexi stumbled into the living room.

"Oh my gosh, they are kissing!" Holland said.

"I think we might have interrupted that part," Lexi said, bumping Holland with her shoulder.

"Wait. Do you two know each other?" Bronte pulled away from Jonah, pointing back and forth between Lexi and Holland.

Lexi shrugged. "We actually just met. I bumped into them in the elevator."

"And she heard me telling Jonah what he needed to do to win you back," Holland added, throwing an arm around Lexi's shoulders. "Lexi put two and two together, and here we are."

"Have you ever met a stranger?" Bronte asked Lexi. No one would ever have guessed the two of them had just met five minutes ago.

"I don't think either of them has ever met a stranger," Jonah mumbled behind her.

"Bronte." Lexi jabbed a finger in her direction. "Jonah is ten times hotter in real life."

Bronte's cheeks heated as Jonah pulled her back to him.

"Can you come back home with me and meet my family?" Jonah's eyes pleaded with hers.

Bronte took a deep breath and stilled her face from the smile she felt growing. "Can't."

Jonah's face fell, and Bronte let her smile break through. She couldn't torture him any longer. "My book. I have to finish it and turn it in."

"Actually," Lexi said, pulling looks from both Jonah and Bronte. Lexi's fingers were flying over the screen of her phone. "I bought you an extra week."

"What?" Bronte's heart pounded so hard she wondered if Jonah could feel it.

"Well, I just sent a nicely-worded email to your publisher, letting them know that you'll have the manuscript on their desk by the twelfth. Whoever heard of turning a manuscript in the first week of the year? Everyone knows publishers are buried under their inboxes for at least the first full week back."

"Well, in that case . . ." Bronte put a finger to her chin.

"You'll come home with me?" Jonah's hands tightened around her hips, his touch the only thing keeping her feet on the ground.

"Let me think about it."

Jonah straightened up and shrugged. She instantly missed his touch. "I guess we're headed home, Holland. I only have a little over a week of leave left, and it seems Bronte is too busy for us."

Both Holland and Lexi started to protest when Bronte grabbed Jonah's wrist and pulled him back to her. "Shut up and kiss me, Jonah White."

"Yes, ma'am."

"We're just going to see ourselves out." Holland and Lexi tiptoed back into the hallway, closing the door behind them.

Not being able to stand the space between them, Bronte rose on her tiptoes and softly pressed her lips to Jonah's. She'd missed the feel of his lips on hers. Missed the fireworks shooting off in her head at his touch.

"Jonah," she whispered, pulling away.

Jonah, eyes closed, found her lips again with his. "We're supposed to be kissing."

"I know," she said in between kisses. "But I need to say this." Before her head was too clouded with his kisses and his sandalwood and citrus scent.

Jonah leaned his head back but left his arms around her, his blue eyes staring into hers.

One could drown in his eyes. "Thank you."

Eyebrows dipping into a frown, he asked, "For what?"

"For coming to find me. For not giving up on us. For choosing me." Her voice wobbled with emotion.

"I will always choose you." His eyes darted between hers. "Can we be done talking now? Because I really want to kiss you some more."

She could only nod as he brought his mouth back to hers, claiming her lips with his own.

Sighing into his kiss, she let his words roll over her. She finally, really, *truly* belonged to someone—and she couldn't have picked a better someone for herself.

Epilogue

Date December 31

Days until Deadline 13

Words to be written 15,743 (and some edits)

BRONTE'S INSIDES TWISTED AS SHE once again stood outside Holland's house. This time, tucked into Jonah's side.

Since they hadn't been able to get a flight back to Michigan until New Year's Eve, Bronte had enjoyed taking Jonah and Holland around Tulsa and showing them all her favorite spots. Jonah had been right about Bronte loving Holland.

"Are they going to be mad I left?" Bronte whispered, thinking only Jonah would be able to hear.

"Trust me," Holland answered, skirting around them. "They would have been mad had we not brought you back. Jonah has been sulking for daaaays."

Bronte looked up at Jonah, and he shrugged. "What can I say? My heart left."

Smiling, Bronte stood on tiptoes to give Jonah a quick peck, but he pulled her closer, deepening the kiss.

"You guys, the parents are coming," Holland warned, slipping into the house two seconds before Jonah's parents bounded out the door, arms open wide.

"Jonah! Bronte!" Renee and George White pulled them into a hug.

Bronte had thought her heart couldn't get any fuller, but she had been wrong. Meeting Jonah's parents had her heart almost overflowing.

During the flight, Jonah had told Bronte all about how his parents had been excited that he'd be moving home. It didn't matter that he still had at least a year of processing before he'd be officially out of the Army. He'd gotten in touch with the Johnsons, and they were working on writing up a deal for him and Oliver to purchase the bookstore. Since it would be a while before Jonah could move home, the plan was for Oliver to return to the island in a few weeks. They wanted to have the bookstore opened in time for the start of the season at the beginning of May. His dad had also talked to Dr. Nova, and she was planning to purchase the clinic.

Bronte couldn't be more excited for him.

"Hurry up, you guys, I'm ready to open more presents!" Holland called over her shoulder.

"What do you mean you're opening more presents?" Bronte asked, bending to pick up her suitcase but stopping when Jonah beat her to it.

"We decided we wanted to redo Christmas so you could enjoy it too," Renee said, putting an arm around Bronte's waist and leading her to the door. Renee only came up to Bronte's chin and smelled as if she had been baking cookies all day. "Jonah told us how you haven't ever had a real Christmas."

Bronte felt her face heat. "Oh, you don't have to do that."

"You're right, we don't have to, but we want to," George said, blue eyes sparkling. He gave Bronte a quick side hug as he walked by with Holland's suitcase that she'd left on the sidewalk. "Come in and meet the rest of the family! We're all here!"

Letting herself be pulled through the house, Bronte tried to swallow down her nerves. When she'd agreed to fly back with Jonah and Holland, she'd thought she'd just be meeting Jonah's parents, but apparently when Jonah had asked her to come meet his family, he'd meant all of them. True to George's words, when she and Jonah walked through to the kitchen and living room, a cheer went up from everyone who sat gathered around the tree.

"You must be Bronte." A woman with freckles sprinkled across her nose and the same blue eyes as Jonah stood and pulled Bronte into a hug. Bronte was too shocked to do anything but hug the woman back.

"Bronte, this is Mika Beth," Jonah said, stepping up behind her. "And that's Halle." Jonah pointed to the woman with chocolate-colored eyes and the same color hair as him, sitting on the hearth in front of the fire. She smiled and waved. "And I think you've already met Amy and Ruby." Amy and Ruby waved from their spot on the floor next to the tree.

By the time Jonah had started introducing her to his sisters, Bronte had forgotten to be nervous. Everyone was so welcoming.

"I hope you don't mind, but we invited Nova to join us as well," Renee said, motioning to the doctor, who was sitting on the yellow velvet couch. "She spent Christmas alone, and we found out she was going to be spending New Year's by herself as well, so we decided she needed to come celebrate with us."

"I love it," Bronte said, lifting her hand in greeting and smiling at the doctor.

"Can we open presents now?" Holland asked.

"The ten-year-old has more self-control than you do right now, Holland," Mika Beth chided.

Someone had put a cup of tea in Bronte's hands, and she was glad for the familiar scent of Earl Grey. But then a panicked thought shot through her. "Jonah, I didn't get anyone anything."

"It's fine," Jonah whispered back, his breath tickling her ear. "They're all presents I ordered that didn't come in time for Christmas, and I put both our names on them. When everyone found out you would be coming home with me, we decided it would be perfect to have another Christmas."

Bronte ducked her head to hide the fact that her face turned red. She couldn't believe someone would do that for her. And here, not only one person was making her feel welcome and wanting to make sure she experienced stuff like Christmas, but an entire family.

Everyone oohed and awed over Jonah's gifts. Blankets for his sisters, and there had even been an extra one for Nova as well. A book of poetry for his dad, and a hand-pottered mug for his mom.

For Bronte, there was a Jonathon Island stocking filled with trinkets and souvenirs from shops around town. More fudge from the Fudge Shop on the Corner from Amy and Ruby, a new leather notebook from Halle, and a tin of tea from Mika Beth—all of which she had a feeling, even though his sister's names were on them, had been purchased by Jonah.

She thought they'd opened all the gifts, until Ruby crawled out from under the tree, a small box in her hands. "This one's for . . ." The girl paused to find the tag. She pushed her glasses up on her face, read the tag, and looked at Bronte. "Bronte."

Bronte barely had time to register that Ruby had said her name before the package was placed in her lap.

"This one's from me," Jonah said, the huskiness of his voice causing Bronte's neck to flush.

"Of course it is." She nudged him as she carefully unwrapped the gift to reveal an old Bible, the words *Little Stone Bible Church* engraved on the front. Bronte looked up at Jonah, eyebrows pulled into a question.

"Don't worry, I asked before I took it, but you said the last place that had felt like home was a church, and I wanted to give you something to remind you that, well . . . you can read the inscription inside."

Bronte ran her hand over the worn red cardboard cover before opening it to the front to read the inscription.

>JM>Bronte, even if you never make it to another church building again, may this book remind you that you will always belong in the Kingdom of Heaven. God didn't make any mistakes, and He will always pick you. Forever and ever.

"Jonah . . ." Bronte couldn't say anything. She hugged the Bible to her chest, knowing that she would treasure the book for always. "This is perfect. Thank you." Her eyes burned with the prick of tears, but for the first time in a long time, they were happy tears.

Jonah leaned in close and let his lips brush hers.

"How romantic." Ruby sighed from across the room. "Although Mom does tell me that kissing spreads germs."

Laughing, Bronte and Jonah broke apart. "Well, Ruby, that's right, and you should be an old lady before you decide to spread germs to anyone," Jonah said before once more kissing Bronte, apparently not caring about spreading germs at all.

"Okay, love birds, break it up." Holland held up her camera. "It's time for a family photo."

Bronte ran a hand over her sweater. "I'll take it so you can all be in it. If you show me how to use it," she said to Holland.

"Absolutely not." Holland messed with the settings on her camera before looking up, flashing a grin at Bronte. "You have to be in it. Nova, you're in it too."

"Yeah." Jonah pulled Bronte onto his lap. "You have to be in it."

Bronte's stomach did the twisty-turny thing it had been doing for the past two days. After stealing another quick kiss, they stood and moved to stand in front of the tree with the rest of his family.

"Get closer so I can get everyone in the shot." Holland motioned with her hands for everyone to scoot together.

The Whites and Nova shuffled closer, and Jonah wrapped his arms around Bronte. Her head had been buzzing all day with . . . well, everything.

"Holland, set your camera on the tripod and get in the shot with us," Renee shouted.

"Hurry, the light's blinking."

Bronte tried to focus on making sure she smiled toward the camera, this being the first time she had been in a family Christmas photo, but Jonah wouldn't stop nuzzling her neck, and it was distracting. "Jonah," she hissed. "We're supposed to be taking a picture." She turned to him, which was a mistake, because as soon as she did, his lips slid over hers.

"Merry Christmas, Bronte."

"Merry Christmas, Jonah." Bronte smiled before Jonah stole another kiss. This one slow and meaningful.

Not that she minded. She would be happy to keep kissing Jonah for the rest of her life.

Thank You

Thank you so much for reading *Meet Me at the Christmas Cottage*. We hope you enjoyed the story. If you did, would you be willing to do us a favor and leave a review? It doesn't have to be long—just a few words to help other readers know what they're getting. (But no spoilers! We don't want to wreck the fun!) Thank you again for reading!

We'd love to hear from you- not only about this story, but about any characters or stories you'd like to read in the future.

Contact us at www.sunrisepublishing.com/contact.

READ ON FOR MORE FROM

Jonathon Island

Return to Jonathon Island Season 2
Find Me in the Story
by Lisa Jordan.

When grief writes your story, can love give you a new chapter?

Eliza Quinn never expected to return to Jonathon Island permanently—but losing her job, her childhood home, and her sense of purpose all in one devastating blow leaves her grasping for anything solid. Enter Oliver Sullivan: the brooding bookstore owner who's clearly allergic to her enthusiasm, her festival ideas, and apparently... her.

Once destined to take the literary world by storm, Oliver has retreated to this car-free island sanctuary after losing everything that mattered—his wife, his unborn daughter, and his publishing career. The last thing he needs is a whirlwind employee who flings open curtains, rearranges his carefully ordered world, and makes him feel things he'd rather keep buried.

But when his sister dumps a last-minute book festival in his lap, Oliver discovers that Eliza's "annoying" optimism might be exactly what his failing bookstore needs. As they clash over everything from window displays to event planning, neither expects the sparks flying between them to ignite into something deeper.

When the biggest literary festival Jonathon Island has ever seen threatens to either save Oliver's bookstore or destroy what's left of his heart, both Oliver and Eliza must decide: Is love worth the risk of losing everything again?

From enemies-to-lovers tension to swoon-worthy small-town charm, this story delivers all the feels of You've Got Mail meets Virgin River.

One

RETURNING TO JONATHON ISLAND hadn't worked out as well as Eliza Quinn had hoped.

She'd come home two months ago from Pittsburgh to help with her mom's recovery from thyroid surgery, but saying goodbye to her family home was harder than expected, especially the stables where she'd spent much of her childhood.

Midafternoon sunshine warmed her chilled face as she dropped another box on the end of the dray wagon to be taken to her parents' new cottage on Rose Road.

Taking a breath, Eliza stepped inside the whitewashed building with a forest green metal roof and inhaled the scents of hay, warm animals, and leather to imprint them into her memory.

Her breath puffed out in front of her as she drew her jacket tighter around her middle.

Even though spring had officially arrived yesterday, a

mid-March storm had swept across Lake Huron last night and blanketed the northern Michigan island in a light snow.

Pegasus, one of the hard-working, dapple-gray Percherons that lived on island year-round, raised his head and looked at her with his dark eyes as he munched hay from his feeder.

She strode inside, reached over the aged wooden stall door, and rested a gloved hand on his muscled neck. "Hey, Gus. How's it going?"

He lifted his head and nuzzled her hand.

"Sorry, I didn't bring a treat with me."

"That's not like you. You always try to sneak treats to Gus and Ginger."

Eliza turned as Dad crossed behind her and dropped a hay bale on the cold concrete floor. She glanced at Ginger, the other Percheron, whose stall was next to Gus's.

"They work hard and deserve treats."

Dad laughed, the carved lines around his blue eyes deepening as he broke the bale apart and dropped a hay biscuit in each stall.

Tall and lean with more silver than dark brown in his short hair and weathered skin from years working outside, her father exuded a quiet strength she always found comforting. Dust and dirt clung to his faded jeans and knee-high boots he wore while mucking out the stalls.

She moved to him and wrapped her arms around his waist, the top of her head coming to his shoulder. Her cheek brushing against his soft flannel shirt, she breathed in the scents of his hard work. "I'm taking a break from helping Mom pack and heading into town to pick up take-out from Kelley's Bar & Grill. Need anything while I'm out?"

Dad's arms tightened around her as he rested his chin on top of her head. "Want me to hitch up the team and drive you?"

"Nah, I can use the walk after packing boxes."

"You planning to head up to the cottage with us after dinner?"

Eliza pulled herself from her father's warm embrace and lifted a shoulder. "We'll see."

"The move's an adjustment for all of us, but your mom and I don't need such a big house and all of this property, but we still want to keep it in the family. Selling it to Asher and Sadie is the right decision. For all of us." He waved a hand toward the four-bedroom house with a stone exterior and wraparound porch nestled in a grove of leafless sugar maples and pines. "I'm sure you'll come to love the cottage too."

Blinking back tears, Eliza forced a smile. "Asher and Sadie will do great here. It's just hard to say goodbye to the only true home I've known most of my life. Mom's all healed now, so once you're moved into the cottage, I'll figure out what's next now that I'm no longer working as Aunt Sally's assistant. Her generous severance won't last forever."

"I hope you'll consider staying on island." Dad caught her chin and lifted it with the calloused knuckle of his index finger. "Your mom and I are winding down, considering retirement."

Eliza batted her father's chest. "You're not even sixty. I don't think you'll ever retire." She waved a hand toward the stable. "The horses, the stable and livery in town, and now the carriage tour business that Asher and you revived . . . well, it's in your blood."

"Sunshine, it could've been yours too, but you turned us down."

Eliza glanced down at the toe of her Dr. Martens leather ankle boot. "It's not the same without Jared. We talked about running the 3Q Ranch together, but . . ."

"But then he was killed."

"Yeah."

Even though she lost her brother over five years ago in a freak accident, there were days when the grief still felt raw.

She'd left the island and spent five years in Pittsburgh with her aunt while her parents clung to each other.

Eliza pressed a kiss to Dad's whiskered cheek. "Well, I'd better head into town and pick up the pizza and wings from Kelley's. Then I'm meeting Sadie at the cottage to get the living room repainted tonight like I promised."

"Thanks, El." Dad's words followed her as she walked out of the stable.

She fished her sunglasses out of her oversized purse and slid them on her nose as she headed down the gravel drive and cut onto Sugar Maple Lane.

She turned toward Henrietta Hudson's white storybook cottage and caught a glimpse of the thawing lake through the bare branches. Sea gulls soared over the treetops and circled over the water, their caws echoing in the quietness of the island in its offseason.

The whistling wind picked up and sent a chill down the collar of her white puffer jacket. Her footsteps crunched in the snow as she hurried down Blueberry Boulevard and passed the post office, a small white clapboard building with trimmed hedges crowned with snow. She waved to Herb Easton, the local postmaster.

Ice slid off the roof of the brick and wood-sided police station that sat in front of the island's small firehouse.

Dr. Nova Lake exited the neighboring medical complex and waved to Eliza. Wearing a long gray wool coat and a light pink hat over her dark hair, she held a medical bag in a gloved hand and hurried across the back lot to the Blueberry Hill residential neighborhood down the slope from the businesses.

Feeling her toes turning numb, Eliza picked up her pace and hurried past Dahlia Drive, Lilac Lane, Zinnia Boulevard, and Poppy Place on her right. Her steps slowed as she reached the cute white clapboard cottage with blue trim and covered front porch on the corner of Rose Road and Blueberry Boulevard.

Her parents' new home. A cottage for two. Not three.

Dad loved that it wasn't far from the livery and stables next to the Island House Inn. Mom loved the large lilac in the backyard trimmed with a hedge border, the weathered picket fence, and the promise of wildflower gardens when summer returned.

Blowing out a breath, she headed for Main Street where sunshine glazed the snow-covered cobblestone streets running in front of the Victorian-style businesses.

Thanks to Dani Sullivan's island revitalization project

last year, the buildings had been repainted in pastel colors with new striped awnings. Soon, the empty flower boxes would be filled with a kaleidoscope of color.

A cyclist buzzed past as her phone vibrated in her back pocket. She dug it out, bit off her mitten, and thumbed open a text from her aunt.

<u>Aunt Sally</u>
Just learned Candace is retiring. Call me.

Several crying emojis followed her aunt's words.

Eliza tapped on her aunt's number and held the phone to her ear.

"El, hey. You got my text." Her aunt's voice sounded in her ear along with the sound of papers rustling.

"Hey, Aunt Sally. Sorry to hear about Candace."

"After thirty years together, I have to find a new agent in the next two months since Candace will be done in June." Her aunt's subdued tone stopped Eliza in the middle of the sidewalk. "Would you do some research and see who could be a good fit? I need someone who will put up with me, you know."

"Yes, you are a handful." Even though Eliza laughed, there was some truth to her words. "You do remember I don't work for you anymore, right?"

"Sorry. Old habits." Her aunt's deep sigh caused Eliza to jerk the phone away from her ear. "Kimberly's doing well, but she's not you."

"Auntie, she's your daughter—she'll pick up being your assistant in no time. You're the one who didn't want me working remotely, remember?"

"I know. I know. But you were the best assistant I had."

Her aunt's voice resonated in her ear. "I've become spoiled and need someone closer to me."

"Someone to be at your beck and call."

"Exactly. You know me—I like things a certain way. Find a job yet?"

"Still looking and figuring out what's next. Being an author assistant to the multi-published, bestselling Sally Jo Wilson will look good on my résumé." Eliza's eyes watered, but she blamed it on the wind blowing across the lake and biting her cheeks.

Her aunt laughed. "I will give you the highest recommendation."

Eliza perched on the edge of a snowy bench lining the sidewalk in front of Blueberry Hill Park and inhaled the scents of yeast and sugar drifting down Main Street from Good Day Coffee—the best coffee shop on the island—along with grilled burgers from Kelley's Bar & Grill.

Her stomach protested the lack of food as an idea took root. She tightened her fingers around the phone. "What if I became your agent?"

"Girl, what are you talking about? You're not an agent."

"No, but I could be. Since Candace lives on island, I could shadow her and learn how to become one." Eliza shifted on the bench and glanced toward the upscale Driftwood Hills neighborhood along the southwestern shores. Candace Bishop of Bishop Literary Management ran her agency from the comforts of her on-island home. "I have connections with publishers and industry professionals after working for you and attending conferences for the past six years."

"Oh, honey, but is that what you truly want?" Eliza pictured her aunt pacing in front of her standing desk—something she did often when trying to talk someone out of something.

Problem was, Eliza didn't know what she did want.

Eliza blew out a breath that clouded in front of her face. As the chill from the metal bench seeped through her jeans, she stood and crossed the street to Main. "I don't know what I want. Maybe this is it?"

"Are you asking me or telling me?"

She lifted a shoulder, then let it fall as she passed the newly reopened Island Bookstore. A red-and-black Help Wanted sign was taped to the glass.

"I don't know. Until I figure out a new career path, I figured I could take on a couple more authors and become their virtual assistants or something."

"Now, see—to me, that's closer to where your heart lies. You get more excited giving authors the exposure they need rather than learning how to broker book deals."

She sidestepped a sandwich board in front of Doug's Market advertising the daily specials, then turned back toward the bookstore. She stopped in front of the door and inspected the sign.

Part-time work available. Inquire within.

The pizza and wings take-out order could wait another few minutes.

"Aunt Sally, I'll call you back." Without waiting for a response, she ended the call, shoved her phone in her back pocket, then pulled the sign off the glass door. Turning the handle, she stepped inside. Bells jangled against the glass.

The warmth of the room that smelled of paper and something she couldn't quite place blanketed her face. She wiped her boots on the black-and-white patterned runner that stretched across the dark wooden floor to the checkout counter. Soft jazz played through a hidden sound system.

Gray curtains covered the lower half of the storefront windows, allowing light to stream through only the upper half. Pendant lights hanging from the tiled ceiling cast a warm glow over the white brick walls, wraparound wall racks, and multiple rows of chin-high shelves arranged behind a cozy sitting area in front of a lit electric fireplace.

Oliver Sullivan, her friend Dani's older brother, looked up from the register, where he added something to the drawer and closed it. He folded his arms over his chest. "Eliza Quinn. Dani mentioned you were back on island. I haven't seen you in what—ten or eleven years?"

She took in his short, dark-brown wavy hair, sharp, well-defined jawline, high cheekbones lined with dark scruff, and those striking blue eyes. Shouldn't he be wearing a stuffy cardigan or something instead of the black polo shirt tucked into black chinos that emphasized his broad shoulders and flat abs?

She'd always admired her friend's older brother who was going to take the literary world by storm. But he was five years older and definitely off-limits. He probably never saw her as more than Dani's pesky friend.

The Ollie she remembered, though—the one with the windblown hair, easy smile, and quick comebacks—

wasn't the one who stood stoically behind the counter and watched her with eyes that had lost their spark.

"Hey, Ollie." She flashed him a wide smile. "The last time I saw you was the summer that the . . . uh . . . you were living on a houseboat—the *Molly Brown*, was it?—with Kyle Munson, your brother Ty, Waylen Barrett, and who was the other guy?"

"Brandon Kelley."

"Right." She fought the cringe that wanted to scrunch up her face and mentally kicked herself for referencing the summer that changed the island forever—the summer the Grand burned.

She waved a hand over the room. "Congrats on the new store. Heard you and Jonah White took it over once Bob and Lucinda Johnson finally decided to sell."

"Only took 'em fifty years." Hands tucked under his arms, he lifted his chin. "What are you doing with my sign? I just hung that up."

Eliza slapped it on the counter. "I'm the answer to your prayers."

She hadn't expected to stay on island once her parents were settled in their cottage, but seeing that Help Wanted sign stirred something inside of her.

She didn't know what it was, but she couldn't ignore her instincts.

Now to convince Oliver Sullivan he needed to hire her.

Oliver Sullivan knew regret too well.

He wasn't about to let a Help Wanted sign earn a place.

Hiring help before the season opened made sense. Get someone trained before business picked up. And Jonah had agreed.

Less than ten minutes after hanging his sign, a dark-haired dynamo blew into his shop like a strong wind and expected to be hired on the spot.

And she'd been the only person in the shop since he opened three hours ago.

"I'm here to save you hours of tedious interviews by giving you the opportunity to hire me right now." Eliza Quinn raised a perfectly arched eyebrow as she leveled him with her brown eyes. "I'm a hard worker. Easy going. I love books. I can work a flexible schedule. Well, except Sunday mornings—church, you know."

"We're closed on Sundays."

"Even better." She pulled off her white knitted hat with a fluffy pom-pom that released a faint crackle as her hair clung to the fibers, untied the bulky matching scarf, and dropped both on the counter, messing up one of his displays. Then she unzipped her white coat, revealing a yellow hoodie with *Just a girl who loves books* written in some sort of script font. Her dark jeans emphasized her long legs and slight curves.

"And I'm never late. In fact, you should give me a key because I'll probably beat you to work."

He scoffed. Couldn't help it. "Not likely."

She didn't need to know he practically lived at the store . . . or at least above it. His eyes shot to the ceiling, then redirected back to her.

He'd known Eliza and her family since they took over

the 3Q Ranch and stables nearly thirty years ago after her grandparents chose to retire. And she used to hang out with his baby sister, Dani, when they were growing up.

Eliza trailed a finger over a round oak table by the checkout counter that highlighted Victor Holt's latest fantasy release, *The Defender*, and then moved and stood in front of the electric fireplace on the right wall and rubbed her hands together. Two armless brown couches held pillows featuring Shakespeare's and Edgar Allen Poe's faces.

She returned to the counter, her footsteps tapping against the polished hardwood floor. "This is a cute place."

He raised an eyebrow. "Cute wasn't the vibe Jonah and I were going for."

"Were you going for dark and tomb-like?" She waved a hand toward the closed curtains. "How can customers see what you have to offer if you close them out?"

"Buttering up the manager won't get you hired any faster."

She looked at him a moment and crossed her arms, hands on her elbows. "I heard about your wife. I'm sorry. Losing someone you love is the hardest thing to endure."

The softness in her eyes arrowed him in the gut. Not pity like so many others. But understanding maybe?

"Thanks. I heard about Jared. I'm sorry. I always liked your brother."

Nodding, she bit her bottom lip and lowered her head. "Everyone did. He was a great guy." Then she lifted her chin, a wide smile on her face as if the past ten seconds hadn't happened. "So, when do I start?"

"I haven't hired you yet." Oliver moved from behind the counter and leaned against the front if it, ankles crossed.

"Minor detail. When do I start?" She stood in front of him, hands clasped.

He ran a hand down his face. "You're persistent."

"One of my best qualities."

"That's debatable."

"Like your hiring process?" She shot him a grin. "What are you looking for?"

"Someone part-time—"

"I can do part-time." Her words came out in a rush. "In fact, I can start right now, if you want."

He stared at her a moment, then lifted his hands and dropped them back to his sides. "Fine, you're hired. But I can't do paperwork right now. I close an hour early on Saturdays for a children's story time, and they'll be here shortly. You're welcome to stay, and then I can walk you through how things are done."

She jerked a thumb toward the door. "I have to pick up an order from Kelley's and run it back to the ranch. Then I can come back."

He waved a dismissive hand. "No need. Come in on Monday. We open at noon during the offseason."

She grinned as she zipped up her jacket. "Thanks, Ollie. You won't regret it."

He held up a hand. "One rule."

"What's that?"

"Don't call me Ollie."

"But everyone does." She headed for the door and waved. "Bye Ol—Oliver."

Bells clanged against the glass as she closed the door behind her.

He dragged a hand through his hair.

What just happened?

That was the most unconventional interview he'd done. If he could even call it an interview.

Was his quiet book shop ready for someone like Eliza?

Blowing out a breath, he pushed away from the counter and opened the curtains in front of the windows. Gray light drifted over the empty display platform.

The scent of paper and coffee-scented candles from a display drifted over him as he straightened a carousel of last-minute purchases to catch customers' attention—bookmarks, magnets, and postcards of the island—and the stack of upcoming events that had been messed up when she tossed her hat and scarf on the counter.

He wandered through the rows of books, his Converses tapping lightly against the walnut flooring as he inspected the shelves. He righted a mug on one of the rotating cases that held mugs with quotes from famous authors, bookmarks, highlighters, and sticky notes.

He moved past the fiction section, walked into the side room, and flipped on the light. The woodland theme came to life as air blowing through the heating vents stirred the mobiles of birds hanging from the ceiling. The Kids Cave as he liked to call it. His twin sister Kate had used her artistic eye and helped him design it.

A lifelike tree trunk sat in the corner with stuffed squirrels and birds sitting on the limbs while a fox sat at the base next to a colorful mushroom wearing glasses and holding a book. Done in a woodland theme, the room held shelves made of tree bark that lined the walls while several small tables and child-sized chairs sat in the middle on a large, grassy, green area rug.

Oliver crossed to the M-section and pulled out the book he planned to read, then he set another copy on one of the easels on top of the waist-high shelves.

"Cute book."

His head jerked up and he found Eliza walking toward him, no hat, and jacket unzipped. "Didn't you have an order to pick up?"

He didn't even hear the door open.

"Mom and Dad took a load to their new cottage and decided to pick it up. Apparently they texted me, but I didn't see it while talking to you. So . . ." She lifted her arms and dropped them again. "I'm back."

He glanced at her, taking in the brightness of her cheeks, the scatter of freckles across her nose, and the light in her brown eyes.

"I heard they sold the ranch and bought a place on Rose." He tapped the hardback book with the watercolor dust jacket of a battered bear sitting in the grass. "The Teddy P. Bear series is classic. I pre-ordered multiple copies of this one, hoping parents will want copies to take home. I reached out to the author for autographed bookplates, and she sent stickers and an activity sheet to go along with the story. The kids will do those after story time."

"Great marketing strategy. Sounds like she knows what she's doing." Eliza picked up the book he'd set on the easel. "Chrissy Monroe. She's one of Candace Bishop's authors.

I met her at the agency retreat last year in Port Joseph that I attended while still working for my aunt."

Oliver lifted a shoulder. "Don't know her. Just emailed when I planned out the books for the month."

His phone vibrated in his pocket. He pulled it out and silenced the alarm that signaled he had five minutes before kids were due to arrive. "Kids will be coming shortly."

He left the Kids Cave and headed for the front of the store.

The door flew open. He caught it before it could crash into the wall.

Three-year-old Maggie Franklin raced past him, her boots leaving squashed bits of snow in her wake.

He was going to need a mop. Or perhaps that would be a good job for his new employee.

He caught Maggie in his arms, then tapped her on the nose. "Good afternoon, Miss Maggie."

She gave him a heart-melting smile as she pushed her blonde curls away from her face. "Hi, Oliber."

Her five-year-old brother Finn raced past them, then stopped, turned around, and waved. "Hi, Ollie."

Oliver ruffled Finn's dark hair, the little boy looking more and more like his deceased dad every day.

Mia Franklin, their mom and his cousin, followed behind. A blue bandanna wrapped like a headband held back her dark hair. She took Maggie from him and smiled. "Hey, Oliver. How's it going?"

"Can't complain. How's that fiancé of yours doing?"

"Cody's good. Busy getting his fishing business ready for opening season."

Oliver's Aunt Mary came in with her grandson Sam, and Mia gestured that she was heading for the Kids Cave.

Aunt Mary flicked her usual blonde ponytail over her shoulder, then wrapped an arm around Oliver and gave him a squeeze. "Afternoon, sweetheart."

"Hi, Aunt Mary." He kissed her cheek, then crouched and held out his fist to the little boy with Down syndrome. "Hey, Sam. How's it going?"

Shrugging, Sam adjusted his glasses, then gave him a rather wimpy fist bump.

Oliver ruffled the little boy's red hair, then Sam shuffled toward the kids' section as if he carried the weight of the world on his tiny shoulders.

Aunt Mary tracked her grandson's movements. "Don't mind Sam. He's been having a rough go of it since he and Ethan returned on island. But he did want to come to story time."

"Maybe he'll feel better after he hears the story."

The door opened again, and Ivy Dawson, owner of Hair Haven Salon, walked in holding hands with her seven-year-old daughter, Zoey. Their matching strawberry blonde hair had been arranged in the same sort of messy bun. Zoey's bangs covered her forehead, while Ivy had loose hairs framing her face.

"Well, if it isn't the Dawson ladies." Oliver smiled at Ivy, then crouched in front of Zoey. "I have a new book, and I think you're going to like it."

Ivy rested a manicured hand on his shoulder. "You sure it's not a problem? I have a quick blowout, then I'll be back to get her."

Oliver pushed to his feet and smiled at the struggling single mother. "Ivy, you ask me the same question each week. It's fine. We'll take good care of Zoey."

Ivy pressed a kiss to Zoey's cheek, then opened the door. She breezed through, then held it for Iris and Violet, six-year-old twins, who drifted over to him as they raced through the door ahead of Doug Manning, their grandfather and owner of the market next to the bookstore.

"Hi, girls." Oliver smiled at them as they shot past him, then nodded to the older man. "Hey, Doug."

"Hey, Ollie." He finger-combed his brown hair that had been teased by the wind. Then he wiped his thick glasses with the hem of his green Doug's Market T-shirt and put them back on his face. "The wind's pretty strong today. More snow is coming."

Shaking his head, Oliver took Zoey's hand and followed them into the other room.

He was ready for snow to be gone for good, but living on island for a large chunk of his life had taught him the weather was as unpredictable as the islanders themselves.

He glanced at Eliza, who chatted with Mia.

"Okay, guys. Grab a rug and have a seat."

The twins chose matching flower rugs, which didn't surprise him. He and Kate, his twin sister older by eight minutes, made a lot of the same choices. Maggie chose a squirrel while Finn chose a fish. Again, not surprising considering Cody's influence over the boy. Zoey chose a mouse and kept her distance. Fitting for the quiet child.

Sam, on the other hand, didn't want to sit with the other kids in a lopsided semicircle in front of Oliver's green reading chair. Instead, he leaned against Aunt Mary and kept his head on her shoulder.

Oliver settled in his chair and pulled out a tattered and matted teddy bear from the basket next to him. "This is Teddy P. Bear. He's very special and well loved. But there was a time when Teddy did not feel loved, and that's what our story is going to be about today. Can you tell me about a time when you didn't feel loved? Or when you felt forgotten?"

He waited patiently while the kids shared their moments. Zoey didn't like it that her mommy had to work so much. Finn grew serious, mentioning not having his dad around for his birthday.

Then his face lit up. "But now I have Cody. And he's awesome. Right, Mom?"

Mia smiled and nodded, but Oliver still caught a shadow that flashed across her eyes.

A shadow he knew all too well.

Unfortunately, grief remained a constant reminder, no matter how much a person tried to move past it.

"Today's book is called *The Day Teddy P. Bear Got Left Outside*. And it's written by Chrissy Monroe. Who can tell me what we call a person who writes books?"

Violet's hand shot into the air. "An author."

"Very good, Violet."

For the next ten minutes, he read the story and paused to answer questions or listen to their comments.

He caught Zoey's eye and raised the book. "Did you like the story, Zoey?"

The little girl shook her head. "I didn't like it."

His heart squeezed at the sad look in her eyes. "Well, I'm going to find a story you do like. Wait and see."

The same conversation they'd had every week for the past month since he started the reading program.

Directing the kids to the small tree trunk table tops, Oliver pulled little metal pails of crayons and colored pencils out of his supply closet. He shared the stickers and activity pages.

Eliza moved away from the doorway where she'd been standing while he read. "Well, that was the most fun I've had on a Saturday afternoon since returning on island."

Her praise warmed something inside of him. "Glad you enjoyed it. I do it every Saturday. A lot of parents read to their kids, which is great because it's one of the fundamental building blocks to their education, but I like to offer additional opportunities where they can socialize with other kids and be exposed to learning opportunities the bookstore has to offer."

"Oliver Sullivan, who would've thought?"

He scowled. "What's that supposed to mean?"

Eliza lifted a shoulder. Nothing. "Just surprises me that you're aware of that."

"Meaning what?"

Her cheeks darkened to a light pink. "Well, not many single guys know much about early learning foundations."

He wasn't single by choice.

Eliza didn't know the half of it.

Not many guys spent six months of their late wife's pregnancy reading daily to their unborn child so he could be the father his kid deserved.

Not that it mattered now.

Grief had a way of rewriting this chapter, no matter how carefully he planned the story.

Acknowledgments

This is the book that almost did me in. But we're here. We made it.

Thank you to Lindsay and Lisa, my editors, who helped this book shine. I really couldn't have done it without your guidance (and let's be honest, I probably would have thrown in the towel if not for your encouragement.) Also, a huge shout out to Kristyn and Katie, my wonderful line editors.

Thank you, always, to Emilie, Natalie, and Stef. More times than once you propped me up and kept me going — whether by helping me brainstorm my way out of a hole, answering my 7,956 questions on Army life (thanks to Natalie's GI Joe—any inconsistencies are totally on me), reminding me to celebrate the little things, or sending me a five-gallon bag of gummy bears to get me to the end of my deadline.

To my family. E, D, and O you are the best kiddos I could ever ask for. I love being your mom. To Andy. You're my rock. There is no way I could do what I do without your support 100% along the way. Also, thank you for being an amazing cook and always keeping me fed with good food.

And finally, to Jesus. For your glory. Always.

Christen Krumm is the author of sweet romance and rom-com for Adults and Teens. She lives with her husband and three kids on their homestead in middle of Oklahoma. She drinks way too much coffee and reads too many books, but creating stories with her Creator is her favorite.

Visit her at christenkrumm.com and listen to her podcast, Exploring the Blank Page on your favorite podcast app.

Jonathon Island

Where faith, family, and romance meet small-town, beachside charm. Whether you spend a weekend at The Grand, take a stroll down Lilac Lane, or cozy up in the Christmas Cottage, you'll fall in love with this heart-warming contemporary romance series, full of second chances and unforgettable love stories!

Check out the full series at sunrisepublishing.com.

SUNRISE PUBLISHING

We solve the problem of what we read next.   Available on Amazon

Have you read our
FREE
prequel novella by
SUSAN MAY WARREN

get your copy here

We solve the problem of what we read next.   Available on Amazon

Home to Heritage

SUSAN MAY WARREN and **TARI FARIS**

with **Mandy Boerma** and **Andrea Michelle Wood**

Sunrise PUBLISHING

We solve the problem of what we read next.   Available on Amazon

WHERE EVERY STORY IS A FRIEND, AND EVERY CHAPTER IS A NEW JOURNEY...

Subscribe to our newsletter for the latest news, weekly giveaways, exclusive author interviews, and more!

follow us on social media!

 @sunrisemediagroup

 @sunrisepublish

 @sunrisepublishing

Shop paperbacks, ebooks, audiobooks, and more at
SUNRISEPUBLISHING.MYSHOPIFY.COM